Books by Nan and Ivan Lyons

Someone Is Killing the Great Chefs of Europe
Champagne Blues

Nan & Ivan Lyons

SIMON AND SCHUSTER   NEW YORK

Champagne Blues

Published by Simon and Schuster
A Division of Gulf & Western Corporation
Simon & Schuster Building
Rockefeller Center
1230 Avenue of the Americas
New York, New York 10020

Designed by Elizabeth Woll
Manufactured in the United States of America

1   2   3   4   5   6   7   8   9   10

Library of Congress Cataloging in Publication Data

Lyons, Nan.
  Champagne blues.

  I. Lyons, Ivan, joint author. II. Title.
PZ4.L9925Ch [PS3562.Y449] 811'.5'4 78-31303

ISBN 0-671-24764-6

The authors gratefully acknowledge permission from the following music publishers to quote song lyrics:
"Begin the Beguine" by Cole Porter. Copyright © 1935 Warner Brothers, Inc. Copyright renewed. All Rights Reserved. Used by permission.
"Bye Bye Blackbird," Lyrics, Mort Dixon/Music, Ray Henderson. Copyright © 1926 Warner Brothers, Inc. Copyright renewed. All Rights Reserved. Used by permission.
"Lady, Be Good" by George and Ira Gershwin. Copyright © 1924 New World Music Corp. Copyright renewed. All Rights Reserved. Used by permission.
"Over the Rainbow," Lyric, E. Y. Harburg/Music, Harold Arlen. Copyright 1938, renewed 1965, Metro-Goldwyn-Mayer, Inc.; 1939, renewed 1966, Leo Feist Inc., New York, N.Y. Rights throughout the world controlled by Leo Feist Inc. Used by permission.
"The Last Time I Saw Paris," Words by Oscar Hammerstein II/Music by Jerome Kern. Copyright © 1940, T. B. Harms Company. Copyright renewed. Used by permission.
"They Can't Take That Away from Me" by George & Ira Gershwin. Copyright © 1936 & 1937 by George Gershwin. Copyright renewed, assigned to Chappell & Co., Inc. International copyright secured. All Rights Reserved. Used by permission.
"Where or When," Rodgers & Hart. Copyright © 1937 by Chappell & Co., Inc. Copyright renewed. International copyright secured. All Rights Reserved. Used by permission.

To Nat and Diane—

for the shirts off their backs

Monday

$\mathbf{O}$N the second floor of the most fabled hotel in all of Paris, Claude Picard, the most fabled concierge in all of Paris, lay awake in his darkened room. Clutched in his hand was a small replica of the Eiffel Tower.

He pulled the blue silk coverlet from his bare body and walked across the room. As he drew back the draperies, the shadows brightened into blue brocade. Blue satin. Blue velvet. The morning sunlight ignited the crystal pendants on the Saint-Louis chandelier as though a flame had been put to them. Still holding tightly to the tarnished metal souvenir, he stared out the window at the original.

Claude had an aquiline nose, prominent lips and olive complexion. His thick black hair fell into a well-mannered wave at the side of his forehead. Although in his fifties, he maintained the proud, muscular build of a young combatant. His torso was hairless. A perfectly bordered dense shrub of pubic hair gave his body an elegant sexuality.

Brring. Brring. He turned from the window to answer the telephone. "Oui?"

"They have refused the car," the woman whispered. "They would not even let the porter take their bags. They are waiting for the bus." There was a pause. "Emma Benjamin is very beautiful."

"She is also very deadly."

"It is almost like the old days, Le Dom."

Claude smiled. "It was easier then. We had only the Wehrmacht to worry about."

"I will not let them out of my sight. Vive la France!"

"Vive la France!" As Claude hung up the receiver, the foyer door opened.

Jean-Paul walked into the bedroom. He had long since overcome his embarrassment at seeing Claude naked. "Bonjour, Le Dom."

Claude nodded as he watched the valet hang a new uniform on his closet door. Jean-Paul walked across the Aubusson, around the lacquer harpsichord and over to the ebony writing table. He opened one of the Baccarat decanters, took a stemmed Clichy cordial glass and poured it three-quarters full of armagnac. He put the glass on the Meissonier silver tray.

"Le Directeur says we must all wear new uniforms today."

Claude drank the armagnac in a single gulp. He winced, and deep lines formed at the corners of his bright blue eyes. "Not all," he said.

"You are very tense, Le Dom. Your fist."

Claude opened his palm. He was still clutching the Eiffel Tower. He stared at it for a moment, at the indentations the metal had made in his skin.

12

"There is a better one outside the window," Jean-Paul said.

"No." Claude smiled. "That one is just for the tourists. Mine is the real one."

Jean-Paul smoothed the bed for Claude's morning massage. The armagnac, the massage and a hot bath usually eased the stiffness in his scarred knee. "Le Dom?"

Brring. Brring. "Not today," Claude said, reaching for the phone. "Fill the tub." Brring. Brring. He waited until Jean-Paul left the room. "Oui?"

"The Simons have arrived at Orly!" the man reported.

"Now they are all on French soil."

"Mon Dieu!" he said breathlessly. "They are drinking champagne as they walk through Immigration!"

"If we let them, they will drink France dry."

"Then we will not let them!"

"Vive la France!"

"Vive la France!"

The bathroom was pale green marble. Jean-Paul was filling the tub. "Le Directeur has been screaming at everyone. The Simons must have this! The Benjamins must have that!"

"Turn off the water," Claude said, eager to change the subject. "Fix the tray, please."

Jean-Paul arranged the tub tray. On it were a telephone, a gold cigarette case from Le Général, a Zippo lighter inscribed "Patton's Third, 28 August 1944" and a Lalique ashtray.

Claude poured half a bottle of Pernod into the bathwater. He put one foot into the tub and swirled it around. He inhaled the licorice scent as he lowered himself into the steaming apéritif.

"Is there anything else, Le Dom?"

"Yes. Return the new uniform to le Directeur."

13

"But—"

"Merci, Jean-Paul."

The boy shook his head and closed the door as he left.

Claude leaned back and slid down until the water covered his chest. He winced. Almost involuntarily, his hand went to the small crater in his knee. Every time he stretched or bent or walked stairs, it was there. A reminder from the past. A curse from a former lover. He thought of the night he lay bleeding in the vineyard at Epernay. Bleeding onto the vines. The noble grapes of Champagne. Had those branches mended from the weight of his leg? Did they ever ache for him?

There was an angry banging at the door. He knew who it was. "Entrez, Pierre."

The door burst open and slammed against the marble wall. Pierre Durac, the plump, mustachioed director of the Hotel Louis Quinze, moaned as he ran across the room like a wounded animal. He flung up the seat on the toilet. He unzipped his pants and began urinating noisily. "On top of everything else, the President of Rumania will arrive tonight! He always stays in 402! But how can I give him 402? The Marchese is still in 402!"

"You should have known better, Pierre. The Marchese is only in the third day of his affair with the Swedish Ambassador's wife. He is good for another week. What about the Princess?"

"Which one?" Pierre asked as he continued splashing into the bowl.

"The one without breasts."

"The British one? No. She has not yet finished her wardrobe. She has another day or two of fittings. And the Shah?"

Claude smiled. "He has not completed his shopping either. Unless he purchases Maxim's, Galeries Lafayette or Notre Dame, he too will remain."

14

"Then what am I to do?" Pierre exclaimed as he zipped his pants and turned around.

Claude smiled. "You are to flush."

Pierre narrowed his eyes. He pressed the lever as though the surge of water would express his anger.

Claude offered him a cigarette. Pierre shook his head. "I cannot cope with the President of Rumania, and the Simons, and the Benjamins, and Marcel's insolence." He paused to reread the inscription on the lighter. "I have just fired Marcel."

"So," Claude said bitterly, "it has begun. The state of siege. And Marcel is the first to fall. The first casualty of the Simons and the Benjamins."

Pierre slammed down the lid and sat on the toilet. "I have been rehearsing everyone since dawn. Marcel kept putting the Mandarin Orange on their tray instead of the Dark Seville! Not once," Pierre said defensively. "But to mock me, he did it twice!"

"You are telling me that Marcel, who fought with us to save France, Marcel the brilliant strategist, was fired because of the marmalade?"

"His strategy this morning was far from brilliant. I put up with Marcel's insults for too many years. I have too much at stake. The Simons can ruin me!"

"It appears they already have."

Pierre began to yell. "He knew the Mandarin Orange was fit only for the Arabs, not for the Simons! There is nothing you can do. You may have helped save France, but you cannot save Marcel! I have a reputation to protect!"

Claude reached for the telephone. "And I have a Frenchman to protect!" He flashed the operator. "In Strasbourg. I want the Auberge du Cygne." Claude held the receiver to his ear. He and Pierre glared at each other. "Bertrand, s'il vous plaît," Claude said.

15

A moment later a soft voice said, "Bertrand."

"Heil Hitler!" Claude shouted. "Wie gehts, Herr Bertrand?"

There was an audible gasp. "Le Dom?"

"Tell me, why is it you never keep in touch, Bertrand? Year after year the Führer's birthday comes and goes but I never hear from you."

Another pause. "That was thirty-five years ago," Bertrand whispered.

"I recall it as though it were only yesterday."

"What do you want of me?"

"I wish to collaborate with you for a change. I understand you are looking for a new maître."

"I am not looking for a—"

"And I have just the person for you. Surely you remember Marcel? Marcel Oriole? He has a sister living in Strasbourg and would like to be near her."

"You cannot do this to me. I am not afraid of you anymore."

"Marcel's number is 231.77.61. Someday perhaps you will do me a favor in return. Auf Wiedersehen." Claude hung up the receiver.

"And so the legendary Le Dom has once again accomplished the impossible."

"You fired an old friend, Pierre. Surely that is enough fun for one day. It is time you went back to work."

"I allow you great latitude, Concierge, because of the past we share. But you cannot continue to resist the fact that this hotel is a business. The Louis Quinze, this fortress of French elegance, survives only because it makes a profit from people with full bladders, tired feet and dirty laundry."

Claude smiled sardonically. "What they say, then, is true. You can take the boy out of the Hilton, but you cannot take the Hilton out of the boy."

16

Pierre turned his back to Claude and leaned over the sink. There was a long pause and then he shouted, "I did not want to fire Marcel!"

"How ironic. You must tell that to Marcel."

"No. It is ironic that le Directeur must confess to le Concierge."

"If it is any consolation, I shall never forgive you."

"I do not require your forgiveness! Or your permission!" Pierre turned to face him. "You are no longer the hero of Champagne. You are now 'the very charming Claude Picard'," he quoted sarcastically. " 'The man who can do the impossible. The greatest concierge in all of Paris'!"

"Enough, Pierre. I know exactly who I am."

"The Simons have always been quite generous to you. An entire paragraph in every edition. Perhaps you are angry with them because they do not know who you *were*." Without a word, Pierre opened the door. He paused before leaving. "Le Dom, it is not *still* the battle of Champagne."

"You are wrong, Pierre. It is always the battle of Champagne!"

Pierre slammed the door. Claude lay back in the tub. He thought of Marcel and Pierre bicycling every night from Epernay to Mailly to count the Nazis who were grouping there. Marcel and Pierre were inseparable. Until the day Marcel forgot the Dark Seville.

Claude was startled as the door opened again. Marie-Thérèse was the ne plus ultra of executive chic. As housekeeper for the Louis Q, she had a staff of nearly one hundred and was equal in position to many top executives.

"Monsieur le Concierge," she said urgently, "there is something I must tell you." She locked the door. She dropped her papers and books.

"Oui?" he asked.

17

She knelt down on the floor and leaned over to him. "I must tell you that I love you!" They kissed.

"You don't love me," he said as she unbuttoned her skirt and took off her blouse. "You love Le Dom."

She took off her brassiere and turned to Claude. "Have you seen him today?" she asked.

"He was here. Briefly."

Marie-Thérèse sat on the edge of the tub to roll down her stockings. "I hope I have not missed him."

Claude sat back and watched as she took off her panties. "He is never gone for long." He smiled and stretched his arms up to her.

Marie-Thérèse slipped gently into the tub. Water splashed onto the floor as he put his arms around her. They kissed. She moaned softly as his tongue met hers. She felt him stiffen against her stomach. "There he is!" she whispered. Her hand slipped down toward his thigh, but instead of reaching for his penis, her fingers touched his knee. She caressed the scar. "If only I had been there with him!"

"It was not the best of times."

She kissed him again. "It was not the worst of times."

He smiled. "What would you have done in Epernay?"

"I would have lived in the caves with him." She leaned forward. "After he came home from a hard day of resistance, I would open a bottle of champagne and pour his dinner."

He lifted his head to kiss her breasts. "He never drank the champagne. It was all that was left of a free France."

"So that is why he never drinks champagne." She rubbed his nipples until they became hard.

"No." Claude pointed to his right knee. "*That* is why he never drinks champagne."

"If only I had been there," she whispered.

He held her face in his hands. "They would have taken

18

you away. They took everything that was beautiful." He sat facing her and fondled her breasts. "They changed the names of streets. Children. Labels on little bottles of spices!" He reached between her legs. "They destroyed picture postcards. Harmless picture postcards of the Champs-Elysées." First one finger inside, then a second. "Any memento of France. They searched everywhere. They even took little souvenirs of the Eiffel Tower."

"Achtung!" she whispered excitedly. She squeezed his penis in her hand. "Achtung! La Tour Eiffel!"

"Der Eiffel Turm!"

Marie-Thérèse straddled his stomach. She guided him inside as she sat down slowly. "Tell me again!" she insisted, digging her fingers into his shoulders. "My darling, how many Nazis were at Mailly?"

"Every night Le Dom would send two men to bicycle from Epernay to Mailly."

Marie-Thérèse squeezed her thighs against his. "You must tell me, dearest. How many Nazis were at Mailly?"

He closed his eyes. Her legs tightened around him. "Pierre and Marcel would count the number gathering for the battle in Normandy."

She raised herself very slowly. "The Nazis, my love. How many?" He moaned as Marie-Thérèse lowered herself quickly. "How many were there?" She held on to the sides of the tub and began rocking furiously. "I have ways of making you talk!"

When he thought he could no longer stand it, he confessed. "Ten thousand!"

"Ten thousand," she shouted, clutching her breasts. "Oh, darling. Yes! Ten thousand Nazis! Oh, my God!"

"The Allies bombed Mailly for eight hours." He pressed his fingers into her thighs. "You could see the flames for miles." Claude pushed the soles of his feet against the edge of the tub. He stiffened his entire body. "If only you had

19

been there!" The pain in his right knee was nearly unbearable. He thrust upward as deeply as he could. "I can see the flames!" he cried out.

"The sky is red!" she gasped. "I can see the flames!"

Small waves of water continued spilling over the side of the tub. Finally they lay still. Almost smiling, he whispered, "It was not the worst of times."

THE most important person in a hotel is the doorman, thought Gaspar the doorman. He is the first to be seen by the arriving guest. His bearing and manner set the tone for the entire staff. If only the people inside maintained the doorman's high standards. God knows, there was little enough else for them to do!

Gaspar inspected his domain. He picked up a stray leaf from the sidewalk and stuffed it into his pocket. Everything was ready. The mats had been swept. The brass hardware had been polished. Every light bulb had been replaced. Not a single streak was to be found on the etched glass doors. Even his most unreliable assistant, God, had lit the scene properly. There was a 22-karat sun in the sky. The emerald green canopy, as well as the arched awnings on each window, stood crisp and fresh as though just plucked from a garden.

21

Gaspar felt his pulse quicken as the sable brown Bentley turned the corner. He slapped his thigh three times to alert the lobby personnel. The car slid to a smooth stop in front of the emerald green carpet. He opened the door.

A woman's bejeweled hands flung out a bucket of ice implanted with a bottle of champagne. "For God's sake, Gaspar, get rid of this slop!" Lily Simon watched as he struggled to catch the bucket. She laughed. It was the carefully cultivated, almost bawdy trademark of her decade as half of America's leading third-rate acting team. Lily, in her mauve silk pantsuit, characteristically tossed back her long red silk hair to look stage left at Dwight.

The other half of the team sported his matinee-idol silver-streaked hair and blue cashmere blazer with the pride of a general wearing his favorite medals. It was Dwight who had provoked their retirement from the stage. At an opening-night party at the Grand Motel in Eureka, Kansas, he declared that nothing worth acting had been written since the death of Philip Barry. He set a match to their Equity cards, which were buried inside his traveling copy of *The Philadelphia Story*. Unfortunately, the room caught fire. The Simons left town before they could be served with a summons. They had been traveling ever since.

Lily put her hand on Gaspar's free arm as he helped her from the car. "Beware, darling!" she warned. "It's non-vintage."

"Don't spill it on yourself," Dwight said as he stepped out. "It's sure to stain your . . . I say!" He paused for a moment and focused a professional eye. "Mmmm. A new uniform. A very handsome new emerald green tunic with snappy gold-edged lapels."

Pierre ran to them, his arms outstretched. "Enchanté, Madame. You have brought with you the sunshine!" He kissed her hand.

22

"You know what *Simon Says*," Dwight Simon said. " 'A good traveler always packs his own sunshine.' " He slapped Pierre on the shoulder.

"No, no, no!" Pierre said, smiling for all he was worth. "A good traveler always packs his own copy of *Simon Says*."

Lily reached into her purse and took out a small tape recorder. "Lily. Paris. The twenty-first. Hôtel Louis Quinze." She cleared her throat. "Dear Reader, for proof positive that not all the treasures of La Belle France are locked inside musty museums, tell the chauffeur to whisk you to the Hôtel Louis Quinze." She smiled at Gaspar, as though alerting him that he was about to receive his Christmas bonus. "After the very attentive Gaspar helps you alight from your pumpkin, you'll know why Cinderella had to settle for second best. If she had but waited for the dapper Pierre Durac, D-u-r-a-c, now in his . . ." Lily turned to Pierre as they walked into the lobby. "Darling, how many years have you racked up here?"

"Fourteen," Pierre answered.

Lily switched on the recorder. "Now in his fifteenth brilliant year . . ."

"No, no," Pierre corrected, with a smile. "My fourteenth brilliant year."

"It will be fifteen brilliant years," Dwight said, "by the time they read this. We're always working a year ahead." Dwight turned sharply and looked down at the floor. He smiled and slapped Pierre again. "Good show, Durac. They picked up the matchbook I dropped as we came in. Glad to see your staff is still on its toes."

The lobby of the Louis Q had six pink marble columns and three immense crystal chandeliers. Thick Oriental carpets sat smugly on the pink marble floor. Lily glanced up at the Gobelins tapestry. Still dictating, she ran a finger across the top of the Orléans fireplace mantel. "If Cinderella had but waited for the dapper Pierre Durac, now in

23

his fifteenth brilliant year as Director, she would have lived happily ever after in the S-h-e-i-k-est oasis on the right side of the Seine. Of course, it remains to be seen who could retain his Seine-ity bedding down next door to the likes of, uh . . ." Lily put her hand to her forehead. ". . . the Shah, Lord and Lady Bethune, the Marchese di Santi, Elizabeth—"

"But that is our VIP guest list!" Pierre gasped. "How did you get that?"

Lily winked at Dwight and walked away. "Claude, darling!" She strode down the aisle between the mahogany-paneled reception area and the elaborately carved desk of the concierge.

The Dutch industrialist stopped arguing with the cashier. The American couple looked up from their *Herald Tribune*. Six Egyptians walking in single file turned their heads. And Claude Picard sighted the enemy. Lily Simon was advancing. She was within shooting range. He kissed her hand.

"Do you know of the attempt on my life?" she asked breathlessly.

"Madame?"

"At the airport. It was nonvintage champagne!"

"I shall notify the Sûreté!"

"To hell with the Sûreté. Book me a plot at Père-Lachaise!"

"Well, Picard," Dwight said, shaking hands. "Are you ready for the invasion of the Simons?"

"I have looked forward to it."

"Tell me, Picard, what suite is the Shah in? Three-oh-five? Our readers must know which rooms to ask for."

"You know I cannot tell you that."

"Well, then, what about the Marchese?" Dwight asked eagerly. "Does he still dine at Allard?"

24

"Allard is a very popular restaurant."

"Darling," Lily cooed, "all we want to know is where the blue-bloods of happiness are hanging out."

"Tonight, everyone will be at the Opéra. It is completely sold out. And after, of course, to Chez Gustave. It has been booked for weeks."

"Wunderbar!" Dwight exclaimed. "I could use a nap. Let's have a night at the opera."

"And then," Lily said, "Chez Gustave." She smiled as she moved in for the kill. "The window table!"

"Naturally," said Claude. Then he parried, "Shall I have them prepare the lobster soufflé?"

Lily laughed. "How do you do it, Claude?"

"Madame?"

"The impossible! Someday you must tell me how."

He looked into her eyes. "Someday."

Pierre interrupted by taking Lily's arm to lead her across the lobby. "And now, while the maids unpack, you must allow me to restore your faith in the nation. I trust the mishap earlier will not spoil your day."

Lily sighed. "So said the Captain of the *Titanic*."

They sat on the gold brocade sofa and chairs facing the fireplace. Lily leaned back. So far, so good. How comforting to find the Louis still up to snuff. "I tell you, Pierre," she confided, "there are easier ways to earn a living."

Pierre stared at her, trying to think of one. "Of course."

"You know, Durac, we've done over thirty thousand miles this year alone."

"At a cost of nearly two dollars per!" Lily took a deep breath. "It's so terribly expensive to be rich these days."

André set down the champagne service. "Good God," Dwight said. " 'Seventy-three? Is there really any more of that left? I thought we drank it all."

"No, darling, that was '66 and '69," Lily said, smiling.

25

Dwight raised his glass in a toast. "You know what *Simon Says:* " 'A day without champagne is like a hunchback without Notre Dame.' "

Lily raised her glass. "To Le Dom!"

"Le Dom?" Pierre was shocked.

"Of course, darling; who else do you think made all of this possible?" She pointed to the bottle of champagne. "To Dom Pérignon himself!"

Dwight looked across the lobby and smiled. "Now, who is that with the Marchese?"

Pierre cleared his throat. "We have rewired completely. First it was the electric razors. Now it is the hot combs."

"Splendid," Dwight said.

"Isn't she an ambassador's wife?" Lily asked.

"Yes, from one of those blond countries. Sweden!" Dwight said.

Lily poked Pierre. "So, darling, you're serving Smörgåsbord in the lobby these days."

"We have also this year installed direct-dial telephones."

Lily sighed aloud. "Well, if the cat's got your tongue, direct-dial me an emergency croissant."

"I thought, Madame, you might prefer tea in your suite."

"Be a dear. I do hate starving on an empty stomach."

"Of course." Pierre snapped his fingers for André. "Tell Philippe to serve tea at once."

André leaned over and whispered, "Their tray was taken upstairs."

"Tea. Here!"

André shrugged. "It may take a few moments."

"Or it may not!" Pierre snarled. He would have to stall for time. "I am intensely interested in hearing about your new project."

"I don't mind telling you, Durac, it's a damn clever idea."

" 'COME TO FRANCE—YOU'LL EAT IT UP!' " Lily exclaimed.

"Damn good slogan," Dwight said. "For once they're using their heads."

"You mean, darling, for once they're using *our* heads."

'They' were North American Airlines. In an effort to capture what NAA considered a long-overdue piece of the transatlantic trade, a major tour package was being developed to cover Champagne, Burgundy and Bordeaux. Dwight and Lily, as authors of the "millionaire's" guide to Europe, were wooed and won on a millionaire's retainer to research the wine country for NAA's marketing team.

"And on this 'Eat France Alive' project . . ." Pierre began.

"Not *alive*," Lily said laughing. "*Up*, darling. *Eat France Up!*"

"Mmmm," Pierre replied, unconvinced. "You have for the first time colleagues?"

"The Benjamins are not our colleagues!" Dwight snapped.

Pierre knew he had struck a nerve, but could not resist. "I hear their *Penny Pincher's Guide* is extremely popular. Of course, with a much different clientele."

Dwight smirked. "One might say, and I would hate not to be quoted, that the Benjamins are the veterinarians of the travel industry."

"Now, now," Lily chided, "let's not speak ill of the dread."

CLAUDE stood against the kitchen door as André, Philippe and Jean assembled the tea tray.

"Damn it!" Philippe called out. "I can't read Marcel's notes."

"What's the difference?" André asked. "She would not

notice if she were on fire. She is already on her second bottle."

"Nothing ever escapes her," Claude said.

"All right," Jean announced. "It is ready!" André, Philippe and Jean hovered over the tray, checking each item. Jean pointed angrily to the crystal dish with the Dark Seville marmalade. "It was for *this* Marcel was fired!"

Claude stepped forward. "No." He replaced the Dark Seville with the deadly Mandarin Orange. "It was for *this* Marcel was fired!"

Philippe picked up the tray solemnly. "I shall deliver this in memory of our fallen comrade." He paused and then raised his eyebrows mischievously. "The marmalade heard round the world!"

LILY scrutinized every move as Philippe arranged the settings. She picked up her tea cup. "I've never seen this pattern before."

Pierre smiled. "It was copied specially for us. It was designed originally for a cousin of Pauline Bonaparte."

"That's good for a paragraph." Lily took out the tape recorder. She cleared her throat and flipped the switch. "New paragraph, Sophie. Imagine, darlings, sitting in a mirrored alcove on a Versailles settee previously occupied by Marie Antoinette's tush, and being surprised by an impromptu tea served in the unique Pauline Bonaparte Limoges. Note: commoners need not apply."

"Durac, how about some copy on the tea?"

Pierre shrugged his shoulders. "It is a blend made for us by Fauchon."

"What's it called, darling? Don't worry, I won't tell a soul."

"It is called Number Twenty-three."

Lily switched on the recorder. "And in case you're won-

28

dering what we drank, it was a blend mysteriously named Number Twenty-three and made exclusively at our favorite Right Bank deli, Fauchon. It was superfluously sweet for our taste. But, all in all, a most pleasant interlude with a dear friend." Lily smiled at the astonished Pierre. She put down the recorder. "Darling, what an absolutely vile brew!"

Pierre sighed. "At least there is a year before Fauchon is forced to change the blend."

"Come now, Durac," Dwight said. "Don't sulk. We've never given an opinion that didn't reflect the tastes of our readers. Just between us, old boy, the fifteen editions of our little literary lark have been instrumental in upgrading the quality of life available to countless travelers."

"Speaking of upgrading the quality of life, how about my croissant?"

"Madame." Pierre picked up the silver tray and held it for her. Simultaneously, he and Lily recognized the pale golden reflection of the Mandarin Orange. Pierre shut his eyes.

"Oh, Pierre," she said sadly.

"All is lost," he murmured.

"What is it, Lily?" Dwight asked.

"The marmalade! Pierre, how could you do this to me? After we have personally guaranteed the Louis for years!"

"I'm afraid we all know what this means," Dwight said with a deep sigh.

Lily narrowed her eyes. She leaned toward Pierre. "The *confiture* is on the wall."

Dwight sat back. "Too bad, old friend. We'll have to redo you from top to bottom."

Pierre broke out in a cold sweat.

Lily snatched her tape recorder. "Okay, Sophie. This is for the locked file. Triple-space, and let's hope we never have to use it." She began. "Red alert to all Our Darlings.

29

For the past ten years we've toot-toot-touted the glories of the Louis Quinze as the most elegant digs in our beloved City of Light. Well, sweeties, don't look now, but despite our kindly kudos, unless things pick up pronto, we might as well move to the wrong side of the arrondissement and stay at the Plaza-Athénée with the poor people. Unfortunately, we've had to adopt 'a phooey-on-Louis' policy this time round. Keep your fingers crossed, Dear Readers, and let's hope the patient recovers." She put the recorder away.

"But it was only the marmalade!" Pierre pleaded.

Lily patted his hand. "Today the marmalade! Tomorrow the toidy!"

CLAUDE walked back to his desk. The deceit he dreaded was nearly over. He had greeted the Simons as their devoted concierge. Le Dom was still a stranger to them.

He nodded to his assistant, Henri. "What trouble have you gotten into?"

"I had six flight confirmations, two flight changes, three requests for special seats, four limousines." Henri read from the next sheet. "I have pickups scheduled so far at Givenchy, Vuitton, Dunhill and Caron." The next sheet. "I have returns to Cartier, Hermès and Ricci." Sheet four. "There were fifteen cables, one telex, four hand-delivered letters and one registered-mail picture postcard." Sheet five. "Seven lunches and so far," he said, picking up another sheet, "only four dinners." He shuffled through the other pages. "No tours. Six hairdresser appointments, two

31

barbers, one pedicure." He sighed. "And last, there is the sad tale of the Princess who wants to attend the Saint Laurent showing."

Claude looked up at Henri for the first time. "There are no seats left."

"I know. That's what I told her."

Claude's lips tightened. "You told her she would be unable to attend?"

"You just said it was impossible."

"Of course it is impossible. But what has that to do with whether I will get her a seat?"

Henri shook his head with the familiarity of one who had been through it before. "I will go to the back room. I will pick up the house phone," he said, anticipating Claude's words. "I will tell the Princess to be ready at two-thirty. I will know better the next time. I will never tell a guest anything is impossible."

As Henri left, Claude took his pad and picked up a pencil. Simon. Opéra. Chez Gustave. He took a deep breath. It was the least he could do. One last cigarette before the blindfold. He signaled for an outside line, dialed and waited for Jules to answer. "Good morning. This is Claude."

"I do not care if you are Giuseppe Verdi! The Paris Opéra is sold out for this performance."

"I need a box for tonight."

"So does Count Dracula."

"I will have the tickets picked up in an hour. Merci." Claude hung up, but kept his hand on the receiver. As he had expected, the phone rang immediately.

"Why must you have a box?" Jules asked.

"Because it is there."

"It is impossible!" Jules yelled.

"I know," Claude said. He hung up the receiver. They had told Claude it was impossible to survive the Germans

32

at Epernay. It was impossible for the Republic to fall. It was impossible to organize a resistance movement. It was impossible to declare a vintage champagne in 1942. And *now* it was impossible to get a box at the Opéra.

He dialed Chez Gustave. "Jacques? Claude Picard."

"Bonjour, Claude. How are you?"

"Very well. Who has the window table for tonight?"

"César."

"No, no. I mean *for* whom?"

"The Israeli Minister of Defense. Unfortunately, it is not merely a king or a movie star. I cannot afford to unseat him with relations so tenuous."

"Of course. If the talks in Geneva had gone better—"

"Or if the arms shipment had been made, then in that case I would not care if I sat the Minister in the men's room."

After he hung up, Claude paused and dialed César, the concierge at Le Château Fontaine.

"Concierge."

"An admirable aspiration, César. But you should not make your dreams public."

"If you are looking for work, Claude, I suggest you call the Comédie-Française."

"César, I need your help."

"Le Dom, you have merely to ask."

"Can you persuade the Israeli Minister to have dinner elsewhere?"

"But it was I who insisted he try Chez Gustave. I presume you need the window table."

"Yes."

"May I ask for whom?"

"No."

"It must be for the Marchese di Santi. I hear he is having an affair with the Swedish Ambassador's wife."

"He is very pleasant for a minor marchese," Claude said.

33

"I had him the year he bought so heavily into soybean futures. He was with that flat-chested British princess."

"She is here too. An unfortunate coincidence."

"Mon Dieu! Why did you not send one of them to me?"

"I would have. But Pierre accepted the reservation without checking my notes."

"How embarrassing for you. And now to be faced with this crisis. The Marchese will never accept any other table."

"It is not for the Marchese," Claude said simply.

"Always so discreet, Claude. I admire that. But I cannot help you tonight."

"I understand. I will have to arrange it myself. Tell me where the Minister has been."

"The embassies, mainly. The first night it was the Elysée, of course. Obviously, the Germans were eager, and for some reason the Swiss—"

"The devaluation."

"Most likely. Then there was a reception at the EEC."

"What kind of food does he like?"

"The Israeli Minister?" César laughed. "What do you think?"

Claude smiled. "Chinese?"

"Of course."

"Merci, César. You have been very helpful." As soon as Claude hung up, the other line rang. "Oui?"

It was Jules. "I can get you two seats downstairs and two seats upstairs."

"I said a box."

"It is not possible. It is *Aida* tonight. For God's sake! It is *Aida!* All of the Middle East has taken the boxes. Tonight the Paris Opéra will have more camels in the audience than on stage!"

"A box, Jules."

34

"I told you. It cannot be done. Even for you!" Jules hung up. Claude reached for his black notebook. He found the number.

"Ambassade Chinoise," the voice said.

"The Ambassador's secretary, please."

"One moment."

"Ho Ping. May I help, please?"

"Bonjour, Ho Ping. This is Claude Picard."

"Ah, yes, the only man in Paris who can secure his laundry without the presentation of a ticket."

"I have an equally diplomatic mission. I was wondering whether the Ambassador and Madame Sooching have plans for this evening."

"Unhappily, the Ambassador and Madame Sooching wish to attend the opera. But it is impossible to obtain even two seats for tonight. I have been sitting here like a thousand-year-old egg."

"Then I assume the Ambassador's calendar is otherwise clear for this evening?"

"As clear as winter melon soup."

"I will call you back, Ho Ping."

Brring. An outside phone. Claude snatched the receiver from its perch on the first ring. "Oui?"

"All right! You win again! Four seats in the orchestra! Together!"

"I said a box, Jules."

"Why are you doing this to me?" Jules screamed. "Why must you always do the impossible?"

"It is the only thing worth accomplishing."

"Indeed. Accomplishing the impossible is worth a great deal. It is worth a big tip. A gift! A lady's favors. Something! It is unnatural to accomplish the impossible for nothing!"

"I take only what is priceless," Claude said.

35

"What is the use?" Jules hung up.

Claude dialed the Embassy. "I have a favor to ask of you, Ho Ping."

"My fortune cookie says you have tickets for the opera."

"If I had tickets for the opera, perhaps even a box, would the Ambassador invite the Israeli Minister of Defense—"

"To see *Aida?*" Ho Ping gasped.

"And then back to the Embassy for an intimate banquet?"

"Do you also wish us to hang a Star of David on the Great Wall?"

"Ho Ping, I wish you to consider the following. The boxes tonight will be overflowing with Arabs. All except one. In this one box will be the Chinese Ambassador and the Israeli Minister of Defense."

Ho Ping paused. "I begin to see. One from Column A and one from Column B."

"It occurred to me that the People's Republic might wish to raise its profile with the OPEC nations."

"In other words, you wish us to bring the Matzoh Ball to Mohammed."

"And then home for a banquet."

"How inscrutable you French are! I shall call the Israeli Minister within the half hour."

"It has been a pleasure," Claude said.

"Inscrutable," Ho Ping murmured and hung up.

Claude reached for the outside phone just as it began to ring.

"If I could get you a box, what would you do for me?"

"I would save your life," Claude said.

A pause. "What do you mean?" Jules asked. "There is no one trying to kill me."

"Not yet."

"In whose name is the box?"

"I will send Jean-Paul for the tickets." Claude smiled. "There is one more thing, Jules."

"Let me guess. You wish to sing Radamès."

"Even more difficult."

"I feel the condition of my health suddenly worsening."

"I am afraid, my friend, you are terminal again." There was a pause. "Jules, we cannot play the game again today, as much as we both enjoy it. I need a second box."

"Le Dom, so far you have accomplished the impossible. Do not ask me to perform the unreasonable."

"I am asking you to save me time. You know I will get the second box."

"I know only that I have solved the mystery of the Phantom of the Opera."

"You are a good friend, I do not forget the help of a friend."

"Unless you wish us both tied to camels and dragged through the Place de la Concorde, I suggest you forget my help immediately." Jules hung up.

Claude paused and then dialed Jacques at Chez Gustave. "If the Israeli Minister were to cancel . . ."

Jacques laughed. "You must be my guest very soon and tell me how you arranged this one."

"With pleasure."

"Now, then, Claude. I can hardly wait. In whose name?"

"Simon."

"Simon!" he exclaimed. Are they back already?"

"Yes."

"But Claude, why did you not tell me? Of course I would have given you the table."

"An oversight." Claude smiled.

37

GASPAR stood in front of the hotel and watched them walk up the block. The tall, thin man had a duffel bag over one shoulder. Ten paces behind him, limping on one shoe, was a very beautiful woman in a tightly belted raincoat.

Emma Benjamin had boyishly short hair. Under her raincoat she wore an old army shirt with sergeant's chevrons on the sleeve and tailored khaki pants. Her lack of makeup and jewelry gave her the air of a very rich woman. Emma was indeed a very rich woman. She kept reminding herself of that as she dragged her duffel bag along the pavement.

"Three buses, Clifford!" she yelled, oblivious to the stares of passersby. "That's why my shoe broke. Shoes from Bergdorf Goodman are not meant to take three buses!"

He stopped and turned around to her. "Who the hell told you to buy shoes at Bergdorf's?"

"What could I do? The Army-Navy Store was out of my size!" She lowered her voice ominously as she held up the broken shoe. "Three buses, Clifford. This is a three-bus crime!"

"The only crime is that you've become a traitor!"

Emma dropped the strings of her duffel. She walked to Clifford and looked up into his brown eyes. "Me?" she asked.

Clifford Benjamin had the open, friendly face one associates with Alpine shepherds. But he was a New Yorker, a street-wise city kid whose first view of a sheep had come when he was nearly twenty and was bicycling his way across Europe. Since then Clifford and Emma had amassed a fortune from the annual editions of *The Penny Pincher's Guide to Europe*. Their best-selling book had become the young traveler's bible. Clifford enthused over each new edition as a means of recapturing his dollar-a-day past, while Emma toiled in order to secure her million-dollar future.

Clifford still got haircuts that took weeks to grow out. He had the rumpled look expected of those who wore tweed jackets with suede elbow patches, chino pants and open plaid sport shirts. As Emma put it, Clifford looked better naked, because something was still left to the imagination.

They had met nearly twenty years before, when Emma, an aging nymphet, was abandoned by the sweater salesman who had taken her to Europe. He dropped her, and a dozen assorted cashmeres, onto a student ship that sped across the Atlantic in a mere ten days. Neither Emma nor Clifford had any money or prospects other than nine nights at sea and the Port of New York ahead. Clifford got a job as copy editor on the first edition of a luxury travel guide titled *Simon Says*. He was fired promptly after telling Simon exactly what he thought of what he said. In the heat of anger, Clifford and Emma wrote a budget travel article to purge themselves of the sybaritic Simons. After a series of such pieces, they were offered an advance with which to research their own travel guide.

As the world's leading "Penny Pinchers," they were North American Airlines' obvious choice to counterpoint the affluent perspective of the Simons. Clifford accepted the offer with no less vigor than the Count of Monte Cristo planning his revenge on Morcerf, Danglars and Villefort.

"Show you a limousine and you go to pieces. Emma, you have the heart of a Czarist!"

Emma shut her eyes tight. Then she raised her arms to the skies and shouted, "Do you hear that, Citizens of Paris? The heart of a Czarist! Me! Emma Lenin! The kid who discovered the cheapest optician in Prague! The day-old pâtisserie in Brussels! The four-dinar bus from the airport to downtown Dubrovnik! Was it not I," she challenged, meeting him nose to nose, "who found the free soup kitchen next to the employment office in Palermo?"

"Aha! That's the point, you closet elitist. You found it, but would you eat there? No!"

"Only because I don't happen to like spaghetti with eyes!"

"They were not serving spaghetti with eyes."

"If it doesn't move and it's cheap, you'll eat it." Emma sighed. She reached out with both hands and held him by the shoulders. "Oh, Cliffy. If only you understood my shoes, we could be so happy together."

"How much did those shoes cost?" he asked accusingly.

She stepped back and spoke loudly, enunciating every syllable. "Ten hundred and fifty thousand rubles!" Clifford turned away and continued walking. Emma picked up the strings of her duffel and began dragging it. "I can

40

see it gnawing at the back of your mind. You could have saved ten hundred and fifty thousand rubles, Comrade, if you had but taken the filthy Imperialist Dog limousine."

He stopped. "For the last time, if I had taken the limousine, *I* would have been the traitor. Just as if I had let NAA force us in First Class. I have a responsibility, Emma."

"To whom?"

"To my readers!"

"Up the readers!" she yelled. "What about your responsibility to me? I already put my time in for the fucking readers this year. I did my six months checking out the homey fleabags and charming greasy-spoons of Europe. This was supposed to be time out for good behavior. I thought I was on parole, Cliffy. At last, a hotel where they have room service and give you free soap!" Clifford began walking again. Emma lifted the strings on her duffel and dragged it along. "Never forget what that great American, Patrick Henry said: 'Give me a limousine or give me death'!"

"All this for one lousy limo, Emma?"

"One lousy limo could have quelled the Emma Revolution. You turnip! You should have suffered through First Class! When will you learn God did not make man to sit three abreast?" Emma sighed and dragged her duffel. They walked in silence toward the entrance of the Louis Q.

Gaspar rushed forward to help. "That's okay," Clifford said politely. "I can manage. Thanks."

As he stepped into the revolving door, Emma called after him, "Be careful, Cliffy! You might turn into a prince." Gaspar reached down to take the strings of Emma's duffel. "Are you kidding? I'm almost at the finish line!"

An astonished Gaspar moved aside as Emma stepped

into the revolving door and pulled the duffel to an upright position in front of her. Slowly she shuffled forward, lifting the bag with each labored step. A bellboy helped guide the doors. She refused to let him take the bag from her.

Clifford stood in the middle of the lobby, searching through his jacket. Emma dropped her duffel at his feet. "I will get you for this one," she whispered. "Someday very soon. Sometime when you least expect it. Maybe during foreplay."

"Bonjour, Madame et Monsieur." It was Pierre.

"Good morning," Clifford said, slapping his pockets. "I have a reservation here somewhere."

"Please," Pierre said. "It is not necessary. We have been expecting the Benjamins!"

Clifford nodded and smiled awkwardly as Emma whispered, "I might even train myself to reach climax before you!"

"Some light refreshment, perhaps." Pierre snapped his fingers. "André, le champagne!"

"No, no," Clifford said quickly. "Nothing to drink for us. We're here to work."

"But Monsieur, you will not be working at the Louis Quinze." Pierre smiled as though sharing a confidence with Clifford. "Despite the harrowing nature of your occupation, now that you are within our discreet little family, you must accept our hospitality." Clifford's eyes began to narrow. Undaunted, Pierre continued, "Now you and Madame will join me in a glass of champagne."

"We would like to register and go immediately to our room," Clifford said firmly.

"Your future," Emma hissed, "holds nothing but night after night of coitus interruptus!"

"As you wish," Pierre said resignedly. "I only thought that while the maids unpacked for you . . ."

Emma began to laugh. She looked at the duffels and

thought of musical-comedy French maids with little white caps delicately hanging up her preshrunk jeans. She imagined their shock at finding a black crepe Givenchy at the bottom of her bag. It was the one dress she packed for every trip. It was still unopened in its original wrapping.

Pierre followed as Clifford stalked over to the reception desk. "Yes, of course, you may go directly to your rooms . . ."

"Rooms?" Clifford smelled danger.

"We have reserved for you the former Ambassador's Suite," Pierre announced proudly.

Clifford held up his hand. "All we want is a double room with private bath."

"But Monsieur," Pierre whispered. "You will not be billed. The airline—"

"I don't care who's being billed," Clifford said loudly. "I don't want the Ambassador's Suite!"

Pierre smiled patiently. "I have explained, Monsieur, that our staff is quite discreet. Indeed, our clientele returns year after year because they depend upon—"

"I just want a double room with bath!" he repeated.

"Je regrette, Monsieur. But we are fully booked," Pierre lied emphatically. "The only accommodation we can offer is the suite."

Emma smiled and put her arm through Clifford's. "Just imagine, Cliffy. If I were pregnant and this were Bethlehem . . ."

Clifford pulled away from her. "Emma, watch it!"

"My dearest darling," she lavished sarcastically. "What does it matter where we are? As long as we're together!"

"I want to know the minute you have a cancellation!" Clifford demanded.

Pierre felt his flesh crawl. He drew himself up and exclaimed, "We have not had a cancellation since the Archduke Ferdinand in 1914!"

Emma turned away. She walked barefoot across the lobby. It didn't matter where she was going as long as it was away from Clifford. Away from another scene. There had been no letup since the airport. Surely he'd already racked up enough points to be anointed patron saint of the Penny Pinchers. Emma sighed. She looked up to see where she was. Someone was staring at her. The concierge.

"You are far more beautiful than your picture, Madame Benjamin."

Emma was caught off guard. Who was he? His eyes. Incredibly bright blue. Much too blue for a concierge. She picked up the brass sign on his desk. "You don't look much like yours either."

"Then perhaps you and I are not what we appear to be."

"That's the first encouraging thing I've heard all day." She held up her shoe. "Look at this!"

"I will have it repaired at once."

Emma leaned across the desk. He had that wonderful olive complexion. Such thick black hair. "No. They're just a cheap pair. Two or three hundred dollars. It's hardly worth having them fixed."

"Perhaps you would prefer I had them copied for you?"

"Are you kidding? That would cost a fortune!"

"I know an excellent shoemaker."

She began to laugh. "Well, unless you know Dr. Manette himself, I don't think there is anybody who remembers this style."

"Pardon?"

"Dr. Manette!" she repeated. "Oh, I haven't thought of him in years. You remember poor Lucie's father? Sitting at his shoemaker's bench?"

"I am afraid Dr. Manette is no longer in business." Claude stared at her. She had surprised him. He had not expected her to open fire with *A Tale of Two Cities*.

44

"Who was your favorite character? That is, aside from Sidney Carton."

"Madame Defarge," he said coldly.

Emma laughed. He did not. She wanted to see him smile. His lips looked as though they had been sculpted. They were perfect, but immobile. "They're my sensible shoes, too," she said uncomfortably. "You'd think they wouldn't go crazy the minute they walked into Paris." Emma paused. "I mean, I wouldn't be surprised if my evening sandals broke. What the hell do they know?"

She was tense, he thought. As though she were already afraid of him. "Do you wish to leave them with me?"

"I really love these shoes."

"Then we must try to save them. I believe we must save the things we love—no matter what the cost."

"Do I need a receipt?"

"Most definitely, Madame." He reached for a bouquet of yellow roses that had just been delivered. Discreetly, he removed the card and presented them to her. "Welcome to the Louis Quinze."

Emma brought the flowers to her face and inhaled deeply. She broke off a small bud and slipped it into his lapel. "It is a far, far better thing that you have done than you will ever know."

Claude watched her turn away. Without taking his eyes from her, he turned up his collar to sniff the bud. She was very beautiful. Far more vulnerable than Lily Simon, but no less deadly.

Emma felt suddenly renewed. She walked brightly across the lobby, where Clifford was proclaiming that he would not tolerate a terrace. "I finally met a man who understands my shoes!" she announced. Pierre looked down at her bare feet in horror. Emma smiled at him and opened her purse. She looked him straight in the eye and asked, "Say, can you change a million-dollar bill?"

45

$\mathcal{A}$S soon as the Benjamins left the lobby, Gaspar walked to the reception desk and raised his hands in disbelief. The bellboy prodded the duffel bags as though he were a hunter uncertain that the animals at his feet were dead. André pointed to the champagne that had never been opened. The cashier poked her head above the barred partition and pressed her nose with thumb and forefinger as though announcing an appalling odor.

Jean left the reception desk and walked across the aisle to Claude. With each step, he slapped the four American passports against his open palm. "Now they are all here," Jean said.

The moment Claude took the passports from Jean, he began to sweat. He turned abruptly, reached for the key to Suite 300 and walked to the elevator. He held up the key to show the operator where he wanted to go.

His hand trembled as he unlocked the Presidential Apartment. Once inside, he leaned back against the door. It was as though he had entered another dimension. All that he saw was real, but did not yet exist. Suite 300 would come to life at four o'clock. The setting would remain in suspension until the Simons, the Benjamins and the people from NAA had their final meeting. He walked from room to room as a surgeon studies X-ray after X-ray.

He breathed in deeply and exhaled. It was the only part of his presence he could leave behind. Anonymity was the most powerful weapon of the guerrilla fighter. It was also his greatest frustration. At least he had been called Le Dom. It was a shred of identity. A nameless name hated by the enemy. A symbol that was guarded by his countrymen. Claude knew that the soldiers to fear were not those who donned bright tunics and tapped tin drums. Far more dangerous were the resisters, the saboteurs, the underground fighters. They wore no uniforms. They never fought for so selfish a reason as saving their own lives.

He stood alone in the middle of Suite 300, inspecting enemy headquarters before his war was to begin. He wished suddenly for a drum.

Marcel Oriole appeared in the doorway. He had changed from his maître's uniform into an old brown suit and a green turtleneck shirt. His face was freshly washed and his white hair neatly combed. In one hand he held a book and in the other a silver tray on which was centered a single éclair.

"Mon ami," Claude said. The two men felt their eyes moisten.

"I knew you would be here. I have brought you one last éclair," Marcel said, sniffing.

Claude smiled as he took the pastry. He motioned for Marcel to sit on the divan while he sat in an armchair. "It is very good, Marcel," he said as he bit into it. "Merci."

Marcel shrugged his shoulders and nodded. "Bertrand called from Strasbourg. He did not say you told him to. But I knew."

Claude lowered his eyes as he continued to eat. "Think of it this way, Marcel. It is time you began to steal from someone else. I am sure Bertrand does not keep such careful books. You will be able to take good care of your dog and your sister."

For a moment, the two men smiled at each other. Then Marcel's lips grew tight. "Le Dom, I am sorry. I—"

"You are a patriot, Marcel! Un enfant de la Patrie. You have fought many other battles. I will fight this one for you."

Marcel sighed. "And if I die before you, who will take care of me in Heaven?"

Claude laughed. "Marcel, what makes you think you'll go to Heaven? After all the men you've killed?"

"I never killed a man," Marcel said proudly. "I killed only Nazis."

"And how you did kill them, mon ami. Between you and Petit Meurice . . ."

Marcel began to cry. "I think of those times. Of how terrible they were. And then I feel ashamed, Le Dom, because I miss them. I miss those times."

Claude stretched his legs. "It was unfortunate we had to kill all the Nazis. I would have preferred to bottle them for storage next to the wine. How satisfying it would be, after Sunday dinner, to bring up a Nazi from the cellar. The ultimate digestif."

There was a silence. Then Marcel said softly, "I wanted to fight for France just once more. To rid her of the Simons and the Benjamins."

"I am sorry, Marcel. But I am concerned about Pierre. He must not suspect anything."

The telephone rang. Both Claude and Marcel were startled. Claude picked up the receiver quickly. Who knew he was there?

"What are you doing there?" Pierre asked angrily.

Claude smiled. "Reminiscing."

"Don't leave the tray in the room," Pierre said. "And get the old fool out before he farts and we are faced with a major environmental crisis."

Claude hung up and then helped Marcel to his feet. They brushed their hands over the furniture, plumped the pillows and removed all traces of their presence.

There were probably other places to say goodbye, but none more appropriate. They put their arms around each other as they stood on the threshold of Suite 300. A tearful Marcel handed Claude a very worn copy of *L'Encyclopédie des Maladies Tropicales*, Vol. 10, X–Z.

HE Mayor of Roquefort had recently come into national prominence after banning the song "Am I Blue?" from all local radio stations. He stood up angrily. "I represent a national treasure as valuable as any in the Louvre!"

Etienne Duvert, the Secretary of Tourism, leaned across his desk. "I have a brother with a vineyard in the Loire valley. Another brother owns a hotel in Cognac. You cannot imagine what is going on in my own family!"

"I, too, am your family, Monsieur le Secrétaire."

"Your Honor," he said intently, "we are, of course, all brothers. Enfants de la Patrie." Etienne banged his fist on the desk, making certain to demonstrate great frustration. "If only there were something I could do!"

"But surely you have influence. They must be made to realize it is an unnatural criminal act to exclude cheese and tour only the wine country. I am perhaps the biggest cheese in all of France!"

"I agree," Etienne said.

"Roquefort is the King of Cheeses. So it was voted at last year's International Cheese Conference. Of course, I did not attend, since it was held, most unfortunately, in Gorgonzola. We must make the world aware that the ancient caves in Roquefort are as picturesque a tourist attraction as the caves of Champagne!"

"I agree," Etienne said.

"North American Airlines must allow the Simons and the Benjamins to include us in their itinerary." The Mayor of Roquefort stood up.

"A wonderful idea," Etienne said, leaning back in his chair.

"But I will need help," said the Mayor.

"Yes, you will," agreed Etienne. He told his secretary to hold all calls.

"I will have to know where the Simons and Benjamins are."

"And you might wish to see their itinerary." Etienne lit a long cigar.

"I have a great deal at stake, Monsieur le Secrétaire."

"Mais certainement," Etienne said, blowing a long stream of smoke. "Exactly how much do you estimate you have at stake?" Etienne swiveled his chair around and stared out the window.

"Five thousand francs."

A puff of white smoke rose in the air. "Surely Roquefort can be sliced thicker than that."

"Ten thousand."

"Tomorrow?"

"Of course, Monsieur le Secrétaire."

Another puff of smoke. Then Etienne turned around slowly and greeted him with a broad smile. "My fellow

51

patriot, as Dom Pérignon is a legend in Champagne, it will be said in Roquefort that after you, God broke the mold."

AFTER the Mayor left, Etienne glanced nervously at his watch. He reached into his pocket and took out the pack of American cigarettes. He repinned to his lapel the small American flag. Straightening his jacket, he walked to the other door, which led to the conference room.

Murphy Norwalk, head of international sales for NAA, looked up as Etienne entered. There were six other men seated around the conference table.

"I'm sorry for the interruption, Murphy, but the Mayor had been waiting for an hour."

Murphy patted his flat stomach. "That's all right. We made the corrections on your copies of the itinerary." He smiled. "Besides, it gave me a chance to tell these Twinkie freaks about the dinner last night."

"I am pleased you enjoyed the meal."

"Enjoyed? Christ, those were the best quenelles I've ever had. You really should have been there, Eddie. You would have come right in your pants."

Eddie shook his head. "Goddamn, you know how I love quenelles. I suppose they were coated with a sauce Nantua?"

Murphy thought for a moment. "Jesus, I don't really know, Eddie. There were mushrooms in it. Struck me, it might have been a sauce Normande." His face brightened. "Then, after the quenelles, they brought out the best fucking Escalopes de Veau aux Haricots Verts I've ever had!" Everyone was silent for a moment. "You know," Murphy said, putting a hand on Etienne's shoulder, "I kept thinking how I used to hate haricots verts as a kid. Can you beat that?"

"Hey, Murph," Sid called out. "You didn't tell us what wine you had. I'll bet it was a Meursault."

Murphy smiled and shook his head. "You guys just aren't gonna believe it." He pointed to Etienne. "This man here had the colossal balls to order a Riesling." He slapped Etienne's shoulder affectionately.

"Holy shit!"

"Jesus!"

"Now, that takes guts!"

"Well, for Chrissake, Murphy. Tell us about it."

Murphy sat back and smiled. He squinted his eyes as he began slowly. "It was young. Very young."

"God," Sid whispered. "I love them when they're young."

"And just cold enough to be cool in your mouth."

"Yahoo!"

"When you looked at it," he said, cupping his hand as though it were the bowl of a goblet, "you thought you saw a greenish tint, but not really." He brought his cupped hands to his nose. "And when you smelled it . . ."

"You're killin' me," Daryll said. "You know I'm a nose man!"

"You could catch the scent of something mighty sweet that had just gone by but didn't stop at all!"

"Christ! Don't nobody ask me to stand up!"

Etienne shrugged his shoulders. "I would be pleased this evening to take you back—"

"Like hell you will!" Murphy said. "Tonight's the night you promised me Langouste avec Beurre Blanc!"

"Hey, Murph," Chuck said. "I wouldn't mind a little piece of that myself."

"Count me in too!"

53

"Beurre blanc! Jesus, I've been off that since college!"

"I'll hate myself in the morning, but you only live once!"

Murphy smiled. "I guess we've got a full house for tonight."

"It is my pleasure," Etienne said.

"Terrific! And then we'll cap off the evening with a big bottle of bubbly," Murphy said. "You know, I'm hoping the day isn't far off when you'll be on our team."

Etienne smiled. "But Murphy, I thought I *was* on your team."

Murphy leaned over. "You bet you are, old buddy. We couldn't have brought any of this off if it weren't for you."

"I spoke to the agency yesterday," Daryll said. "They've already been authorized to double the ad campaign for the first three months."

"We've got six publishers bidding on subsidiary rights."

"Seventy-five major tour operators are co-oping ads with us."

"Four hundred and sixty-one affinity groups have already signed up."

"We've nearly firmed a landmark agreement with the National Liquor and Wine Dealers' Association to have travel brochures with recipes displayed in liquor stores throughout the country!"

"You know, if this works, we plan to offer 'EAT IT UP!' tours in every fucking country. NAA will be the first airline to provide international gourmet tours, both à la carte and prix fixe."

Etienne nodded. "You must be very pleased."

"No small thanks to you, fella." Murphy stood up. Everyone shook hands and began leaving the room. Murphy took Etienne aside. "One last question."

"Yes?"

"Color."

"Ah, yes."

"Did you decide?" Murphy asked.

"I thought red."

"A good choice. I'll have it parked downstairs for you."

"You are very generous."

"Yes," Murphy said. "I am."

IN 1944, Heinrich Himmler planned to dynamite the champagne cellars of Epernay if it became necessary for the Nazis to retreat. He wanted to give German manufacturers of sparkling wine a head start during the postwar period. Himmler's plan was never carried out because a surprise attack by Patton's Third Army liberated Epernay. And because the location of the dynamite was known to a local resistance leader whose code name was "Le Dom," and to his aide, Petit Meurice.

On the southern slopes of Epernay, there is a three-story building beneath which the world-famous champagne of Pommel et Bonnard is made. At the point most wines are merely cellared to mature, the making of champagne just begins. Hundreds of pairs of hands process the bottles stored in Pommel's eleven miles of underground cellars. The largest of those hands belonged to Petit Meurice.

It was his job to begin the delicate process of coaxing the sediment down toward the cork. Petit Meurice walked along narrow aisles in a cold, dank cellar wedged out of whitewashed limestone-and-clay walls. He twisted, two at a time, thirty thousand bottles a day.

Petit Meurice, the head remeueur for Pommel et Bonnard, gave each of the thirty thousand bottles a day a one-eighth turn and, simultaneously, angled them to slide the sediment down to the cork. Once the sediment collected in the neck of the bottle, the old cork was removed by the dégorgeur. Only after the new cork was put in, could the crystal-clear wine be called champagne.

The man who worked alone in the deepest cellar, turning thirty thousand bottles a day with the precision of a diamond cutter and the grace of a ballet dancer, weighed over three hundred pounds. Under his tan leather apron, blue jacket and coveralls, he wore a sweater, a heavy shirt, long underwear, two pairs of socks and rubber boots to protect his feet from the rats as well as the cold.

His pumpkin of a head was covered with a plaid woolen scarf tied under his chin. Over the scarf was a lamb's-wool–lined leather aviator's cap taken from the body of a Nazi pilot over thirty years before. The earflaps came down on the sides of his head, and the chin straps fell to his shoulders. A huge moustache underlined his bulging black eyes. The hands, which could not be covered, were huge, red and rough—except for the fingertips, which thirty thousand bottles a day had worn smooth.

In the dim light of the overhead bare bulbs, Petit Meurice, with his earflaps, had the appearance of a huge cocker spaniel. A huge talking cocker spaniel.

"I don't care what they say!" he shouted. "Rita Hayworth was a ridiculous partner for Fred Astaire! Where was Ginger? Was she so busy she couldn't be in *You Were Never Lovelier*? Eh?" He glanced for a moment at the brick wall and then continued turning the bottles. "Rita was fine for Gene Kelly in *Cover Girl*, but she was never the right type for Fred. I don't care what anyone says!"

He began to hum a few bars of "Cheek to Cheek," tapping his toes as he walked from one rack to the next, turning the bottles with both hands. "Even Judy wasn't right for him. Not elegant enough. Like putting Piaf with Chevalier. No! No! No! What kind of minds do they have in Hollywood? They had the team of all time!" He stopped for a moment and hummed "The Continental," taking a few steps from one side to the other. "And in they drop poor Rita. Too sexy." He laughed loudly. "Ah, too much the bedroom, not enough the ballroom. But Ginger, she had both! Eh? What do you think?"

Petit Meurice glanced again at the brick wall while he turned the bottles. He was talking to the bodies of Gruppenführer Rastenberg, Oberleutnant Koenig and Unteroffizier Shtell, whom he had strangled and buried in the wall thirty-five years ago.

"I would have liked to see Fred with Jeannette Mac-Donald. Now, there was a real lady. She had such humor and grace. Ah, but somehow everything seemed to fall apart after *The Story of Vernon and Irene Castle*. What is one to do? Eh? Nothing goes on forever, does it? Nothing good. Nothing bad. Always something new."

Petit Meurice stopped. He had reached nearly the end of his daily quota. He walked along the racks through the cellar to his special place. He looked around. Of course, there was no one there. But he had long ago learned, mainly at the expense of the Gruppenführer, the Oberleutnant and the Unteroffizier, that you just couldn't be too careful.

His hands were so cold they didn't feel the intense heat

of the bulb as he reached up for it. At once the area was black. Moving carefully, he felt along the wall for the metal marker. He loosened the screws and then put his hand behind the marker to unlock the hidden door. Click. He pushed open the ten-inch-thick panel and walked inside. He screwed in the light bulb he had taken from the corridor.

A small room had been carved from the limestone walls. It was here that Hubert Pommel perfected his secret formula for blending the wine that was to make the house famous. Iron bars, which once protected the sample blends in his work area, ran from wall to wall.

A table and four chairs were in the center of the cell. Petit Meurice smiled as he took an envelope from his inside breast pocket. Determined not to crease any of the small white place cards he had lettered the night before, he set them carefully in front of each chair. Mrs. Simon. Mr. Simon. Mrs. Benjamin. Mr. Benjamin.

CLIFFORD raised his head to admire Emma's breasts. The windows were wide open, and the pale blue silk curtains fluttered in the breeze. A very white sun filled the room. Clifford could feel it on his bare back as he crouched on his knees over Emma. She was staring at the yellow roses the concierge had given her.

"They claim the first champagne glass was molded on Marie Antoinette's breast," Clifford said. "That's why they're shaped that way."

"And here I always thought Bloomingdale's was responsible."

"Emma?"

"Yes, Clifford?"

"They should have waited for you." He put his head on her breast. "Emma?"

"Yes, Clifford?"

"Why do you think people make love at night instead of in the morning?"

"I don't know, Clifford. Maybe it's cheaper at night."

He lifted his head and looked at her. She was smiling. He sighed and sat up to show her he was erect.

"Now, that's just gotta be from Bloomingdale's" she said pointing to his penis.

"Wrong again, kiddo. It's strictly Sex Fifth Avenue." He moved up to put his penis beween her breasts. She stroked it absently as though petting a kitten. "I was hoping for more than a Walt Disney fuck," he said.

She smiled and put her arms up to him. "Darling, you are a hopeless G."

"What does that mean?"

"G-rated sex, Cliffy. All ages admitted."

He leaned over and held her face in his hands. "What's wrong? You're not the old you."

"I *am* the old me. That's what's wrong."

Clifford kissed her gently. "Hey, kiddo, what's the matter with you? Didn't I promise we'd spend our lives in Never-Never Land and never never grow old? Em, baby, you had the incredible good fortune to marry one of the original lost boys. Who, I might add, just happens to be in the middle of one of his most terrific hard-ons."

She took hold of his penis, raised her head and kissed it. "Cliffy, they must have run out of fairy dust. Somehow I got to be thirty-six."

"You just think you're thirty-six. It's because the evil Captain Shnook put us in this dungeon." Clifford sat back on Emma's stomach and pointed to the ceiling. "It's those cherubs up there. The velvet drapes. The plush carpets. The marble toilet. A bedroom with a desk, yet, and a lounge. And then the fiendishly clever touch of a living room! My God, it's enough to make *anyone* feel thirty-six! Fear not, my darling, I'll take you out of all this."

61

She smiled. "It's not the room, Cliffy."

"You're right." He jumped off the bed and ran over to the room-service cart, pointing out each item. "First champagne, then caviar. Lobster. Pâté. A double portion of truffles. What a fool I am! You've been poisoned! I should have known, Tink. You ate everything to save me! That's why you're growing old!" Clifford knelt on the floor and spread his arms. "Oh, please, if you believe in Emma and don't want her to grow old, applaud." He looked at her. "Applaud!" he urged. There was silence.

Emma got up and put her arms around him. "Clifford, I am a very rich thirty-six-year-old woman. And you are a very rich forty-two-year-old lost boy."

He smiled and lay back on the carpet. "Isn't that the cat's ass? You know, Em, I never did it for the money. I still don't!"

"But I do. Even though it didn't start out that way."

He sat up. "I remember how we began. It was so wonderful. No one had the idea before us, Em. We staked out a piece of the world and made it ours. We proved travel isn't just for rich people. Together we proved good times don't depend on champagne and caviar."

"You bet, Cliffy," she said sadly. "We sure proved that one."

"It's not just a job, Em. It's a whole view of life."

"But it's the same one we had fifteen years ago."

"And I still believe in it! You didn't always think that view was so terrible. You used to love it as much as I did."

"Darling, we had the best times ever. We were pioneers. Thumbing our noses at the Establishment."

"What's wrong with that?"

"Nothing. Except now we are the Establishment." She put her hand to his face and lay down next to him on the carpet. "Youth is a great place to visit, Cliffy. But I can't live there anymore."

"Then where do you want to live?"

"Anywhere. As long as it's in the present tense."

There was a long silence as they both lay naked on the carpet, staring up at the cherubs. "Emma." He moved closer and looked into her eyes. "Emma, forget about the goddamn money," he pleaded.

She raised herself on one elbow. "Listen, you mushroom, I worked as hard as you did. I stayed in every one of those goddamn rooming houses. I ate every one of those Oliver Twist meals. Without one word! I worked hard for my money, Clifford. And I didn't even have the kick of playing Peter Pan. It's dishonest not to want to spend it. And it's even more dishonest to ignore it. What's wrong in keeping pace with your own success?"

"You mean, keeping pace with you."

"I told you. They ran out of fairy dust."

He leaned over her. "Emma, I love you. I want there to be adventure always."

"You can't be a virgin every time."

"Next thing you're going to tell me there's no Santa Claus."

She smiled. "Cliffy, you are a pineapple! Instead of complaining about the cherubs, why aren't you letting them watch while you eat lobster on my belly? Why aren't you chasing me across the goddamn plush carpets, pouring the goddamn champagne in my goddamn hair? Oh, Cliffy, why don't you carry me into the living room and feed me caviar with your fingers?"

"You mean you wanna do it in the living room?"

"We used to."

"Yeah, but we were kids then." Suddenly he realized what he had said.

She saw how painful the moment was and reached out. "Cliffy?"

"What is it you want, Emma?"

"I want you to ask me what I want."

"All right." He lay on top of her. He moved her legs apart. He brought her hand down to guide him inside her. "Take hold of my cock. Now tell me what you really want."

"No, Cliffy. That's not fair."

"Take hold of it, Em. Ease it in. I'm asking you what you really want. Tell me. Make believe it's the first time."

She pulled her hand away. "You're asking because *you* need to know."

"It doesn't matter," he said, entering too quickly, "I'm still asking!"

Emma moaned. "Your rules again, Cliffy. It's always *your* game."

"Is it terrific, Em? How is it? I'm asking you! Me! Clifford! Not some fairy Peter Pan!"

She stretched to catch sight of the yellow roses, but could not see them. Emma reached around him and brought her hands together. She began to applaud slowly. "Doesn't anyone here believe in Emma?"

DWIGHT lay on a pink velvet sofa dressed in the robe he had worn onstage in *Private Lives*. Lily sat on the love seat. She wore an embroidered blue satin kimono, and between sips of champagne, she was mending a torn seam in her cranberry velvet evening skirt.

"Eight dollars!" Dwight said as though passing sentence.

Lily sighed and poured more champagne into her glass. "Oh, Dwight. I thought we left all that behind in London."

He held out his glass, and she filled it. "Lily, darling, you simply cannot escape reality. Our liquid assets total eight dollars. Blame not the messenger for the message." He drank the champagne.

Lily reached over and snatched the four ten-franc notes from him. Defiantly, she tore them up. "There. Now that's not half so depressing!"

"Lily, that was our last eight dollars!"

65

"Dearest, I simply will not allow you to waste time worrying about eight dollars. Better to worry about larger sums. So much better for the ego, darling!"

Dwight slumped back on the sofa. "How do you plan on getting your ego to dinner and the opera tonight without that eight bucks for cab fares!"

"Pshaw," she said, pronouncing the "p" with vigor. "This is a job for SuperLily!" She picked up the phone. "Concierge, s'il vous plaît. . . . Merci. . . . Claude, mon cher, Monsieur Simon et moi, nous voudrons un Rolls-Royce avec chauffeur pour ce soir. . . . A quelle heure? . . . Très bien." She smiled at Dwight. "Oh, Claude. Encore du champagne, s'il vous plaît. . . . Merci, darling." She hung up the receiver. "So you see, my love, the only thing eight bucks can buy us is a taxi.. No bucks gets a Rolls and more Champagne."

Dwight leaned over and extended his hand. "You must marry me!"

"But Count Vronsky, I am, I fear, already married." They laughed, and as Lily sat down, she handed him the room-service menu. "Have a sandwich on the expense account, Your Highness." Lily continued her mending.

"My God, how I hate club sandwiches."

"But they're so wickedly expensive, darling."

"I don't care. Even though I always order them, I hate club sandwiches." He looked up at her. She was still mending. "Why don't you give that to the maid?"

"Because the label says, 'Save Marie Antoinette'!"

"Mmm," Dwight mumbled. He snapped his fingers. "Why not good old breast of chicken?" The telephone rang. "It must be New York."

Lily raised her eyebrows. "Places, please!" She went to the other phone. "Good luck, darling!"

Dwight blew her a kiss and said, "Break a leg!" Then he

66

reached for the phone. "Curtain going up!" They each lifted a receiver.

Charles Evron, their publisher, shouted, "It's too late this time, Lily! Not one goddamn syllable can be changed!"

"Charles, darling, how are you?" Lily asked.

"Last year it was the plumbing in Monte Carlo. The year before it was the kitchens in Baden-Baden . . ."

"How is dear Miriam?" asked Dwight.

"Marjorie! Miriam was my second wife. You know what time it is here?"

"My dear Charles, we have a reputation to uphold!" Dwight said.

Lily pointed thumbs up and winked at Dwight. "A public trust!" she exclaimed.

"Do you know what time I went to bed last night?"

Lily took a deep breath and cleared her throat. She put one hand to her forehead. "Charles," she began slowly, "Paris has fallen!" Dwight blew her a kiss. Lily bowed.

"Oh, Jesus."

"It's the Louis Q."

"It collapsed?"

"It might as well have, darling."

"Lily and I must have twenty-four hours more," Dwight said.

"But the book is going on press tomorrow."

"Charles," she said, clutching at the phone cord, "we must protect our readers."

"But Lily—"

"I will not have their faith in us violated for the sake of the printers' union!" Lily protested.

Charles paused. "How's the weather?"

"Darling, there's only so much I can be responsible for."

"By the bye, Charles . . ." Dwight began.

"How much?"

"We're broke again, darling," Lily said.

"You've been broke again for years."

Dwight took a deep breath. "Charles, the bank in London's rather testy about the mortgage."

"How far behind are you?"

"Three measly months," Lily said.

"Would you send them a thousand for goodwill?"

"Yes, Dwight."

"And then, darling, we have not a sou in our knickers."

"I thought NAA was paying all your expenses."

"They are. But, darling, not even Zarathustra could anticipate all of *our* expenses. We need mad money."

"I'll cable you a thousand."

"She said mad, Charles, not slightly pissed."

"How much, then?" he asked wearily.

Lily held up three fingers. Dwight shook his head No and said with a flourish, "Five thousand."

"You two use up your royalties faster than you earn them. You spend money as though it were a disease."

"It *is* a disease, darling."

"Let's face it, Charles. We're terminal."

"Hopeless."

"No cure in sight."

"What in the hell would you two do if your books didn't sell?"

"God knows," Dwight said. "We'd probably be broke!"

SOMEONE knocked on the door. "Lily, there's someone knocking on the door," Dwight called.

"Well, we know it's not opportunity," she said through the closed bathroom door. "Be brave, my darling. I'm still soggy."

"But I was lying down," he muttered. "All right, I'm coming." He opened the door.

68

"Monsieur Simon." It was Marie-Thérèse. "I am so happy to see you. I was wondering if perhaps there was something I might do for you?" She looked into the room. "Or for Madame?" Dwight pulled her into the vestibule and closed the door behind them. Marie-Thérèse threw her arms around him. "Chéri, I thought I would have to wait for the next edition!"

Dwight glanced nervously over his shoulder. "You mad, crazy, wonderful little fool!" he whispered. "I must be with you. This afternoon. I'll get away somehow. Around six."

"I have missed you so."

"And I you, you impetuous imp. But go. You must!" he implored. "She'll be out any moment!"

Marie-Thérèse took Dwight's hand and placed it on her breast. "I was wondering, Monsieur," she said loudly, "how you were feeling." Marie-Thérèse opened her mouth and lifted her face. They kissed. Dwight's hand moved inside her blouse.

"Well, darling," Lily said posing in the doorway. "So you've decided on breast of chicken after all."

Dwight turned and stretched his arms toward Lily, as if his empty hands would exonerate him. "Lily, dearest, it's Marie-Thérèse!"

"Practically one of the family," Lily said.

"Well, that's exactly it!" Dwight exclaimed. "I was merely thanking her for the VIP guest list."

"The quintessential tit for tat," Lily proclaimed.

"How well you are looking, Madame." Marie-Thérèse did not attempt to button her blouse. Nor did she take her eyes from Lily.

"How well I am seeing, Mademoiselle." Lily turned to Dwight. "Darling, did we bring the nylons and Hershey bars for her?"

"I must go," Marie-Thérèse said, reaching for the door-knob.

69

"Really?" Lily asked. "I had hoped you would stay and take a nap with us."

"Monsieur." Marie-Thérèse nodded to Dwight and gently closed the door behind her.

Dwight straightened up. "That was quite an unnecessary performance!"

"I was about to give you the same notice. But then, darling, it's been said about you so often." She paused. "The Anderson play, wasn't it?"

"I wouldn't ring up the curtain on that one, Lily! Lest you remind *me* of some equally forgettable moments." He began to cough.

"You loathsome beast!" Lily walked across the room to the window. She raised one arm, framing herself in the entrance to the terrace. "Everyone adored my Camille."

"The only one who adored your Camille, my dear, was the critic from the *Harvard Business Review*, for whom you personified conspicuous consumption."

"Wretch!"

"Doo-doo unto others, Lily, as they doo-doo unto you." She leaned her head against the door, staring out onto the rooftops of Paris. Dwight put his arms around her. "It's Paris, Lily."

"I know," she said wearily. "Land of the C–cups."

"Darling, you musn't get overwrought."

"God knows, Dwight, there's enough to be wrought over!"

"Lily. Don't. Look out. Ahead. Never back, darling. Out there is our beloved Paris." He kissed her. "No one can ever share the stage with you. I merely wanted to prove that my Lily's titties were still the best."

She pulled away. "Old Lily's titties, you mean."

"Indeed not!"

"Lily's old titties?"

"Stop it!" he exclaimed.

"You stop it, Dwight! You've been president of the Tittie Research Society long enough."

He smiled as he held her close. "I like to keep a hand in."

"Don't, Dwight. It's the wrong time. The wrong year in my life for that. Lily needs you, darling."

Dwight poured them each a glass of champagne. "And I need you." They clinked glasses.

Lily drank the last of the champagne and leaned back on his shoulder. "Look," she said staring out at the sky. "That cloud. Isn't it the most perfect one God ever made?"

A pause. "It is lovely, dearest. But see over there? The cloud that's almost a full circle? That's the perfect one!"

"Oh, no, Dwight. It's such a banal little cloud. It doesn't have the elegance by half of that one, or that one. Oh, see, darling? All the way up there? *That one!*"

THE Simons and the Benjamins traveled in different circles. But at four that afternoon, as the Benjamins came out of Suite 550 and were locking their door, the Simons walked out of Suite 500. After a moment of quadraphonic panic, Lily began to laugh. "My great Aunt Fanny! You won't believe who just crawled through the looking glass."

Emma sighed. "Hello, Lily. Dwight. We heard you were staying here. A little vulture told us."

"Clifford."

"Dwight."

"Lily."

"Clifford."

"Emma."

"Dwight."

"Well, here we are," Lily said. "Off to see Daddy War-bucks with Sandy and Little Orphan Annie."

"I don't know why I can't get this damn door locked," Clifford said, turning the key noisily.

Dwight approached Clifford, who held up his hand and gestured No, thanks. As she waited for Clifford to lock the door, Lily entwined her arm in Dwight's. "I am so pleased we ran into you right at the start. I've been absolutely dreading it, Emma dear. Oh, the sleepless nights! Worrying where, oh, where will we meet them? Will they have just been caught shoplifting? Or sneaking into a theater? Or snatching the waiter's tip from someone's table?" Her smile began to fade as she watched Clifford battle with the door. "It's such a relief, my darlings, to come across you here. Here, where we can spend a few amusing hours together while Clifford locks the door."

"At least you're getting some mileage out of the meeting," Emma said. "I wouldn't want your tongue to rust."

Lily laughed. "I always knew you were the clever one, Emma. I'll bet you can lock a door just like that!" she said, snapping her fingers.

"Jesus," Clifford muttered as he continued to fumble.

"You're looking very well, Dwight," Emma said, turning away from Lily.

"Never better, thank you." He looked at Emma's khaki skirt and blouse. "Good to see you haven't let success go to your head."

"Don't be ridiculous," Lily said. "Of course she has. She's wearing shoes!"

Clifford stood up. "Look, as you may have noticed, I am having some difficulty with this damn door. You don't have to wait. We'll see you downstairs with Murphy."

"Desert a chum?" Lily was shocked. "Never! Besides, I'd hate to leave just when you're getting really rattled and angry."

"I am *not* getting rattled and angry," Clifford yelled. "I am just trying to lock this fucking door!"

"And so you will, my darling," Lily cooed. "You will! I have every confidence that someday you will lock that door."

"Cliffy . . ." Emma moved toward him.

"No," he said sharply. "I'll do it myself!"

"Let me try!" she said between clenched teeth.

"Why don't you go downstairs with them? I'll meet you."

"Nonsense!" Lily said. "The days are simply flying by. Besides, someone will eventually come searching for us. It's not as though we'll be spending the rest of our natural lives here."

"Got it!" Clifford said, finally removing the key from the lock.

"Bravo!" Lily cheered, striding across the corridor. "And as a reward, Clifford, we're going to let you press the elevator button all by yourself." Emma held tightly on to Clifford's arm as he pressed the button. "Hoo-ray," Lily articulated slowly.

As they waited for the elevator, Dwight said, "It is ironic we four should be together again. Opposite ends of the spectrum."

All eyes watched as the floor indicator moved toward 5. "Rather like the pits and the pendulum," Lily mused.

The elevator doors opened, and all four stood in place. Clifford and Dwight moved back slightly to allow Emma and Lily to enter. But Emma and Lily hesitated.

"Is it to be age before beauty, or pearls before swine?" Lily asked.

Emma sighed and took hold of Lily's arm. They walked in together. Clifford got in last, turned to the operator and said, "Three."

From the back of the elevator, Lily added primly, as

74

though reproaching an ill-mannered child, "S'il vous plaît!"

MURPHY rented Suite 300 because it had a conference room. Tan and trim in his Cardin striped blazer, he checked the buffet table with Etienne while Sid, Eddie, Daryll, Chuck, Norman and Fred filled their plates.

"Magnifique!" Murphy said. "The cheeses will be perfect with the wines."

"Especially the Roquefort," Etienne said. "You know, it is a national treasure as valuable as those in the Louvre."

"Hey, Murph, you just gotta try this triple crème," Daryll said with his mouth full. "It's the best goddamn Boursault I've ever had!" Daryll was licking the soft white cheese from his fingers. "Jesus," he said wondrously, "that is every bit as good as my wife!"

"I should be so lucky!" Sid said. "I married a Cheddar."

"Say, what is this? Is this a Pont-l'Evèque I see before me?" Eddie asked. "No, wait a minute. Wait one fucking minute. This is no Pont-l'Evèque! Holy shit! This is a Maroilles!"

Norman cut a piece of the Camembert. "I've been meaning to ask you for some time," he said to Chuck. "Do you really believe Marie Harel invented Camembert?"

Chuck sighed. "You know, Norman, I'd like to enjoy just one meal without your getting me all churned up."

Norman held up his hand. "All I want is a simple yes or no."

"Well, goddamn it, there *is* no simple yes or no, Norman. I want very much to believe that in 1790 Marie Harel invented Camembert. But, let's face it, old buddy." He lowered his voice. "I don't think the world will ever know for sure."

75

"Maroilles! Unbelievable!"

"I've never tasted Maroilles."

"What are you? Some kind of Korean orphan?"

Murphy nodded proudly as his men enthused over the cheeses. Smiling, he selected a bottle of Lafite-Rothschild '45 from among the dozens of fine bordeaux, burgundies and champagnes. "I don't know how you French kids first learned about 'Vive la différence,' but when I was old enough to know, my Dad took me aside. He never tried to make me feel guilty about wanting to go one way or another. He just told me the facts and let me decide for myself." Etienne nodded. "That smart old son of a bitch didn't even hesitate. He just looked right down at me and said, 'A Bordeaux bottle has shoulders.' Jesus, I can remember as though it were yesterday." Murphy laughed. "But the real corker is that *my* kid never came to ask me at all. Goes to show you how times change. Goddamn if he didn't just walk right into the sauna and ask his mother."

"Roquefort is generally recognized as the King of Cheeses," Etienne said. "I hope the Simons and the Benjamins are prepared to recognize the natural affinity of cheese and wine."

"Listen, Et," Murphy said with a broad grin, "you can count on them. I hired those jokers because they're the best money can buy. Real pros."

There was a knock at the door. "My God, both at once?" Murphy exclaimed. "How the hell can I tell both of you you're the most beautiful woman in the world?"

"Why don't you just tell it to *me*?" Lily said, turning a cheek for him to kiss.

"Because, you gorgeous creature, you've heard it so often!"

"And for so many years," Emma added.

"My sweet Emma." Murphy put his arms around her. "Not even a hint of jet lag in those baby blues."

"Expense accounts bring the roses to my cheeks," she said, kissing him.

Etienne walked between Emma and Lily and took them inside. "Did you know the caves of Roquefort are as picturesque as the caves of Champagne?"

"I must say I like your blazer," Dwight told Murphy. He felt the lapel. "Very good work, that."

"Would you believe it's off the rack at Cardin?" Murphy leaned over and whispered, "Why don't you just go in there and pick one out? Put it on my account."

"Very generous of you, old man."

Murphy smiled. "Yeah." Then he turned to Clifford and shook his head. "What the hell am I going to do with a crazy kid like you?" he asked. "You think I don't know all about that monkey business at the airport?"

Clifford sang, "I gotta be me!"

"You are some kind of guy, Clifford. I want you to know how much I admire a man of integrity."

"Does that mean I don't get a free blazer?"

"You get whatever you want, old buddy." Murphy smiled and put his arm around Clifford as they walked into the conference room. "Dwight, Lily, Emma, have you met all the guys yet?"

"No," Lily said. "The only name I've heard so far is Marie Harel."

"Guys, as though you didn't know, here are Lily and Dwight Simon, Emma and Clifford Benjamin. The superstars of our show." The men applauded. "And now, I want the dirty half-dozen to introduce themselves to you. Eddie?"

"Eddie O'Casey. I'm head of NAA's Package Component Group. I coordinate the efforts of all these other guys and work with our Commercial Sales Head and Direct Sales Head."

"Norman O'Connell. Within the Package Component

Group, I'm Executive in Charge of Hotels. I'll be working with the hotels you select to make certain they adhere to your standards."

"Daryll O'Brien. I'm Executive in Charge of Sightseeing. I'll be scheduling tours, indoctrinating the guides and making sure all ground transportation is up to snuff."

"Chuck O'Hara. Exec in Charge of Meals. I'll be the liaison with the chefs at all hotels and restaurants to make certain your menus are followed."

"Fred O'Toole. Executive in Charge of Optional Extras. I work with the other guys here to make arrangements for special side trips, room supplements, extended tour packages."

"Birnbaum. Sid Birnbaum. What do I do? I run from one country to another like a chicken without a head. I'm the conniver who makes all the contacts with England, with Holland, with Italy, Switzerland, Spain and, God forgive me, with Germany to sell the land portion of the tour to foreign wholesalers. If my name was O'Birnbaum, I'd have a desk job too."

Murphy stood up. "The cream of the industry," he said, gesturing toward his staff. "The best money can buy. Thoroughbreds. Each champing at the bit for you to give him the signal. One month from today, with your reports in hand—"

"We have six weeks" Emma said.

Lily nodded. "A contract is a contract."

Murphy shrugged. "Okay. So I'm anxious. You know how much we all have riding on you guys. I tell you, I've never seen the tail wag the dog as furiously before. All we had to do was announce COME TO FRANCE—YOU'LL EAT IT UP! AN A LA CARTE OR PRIX FIXE TOUR OF THE WINE COUNTRY WITH THE SIMONS AND THE BENJAMINS."

Emma smiled. "That's easy for you to say."

Murphy raised his glass. "Let's drink a toast. To the reoccupation of France!"

"I wouldn't put it into print quite that way," Dwight said.

"I'm not going to put it into print, I'm gonna light up the sky with it!" Murphy snapped his fingers. Eddie and Daryll opened a closet door and wheeled out what appeared to be a sculpture covered by a large cloth. "A toast!" Everyone raised his glass. Murphy pulled away the cloth and shouted, "To the Hotel Simon-Benjamin!"

A small battery-operated pink neon sign flashed, SIMON-BENJAMIN, SIMON-BENJAMIN atop the model of a green-tinted glass building. There were little cars and little buses and little people and little trees in front.

"Jesus," Clifford muttered.

"My God," Lily moaned.

"I knew you'd love it!"

Dwight leaned across the table toward Emma. "Did you know about this?"

Emma sighed. "If I had, I would have insisted upon Benjamin-Simon, Benjamin-Simon."

"I give up. What *is* that thing?" Lily demanded.

"Lily, it's our way of saying Thank you. New York has given me the go-ahead on buying the old Hôtel Mono-pole . . ."

"That fleabag?" Lily asked.

"Too overpriced," Clifford said.

". . . to be renovated as the flagship in our fleet of ho-tels."

"You cannot use our names without permission," Lily said.

"My contract doesn't say anything about this!" Clifford yelled.

"Guys," Murphy pleaded. "I just want you to listen to

79

me for a minute. Just listen." They nodded. "This hotel will be the first night's stay in Paris for your people."

"Whose people?" Dwight asked.

"Yours!"

Murphy pointed from Lily to Clifford. "Both of yours. Together."

Lily cleared her throat. "Murphy, darling, there's something I'd like to say to you in private."

"Me too," Clifford said.

"Go right ahead." Murphy smiled at his team. "They're all family."

"Not *my* family," Lily corrected. "Alone, Murphy!"

He shrugged his shoulders. "Guys?"

Lily walked to the buffet and poured herself another glass of champagne. Clifford waited until they all had left and closed the door. Emma slumped back in her chair. Dwight cleared his throat and said, "Let us pray."

"We've already been preyed upon," Lily said.

"You can't do it! Legally, you cannot do it!" Clifford shouted.

"Not without your approval," Murphy said. "I know that."

"Good." Lily sat down. "Then have the Executive in Charge of Neon Signs change it."

"To what?"

"Have him change it to the Hotel Leopold and Loeb!"

"Lily! Clifford!" Murphy began to pace. "Give me a chance! Give me a fighting chance!"

"Let's give the kid a chance," Emma said. "Let's give Murphy just enough rope. We might as well be democratic about it."

"Dear Emma," Lily oozed. "One can always count on you for the common touch."

"Go ahead, Murphy. Hang yourself!" Clifford said.

"The plan is to renovate the first two floors into efficien-

80

cies. No frills. A series of no-nonsense motel units. The upper three floors will be fully restored to their former elegance. Fireplaces. Crystal. Satin. TV. The works. I want to create a hotel that reflects the very essence of this tour."

"You have, darling," Lily said. "The Hôtel de la Merde."

"It's a stupid idea!" Clifford yelled.

Emma folded her arms and looked at Murphy. "What he's saying is 'Let my people go'! "

"By all means, let them go!" Lily urged. "I won't have theirs staying in the same place as ours!"

"It's simply out of the question," Dwight said.

"Not to mention what they'll do to the hotel. Good God, you'll end up with graffiti over the fireplaces and the bar will be filled by riffraff with shopping bags ordering Harvey Wallbangers. I won't be party to that!"

"Cool it, Lily!" Clifford shouted. "At least we're not in business just to tell fat dowagers where they can find clean toilet seats."

"I feel faint," Lily said.

"Some champagne, darling?" Dwight got up.

"I drank all the '66. What's left?"

"The '73."

"What the hell! It's an emergency." She drank it in one swallow and then tore up her copy of the itinerary. "You have breached our contract. It was made patently clear during those endless legal sessions that we would have total autonomy and that our names—which, as you have already conceded, are major factors in wagging the tail of, as you so aptly put it, this dog of a tour—would not be used in connection with recommending any hotel or restaurant that did not meet with our approval."

Dwight stood up. "Under such conditions, you will not be entitled to a return of the advance already paid, and we shall, in addition, sue you for misrepresentation."

Clifford stood up. He crumpled his itinerary. "Same

here. You're not going to create a schizophrenic hotel with my name behind it, much less over it. The whole purpose of what I've been doing all these years is to teach my readers they don't have to take second best."

Emma stood up. "As far as I'm concerned, you can have your damn advance money back. Clifford's right, you know. I'll have some of that champagne, Dwight."

"Of course, my dear. What a shock this must be. Even to someone like you." He handed Emma a glass. "I hope you don't mind. It's vintage."

Murphy leaned back in his chair. He put his feet up on the table. "And now, are you all through?"

"You'll be hearing from our lawyers," Clifford said angrily.

"I won't be hearing from anybody's lawyers." Murphy lit a cigar. "Now I suggest you four park your asses on the velvet and listen to the Norwalk facts of life. Your contracts call for services in the provinces of Champagne, Burgundy and Bordeaux. Your job begins when you leave Paris." One by one they sat down. Murphy continued calmly. "You don't have shit to say about where anybody stays in Paris. I happen to like this idea for a hotel. I want it. I'm gonna get it. New York has approved my plan, which, as you will find on rereading your contracts, is exclusive of the area covered by your services."

"We must have some recourse," Lily said.

"Lily, you said it all before," Murphy reminded her. "A contract is a contract is a contract. You got six weeks. Count 'em. Starting the day after tomorrow. You've got no say on where they stay in Paris, what color planes we use or the grade of toilet paper we put in the can. We're paying our big bucks to hear you talk about the wine country. Period."

Clifford got up. "*The Penny Pincher's Guide* is not required to endorse any establishment on the wine tour."

82

"Nor is ours!" Lily said. "And you may be certain every future edition of *Simon Says* will urge readers to avoid Murphy's Monstrosity like the plague—which, with its new clientele, will more than likely break out there."

"Goddamn it, Lily," Clifford yelled. "Cut that crap!"

"Oh, shut up, you tawdry twerp! You're the one whose fault this whole thing is. You and your band of cheap gypsies."

"Stow it!" Murphy said, banging his fist on the table. "You weren't hired to approve what we do in Paris! You don't want us to pay for your name? To hell with you!" He took out the batteries and removed the sign. Then he pointed at Lily. "I don't want your kind of people staying here." He pointed at Clifford. "And I don't want your kind either. I want *my* kind. People who don't read. And there are a helluva lot more of them than both of you have put together." He reached in back of the model and plugged in a new sign. CHATEAU NORWALK, CHATEAU NORWALK. He spoke softly. "I don't give a fast fuck what you write in your books about my hotel. The Dumbos who take our tours don't read books. If they did, they wouldn't take our tours."

There was a very long silence. Murphy's logic was inescapable. He stood up. His smile returned. "I'm sure once you've thought about it, you'll understand we're not at cross-purposes. Now, we at NAA realize just how tiring air travel can be. I'll make your excuses to the guys. But before you leave, I thoughtfully prepared a few tokens of NAA's appreciation." As though banging the last nails into their coffins, he slammed down small packages in front of them. "Alligator notebooks. One. Two. Three. Four. Eighteen-carat gold pens. One. Two. Three. Four. Engraved luggage tags. Mrs. Simon. Mr. Simon. Mrs. Benjamin. Mr. Benjamin."

As far as the world was concerned, it was Claude's dinner hour. Everyone knew that if he didn't eat at the Louis Q or wasn't dining with the maîtres who favored his reservations, he always ate at the Café Zola. With its coterie of regulars, the Zola served as a private club for local businessmen and their families. It was too unyielding a setting to attract passersby, much less tourists. It was at the Zola that friends met friends, played belote or chess, argued politics, made a business deal or sat peacefully and read newspapers speared on wooden poles courtesy of the management.

Emile Zoladz, the management, leaned in the doorway, his arms folded across his broad chest. For nearly twenty years, Claude had never paid for a drink or a meal at the Zola. He accepted Emile's hospitality, knowing that to refuse would insult the boy whose parents he had saved from the Nazis. The Zola, with its bourgeois voices fighting and laughing and belching, was as much a part of his France as the elegance of the Louis Q.

Claude approached Emile, who smiled and winked at him. "Bonsoir, Monsieur le Concierge."

"Bonsoir, Monsieur le Propriétaire. And what is on the menu to give me indigestion tonight?" Claude shook hands with Emile while his eyes searched the faces of those at the outside tables.

"I think you will find all of your favorites tonight," Emile said, nodding toward the dining room. He leaned over to kiss Claude on both cheeks. "They are inside," he whispered.

Claude narrowed his eyes as he walked into the dimly lit room. The inside of the Zola was cavernous. He walked down the center aisle toward his usual table against the wall. Next to the Lebrun family, with their crying baby, was a nervous man with a nervous white moustache. He picked at an omelette. A worn copy of Vol. 8, R–T, of *L'Encyclopédie des Maladies Tropicales* was at the side of his plate. EDOUARD LIBOR. WAITER. CAFE VICTORIA. EPERNAY. 1942. STOLE FOOD FROM SUPPLIES REQUISITIONED BY GERMANS. CURRENTLY WAITER. CAFE VICTORIA.

Claude turned away and nodded to Armand, the taxi driver, and his dog Gervaise, who sat like a haughty wife with her nose in the air sniffing as each waiter walked by. A handsome woman in her sixties, smoking a thin cigar and sipping a crème de menthe, tapped her fingers on Vol. 3, E–F. ISABELLE TESSIER. TELEPHONISTE. EPERNAY. 1943. PUBLISHED UNDERGROUND NEWSPAPER. CURRENTLY TEACHES KINDERGARTEN.

Once seated, Claude motioned to the waiter. At a back table, the man with Vol. 6, M–N, blew his nose. ANTOINE BAUDIN. GARAGE MECHANIC. EPERNAY. 1943. STOLE PARTS

85

FROM GERMAN CARS. INSTALLED TIME BOMBS ON TROOP TRUCKS. CURRENTLY OWNS GAS STATION.

Across the aisle, the old-maid Dupire sisters were already into their nightly drunken argument about which one Father loved best. The man at the table next to them pretended to be scanning the pages of Vol. 4, G–I. The book was upside down. NICOLAS PLANCHET. TOWN ACCOUNTANT. EPERNAY. 1940. ALTERED GERMAN RECORDS TO SIPHON OFF FUNDS FOR THE RESISTANCE. CURRENTLY HEAD OF RECEPTION. HOTEL SAINT-PIERRE.

The waiter brought a bottle of Pernod, a bottle of Perrier and a stemmed glass. Claude always substituted Perrier for water. Although he refused to drink champagne, he loved bubbles.

"There have already been three deaths from the Boeuf Bourguignon," the waiter said, putting down the Pernod. "If you wish modest odds for survival, order the chicken, which I myself ate earlier and from which I suffered only a mild rash."

Claude poured a drink without looking up. "The boeuf."

"A perfect choice," the waiter said, putting down a plate of beef stew. "I thought you might be in a hurry."

Claude smiled and drank his Pernod in a single gulp. He watched a distinguished-looking man in a black cape meticulously filet a large black olive as he avidly read Vol. 9, U–W. LE COMTE DE MONTAIGNE-VILLIERS. HEIR TO CHAMPAGNE FIRM. EPERNAY. 1943. CONFIDANT TO THE GERMAN HIGH COMMAND. DOUBLE AGENT FOR THE RESISTANCE. CURRENTLY HEAD OF CHAMPAGNE FIRM. By the time Claude was ready for the stew, the waiter had returned with a carafe of red wine.

Vol. 5, J–L, spilled his cup of coffee. ROBERT DEROT. SCHOOLBOY. EPERNAY. 1943. DELIVERED MESSAGES. NEWS-

PAPERS. CURRENTLY CHEF–OWNER. CAFE DEROT. Robert looked up, and their eyes met. Claude turned away.

At the table next to the black wife and Vietnamese husband who came once a week for dinner was Vol. 7, O–Q. He was folding and refolding his napkin. JOSEPH VITRY. CHAMPAGNE SALESMAN. EPERNAY. 1943. SABOTAGED SHIPMENTS DESTINED FOR BERLIN. CURRENTLY TAXI DRIVER.

Claude looked up as the fat man turned sideways and squeezed through the doorway. Dressed in a cream-colored suit, wearing a brown cap and carrying Vol. 2, C–D, Petit Meurice walked down the aisle toward Claude. E–F was watching. G–I, J–L, M–N, O–Q, and U–W were watching. R–T's eyes widened as the volume they were waiting for took one heavy step after another on his way toward Claude's table. The Lebrun baby continued to cry. Gervaise, the dog, continued to sniff. The Dupires continued to argue. But the others, those who knew the man whose footsteps made the floor squeak, sat frozen until he reached Claude's table.

Petit Meurice stopped for a moment. He looked directly at Claude and smiled broadly. He raised his eyebrows, rolled his eyes and sang in a whisper, "Oh, yes, let them begin the beguine, make them play!"

Claude watched Petit Meurice walk to the back as though heading for the rest room. G–I, J–L, O–Q asked for their checks. R–T stood up. U–W crumpled his napkin. E–F left something extra for the waiter. And M–N cancelled his dessert.

THE basement of the Zola had been converted. The cans of oil and tomatoes and juice, the cartons of paper napkins, the cases of beer and wine and water had been cleared away. They were neatly stacked to make

87

room for a table with one chair at the head and four on either side. Tacked to the center wall was a large map of France on which the area of Champagne was outlined in black. Large photographs of the Simons and the Benjamins were taped to the cartons.

The chair at the head of the table was empty. To the right of it, Petit Meurice sat pouring some wine into his glass. He was always served first, as one would feed a hungry attack dog before sitting down to dinner. A few coughs developed as cigarettes were lit. Smoke began to curl around the single naked light bulb.

Edouard pointed accusingly at Petit Meurice. "I want to know why he came First Class!" Petit Meurice looked up. He was accustomed to being referred to in the third person.

"Because Lucas is still afraid of him!" Robert said. "And if you had been at the station early enough, we would have all come First Class!"

"Did you want the guns? Or perhaps you think we could pull this off without guns?" Edouard yelled.

"First Class," Le Comte muttered. "And you wonder why I am concerned about the future of France."

Edouard pointed again at Petit Meurice. "I killed as many Nazis as he did. He should have been in Second with us."

Nicolas took the wine bottle from Robert, who said, "The vin ordinaire compares himself to the grand cru!"

Isabelle smiled a thank you as Le Comte poured wine for her. "The Maquis helps those who help themselves." She turned back to her crocheting.

Edouard shook his head angrily and again pointed to Petit Meurice. "I thought we were all equal!"

Robert sighed. "You are equal to no one." He turned to the others. "You are a waiter. A form of life overlooked by evolution."

88

"It is that kind of intellectual bigotry which has plagued my profession. Every night we must face the same enemies. We are blamed because the chef cannot cook. And we are blamed because the customers do not know how to order. And once again, I was given the wrong order." Edouard stood up and bent his arm at the elbow as though he had a waiter's napkin over it. He spoke mockingly. " 'Waiter, I want two loaded guns.' 'Yes, sir. Would you like anything with your loaded guns?' 'Oh, no. Just two loaded guns will be fine. Oh, waiter—I've changed my mind. Bring me four loaded guns.' 'Four. Yes, sir. Would you like anything with the four loaded guns?' 'No, I don't need anything with the four guns.' 'Yes, sir.' 'But waiter, what is this?' 'It is what you ordered, sir. Four loaded guns.' " Edouard put four guns on the table. " 'But waiter, where are the extra bullets?' "

There was a loud thud as Joseph dropped a bag of bullets onto the table. "Here are the extra bullets."

"You didn't order extra bullets!" Edouard yelled. "I would have gotten them if you had ordered them!"

"You see what I mean?" Robert said. "The waiter's mentality. They say the same thing when they bring the soup without a spoon. Stupid! Stupid! They are all stupid!"

"How dare you?" Edouard yelled at Robert. "If anyone is stupid, it is you! Mon Dieu, what do chefs know of reality? You know nothing about life. Like morticians, all you do is rearrange the dead."

"The only thing worse than dealing with waiters was dealing with the Nazis," Robert said.

"How the hell would you remember?" Antoine asked. "You were only ten years old at the time."

Le Comte put his hand on Robert's arm. "You were a beautiful child."

Robert moved his arm away uneasily. "I was only ten!"

Isabelle smiled. "That was one nouveau Beaujolais you missed, Comte."

"There were distractions." He shrugged. "The Gestapo. I had a great deal to lose."

"And now?" Antoine asked.

Le Comte smiled. "I still have a great deal to lose. The tourists are just as deadly an army. They will change Epernay as much as the Germans."

"They will be worse!" Antoine said. "The Germans paid for nothing. We hated them for what they took. But the tourists will pay and pay and pay. We will grow to depend on them. I do not want them at my gas station!"

Nicolas sneered. "Of course. Why should he bother with tourists when he makes all the money he needs selling stolen cars?"

Antoine laughed. "You know why he is angry? It was not enough I gave him free gas for the trip. He wanted a complete tune-up and a new spare."

"What if I had broken down?" Nicolas argued.

"That is not my problem. Do not presume we are friends merely because we have the same enemies. We live in the same town and I do not see you from one war to the next. I tell you what I will do. I will give you free gas every time you give me a free room at your hotel."

Isabelle looked up from her crocheting. "Cher Antoine, why do you need a room at the Saint-Pierre?" She smiled at him. "Are you still fucking around with your sister-in-law?"

Antoine sighed. "And they let her teach our children!"

"I only teach them to sing 'Frère Jacques' and to read *Pierre Lapin*," she said. "I do not teach them how to knock up their brother's wife."

"You stinking old hag!" Antoine yelled.

Isabelle jumped up and held her crochet hook like a dagger at Antoine's neck. "That is no way to speak to a woman my age. If you do it again, Antoine, I will cut off your balls."

Le Comte smiled. "I suspect it can be done with a cuticle scissors."

Antoine pulled away from Isabelle and straightened his collar. "What is wrong with you? He is a pervert, but you say nothing to him. It is because he is rich!"

"Don't be ridiculous," Isabelle said. "It is easy to understand his liking young boys. But liking to fuck your sister-in-law I cannot understand."

Antoine was enraged. He reached across the table and grabbed one of the guns. His hand shook as he turned around and aimed directly at the picture of Dwight that was taped to a carton. He pulled the trigger. A bullet ripped between Dwight's eyes. A moment later, to the shock of everyone, red liquid began pouring out of the hole in Dwight's head. They got up from their chairs, eyes fixed on the oozing picture. It made no difference that it was tomato juice. Antoine had made them remember the reason they were all there.

No one heard Claude enter. He stood at the top of the stairs. Even he was shocked by the sight and waited without a word until the can had emptied itself down the middle of Dwight Simon's head. "I see your aim has improved."

They turned as one to look up at him. "Le Dom," Antoine gasped.

Claude smiled. "Fortunately for Herr Fruchtmann, you were not so accurate in 1941."

During the occupation, the Nazis had assigned a member of a German wine-making family to control the production of champagne. The manufacturers were relieved that the "Führer of Champagne" was at least a wine-maker. Others, like Antoine, took every opportunity to try to assassinate him.

91

Le Comte raised his fist. "It was stupid to shoot at Fruchtmann! Better to have had him in charge than some beer-drinking swine!"

"Better still to have no one in charge," Claude said. He came down the steps and embraced Isabelle.

She kissed him. "Did I ever tell you what a good lay Fruchtmann was?"

"Every time we made love you told me."

Isabelle smiled. "That often?"

Claude walked around the table shaking hands. He kissed Petit Meurice on both cheeks. "So. I understand you rode First Class?" he said.

"How do you know that?" Antoine asked.

Claude shrugged. "There are spies all around us!" He took his place at the head of the table. They all watched as he reached into his pocket and took out an envelope. He held it up. Everyone smiled. "I have finished the letter. As soon as we have completed our business, I shall read it to you." He nodded to the picture of Dwight. "And to you as well." He put the letter in the center of the table.

"First, you must tell us what the Penny Pinchers are like," Isabelle said.

Claude tensed. "We have never allowed ourselves to become involved with personalities in the past. It is no different now."

"I told you she was very beautiful."

Claude looked up at the picture of Emma. Then he turned quickly to Antoine. "Let us get to business."

"The van has been repainted. I got false license plates from my cousin in Avignon."

"Lucienne?"

"Yes. You remember her?"

Claude smiled. "Very well."

"How well?" Isabelle interrupted.

92

"Isabelle, it was thirty-five years ago!"

"Thirty-five years, thirty-five minutes. It is all the same when you look back."

"You speak as though nothing had happened in between."

"Nothing *has* happened. I teach the same things to the same little children. Only the faces change. You make the same reservations for the same tourists." She pointed to Edouard. "He serves the same shitty food." She shook her head at Petit Meurice. "And for him with his bottles, it is the worst of all. There are not even faces that change."

"*I* have changed!" Nicolas said. "I was not always head of reception. And now I have a chance to buy the hotel!"

"Plus ça change, plus c'est la même chose." Isabelle shrugged. "You are still fighting for your big chance in life."

"Of course I am. Do you think Chabanne will sell to me if he can sell to NAA? He will hold out for a price higher than I can afford."

Claude picked up one of the guns from the table. He turned to Edouard. "These cannot be traced?"

"Not unless they can find the SS records."

Claude looked up at Robert, who reported, "The food will be superb! I am preparing all my regional specialties." He sneered at Edouard. "And since we have decided upon a buffet, I know the service will not ruin the food."

"Isabelle?"

"The mattresses have already been delivered." She reached into her bag and took out four crocheted ski masks. "These are Nicolas's and Edouard's favorite colors." She looked at Claude with a sudden urgency. "For God's sake, give me a gun! The Isabelle who was in the caves, fighting by your side, that Isabelle would not be crocheting ski masks!"

Claude reached across the table. "Isabelle, it was you who taught us that all successful machines have replaceable parts."

"At the time, I did not believe I was the part that was replaceable."

Claude sighed. He turned to Le Comte. "The shifts?"

"I have compensated quite easily for the loss of Marcel. Naturally, the big problem was that we do not want everyone reporting sick for work on Wednesday. There are no difficulties with Joseph, Antoine and Robert, since they are self-employed. Edouard does not go in until late, and Isabelle finishes early. I feel we have maximum flexibility." Le Comte pointed to Petit Meurice. "He and Nicolas are set for the night shifts, and I've given instructions on how everyone is to be picked up and dispatched."

Joseph put his briefcase on the table. "I have made my arrangements with Emile to pass on their personal effects."

"And I shall give Emile the letter after I have read it to you," Claude said. "It would seem, mes amis, we are ready!"

"There is one thing more, Le Dom." Joseph opened his briefcase and took out some papers. "I would like everyone to sign a release."

"A release?" Claude asked.

"Against litigation for invasion of privacy. We will have a very important and," he added with a smile, "a very salable story to tell. We must protect the literary rights, television, films . . ."

"What are you talking about, Joseph?"

"I'm talking about money. Hundreds of thousands of francs. Maybe millions. Don't you realize what a great story this is?" Joseph stretched his arms in the air as though framing headlines. "Champagne Heroes Defend France for Second Time."

Claude got up from his chair. "To whom have you told this, Joseph?"

"Aside from your penis," Isabelle added.

"No one!" Joseph was suddenly frightened.

"Who?" Claude demanded. "You were to talk to no one outside the group. Joseph, you are a fool!"

"I could be ruined," Robert said. "What have you done to me?" he yelled. "I was only ten years old in 1943!"

"Stop reminding me!" Le Comte said.

"Le Dom was my hero. He saved my life," Robert said. "I swore there was nothing I would not do for him."

Nicolas leaned across the table. "But now you are sorry you made your vow? You are perhaps doing too well, Robert?"

"I make a living," he said defensively.

"It must be a very good living to give you second thoughts on such a vow."

"Yes! It is a good living. I have a good life."

"So do I," Antoine said. "But we are not talking about money. We are talking about the honor of our country."

"Save that bullshit for your sister-in-law," Isabelle said.

Antoine pointed his finger at Joseph. "I warn you. If the police start coming around—"

"You are worried about the stolen cars you sell!" Joseph shouted. "That is all you care about!"

"The authorities will have no leads," Claude said. "We have dealt with these problems before."

Joseph sat down. "You don't understand. There is money to be made if we succeed."

"I do not wish to make money from this success."

"But Le Dom, you *never* wish to make money! You are the only concierge in the world who does not wish to make money. But I am not an idealist like you. Or a criminal like Antoine. Or a bored old woman. There is a fortune to be made here!"

95

"To whom have you spoken?" Claude asked.

"You are all so wound up in your petty little lives you do not see what is happening. We have planned an incredible event. It is breathtaking! Unique in the history of the world! There is a story behind it that can be sold without threatening our anonymity."

"I want the name."

"Trust me," Joseph pleaded. "I too risked my life in 1943. I am one of you."

"You never risked your life, Joseph." Isabelle blew a long string of smoke. "And certainly not for France. You were hungry. The Maquis had food. You joined the Maquis."

Joseph pushed out his stomach. "Tell me, am I here today because I am in need of food?" He laughed angrily as he patted his belly. "You think I am still hungry?"

"Yes, you are still hungry, Joseph. But this time for money."

Claude reached across the table and picked up one of the guns. Without hesitating, he placed the muzzle against Joseph's head. Everyone stood up. Joseph looked helplessly around the room. "Louise Vigran," he said flatly.

Claude walked back to the head of the table. He put down the gun. "Please be seated. It appears we have some new business." He put his hand on Petit Meurice's shoulder. "Do not return to Epernay. Stay in Paris. Tomorrow you will meet with Mademoiselle Vigran."

"My God, no! Don't send him!" Joseph pleaded, pointing at Petit Meurice. "She has done nothing!"

"Meurice will not harm her. He will merely persuade her to remain silent."

"I beg of you, Meurice. Do not hurt her. It is not her fault!"

"I will not hurt her," Petit Meurice said. "I will merely persuade her to remain silent."

96

"How?" Joseph screamed. "How will you do that?"

Petit Meurice stood up. "I will bid her a very proper Bonjour. And then . . ." he widened his eyes, broke into an enormous grin and said, "I will tell her, 'Oh, sweet and lovely lady, be good. Oh, lady, be good to me'!"

"What have I done?" Joseph cried.

"Nicolas, you will drive the car instead of Joseph."

"Yes, Le Dom."

"What will I do, then?"

"Nothing. You will go nowhere. You will see no one," Claude said.

"Do you intend to make me a prisoner in my own home?"

"You are not going home. You will remain here, Joseph."

"Where?"

"Here. In the basement."

"Here? Until when? For how long?"

"Until tomorrow. You will then be put on a plane. And God help you if you ever speak of this or if you ever set foot in France again."

The others sat frozen as Joseph pleaded. "Le Dom, you cannot do this to me! You must not send me away!"

"You dishonor your country, Joseph. You dishonor our dead. You are a disgrace to all of us."

"But I am one of you! You cannot forget I am one of you!"

"I have not forgotten. That is why I did not kill you."

All eyes were on Joseph as he ran to the stairs. No one moved to stop him. He had gone up only a few steps when he realized there was no place to run. He sat down and sobbed.

Claude leaned forward across the table. He raised his glass. "A toast before I read the letter." All rose. They lifted their glasses. "This time there is no Vichy to tell us not to fight. We *will* fight! We *must* fight! We did not save France from the Germans to give her to the Simons and the Benjamins! The France of Pasteur and Curie, of Lautrec and Cézanne will defeat Emma and Clifford Benjamin! The France of Rousseau and Voltaire, of Proust and Balzac will defeat Lily and Dwight Simon! Mes amis, enfants de la Patrie!" he shouted thrusting his glass forward. "Vive la France!"

As one, they echoed, "Vive la France!"

And then Isabelle added, "Kill the fuckers!"

Tuesday

CLAUDE threw down the morning telegrams impatiently. Henri held out the phone, rolled his eyes in despair, and said, "She wants my boss."

"Madame Johnson. Bonjour."

"Who's this?"

"I am the chef concierge."

"I don't want the chef!" she interrupted. "I want the head concierge!"

"Madame, I *am* the head concierge." Claude sighed and shook his head. As he looked up, he saw Emma. She was smiling at him. "Chef in French also means head." He put his hand over the receiver. "Bonjour, Madame," he said quickly. "Your shoes will be ready this afternoon."

Emma wondered whether he was married. "What time this afternoon?"

Claude covered the mouthpiece again. "Late." Had she made love with her husband last night?

Emma pointed to his lapel and whispered, "How is your flower?"

"I have a very dear friend in New York who told me I dasn't leave Paris without eating a duck at the Tower of Silver."

"The name is La Tour d'Argent. That is what we call it here." He motioned to Emma that he didn't understand her question.

"La Tour . . . what? Anything to make it more difficult!"

"Your flower," she whispered. "How is it?"

Claude thought Emma was asking him how his flower was.

"Listen, do you know how to say 'duck' in French?"

" 'Duck' is c-a-n-a-r-d. However, 'duckling' is 'caneton.' C-a—"

"My friend said duck. She didn't say duckling. You don't think I'll wind up with a Long Island duckling after all this?"

"No, Madame." Claude raised his eyebrows for Emma's benefit. "There is no Long Island in Paris." Emma leaned on the desk and smiled as she shared his exasperation. Claude never took his eyes from her as he spoke into the receiver. "It is a very fine restaurant. I know you will enjoy dining there. Do you wish me to reserve a table? Perhaps for eight?"

"Eight? No. Two! Just the two of us. I hope this isn't another one of those charmers where everybody sits at a long table and passes the salt all night."

"No, Madame. It is a very elegant and very romantic restaurant." He was still staring at Emma. "It is very beautiful."

Emma looked away. How embarrassing! How wonderful!

102

He knew he had gone too far. "At what time, Madame?" Claude asked, turning from Emma.

"Better make it late. I'll be shopping all afternoon. Better make it six-thirty."

"Merci, Madame." Claude hung up the receiver and cleared his throat. "Madame Benjamin?"

Emma was defensive. "I just stopped by to tell you that my flowers are still in the pink."

He smiled uneasily. "Merci, Madame." He wished she would go away.

"Usually all I get are terminal tulips." She shrugged. Trying to fix her eyes anywhere but on him, she looked down at her watch. "Say, do you know of anyone who fixes watches?"

"Certainly. What is the problem?"

"Well, you see, it's Mickey's little hand. It doesn't glow in the dark anymore. You know Mickey Mouse?"

Claude tried not to smile, but his face broke into a broad grin. "Not personally. He was used as an insignia during the war."

"I'm sorry," she said quickly. "I didn't mean to bring up unpleasant memories."

"The memories are not all unpleasant." He stopped smiling, wishing he could explain. "I will be happy to have the watch repaired, Madame."

"But I need it back today."

"Yes, Madame."

"Because we leave in the morning."

"I know."

She paused. "I like to see his little hands at night."

"Of course."

"But now I never know if it's a quarter past three or four or five." Emma shrugged. "Sometimes I wake up and don't even know where I am. I mean because of all the traveling. Do you travel very much?"

103

"No."

"You and your wife?"

"I am not married."

"I didn't mean to pry."

"Of course, Madame." They stared at each other for a moment. "You *are* much more beautiful than your picture."

"You said that to me yesterday."

"I know. But I have since seen another picture."

"Oh, well, everyone looks better than their passport pictures." She began to undo her watchband. "I know it seems silly, but Mickey means a lot to me." She handed it to him. "It's my engagement watch from Clifford."

"Then we must protect it at all cost." He smiled as he stepped from behind the partition.

It was as though Emma had never seen him in person. He was much more attractive with legs. Taller. Whole. A man. She felt an excitement merely walking across the lobby with him. "Please follow me, Madame."

Claude led the way to a small room off the reception area. Emma began to laugh as he slowly pushed aside the heavy steel door concealing rows of safety-deposit boxes. He opened box number 4. "Luckily, the Baroness left early this morning."

"The Baroness? You want me to put my Mickey in there? Where once a Baroness kept her tiara?"

Claude smiled. "Is Mickey any less important than her tiara?" He took out the box and opened it. "We will take no chances. I shall accompany Mickey to the jeweler myself."

"Oh, no. I didn't mean for you to do it personally."

"It is no trouble. The jeweler is across the street from where I lunch."

"Where's that?" Emma asked.

"The Café Zola." Claude's voice tightened. "But I do not recommend . . ."

"It sounds wonderful." He held out the key to box number 4. As she reached for it, her hand touched his. "No. I trust you," she said, suddenly pulling back. "You keep the key." Emma turned her back to Claude. Over her shoulder she asked, "Who's in the box next door?"

"No one of interest. Credit cards. Traveler's checks."

"Number 6?"

"The Shah."

"The Shah!" Emma rubbed her hand on the door. "Must be lots of oil in there."

"No. That is where he keeps the caviar. The oil is in 7, 8, 9, 10, and 11."

"He has six safety-deposit boxes?" she asked, shaking her head. "What do you think he really has in there?"

Claude pointed from door to door. "In this one the United States, in this one Europe, in this one China . . ."

Emma began to laugh. She pointed as if putting a pin in a map. "Who's in 24?"

Claude shut his eyes for a moment. "The Marchese."

She was giggling. "Then it must be filled with fettuccine."

Claude sniffed the door. "No. Too much garlic."

"And 25?"

"A princess."

"That's easy. A glass slipper. Twenty-six?"

"The head of the Soviet Academy of Sciences."

She knocked on the door. "What could he possibly have in there?"

"Shhh! The head of the Polish Academy of Sciences."

Emma traced the outline of the door as though measuring it. "He must have a very small head." They were both laughing. "Where is your Café Zola?" she asked suddenly.

105

"I do not think you would enjoy it."

"Why? If you eat there—"

"Madame, it is not a place for—"

"Oh, c'mon," she prodded, looking for a pencil in her purse.

"It is difficult to find without a taxi."

Emma sighed. "Damn! I'm not allowed to take taxis."

"Or limousines," Clifford said, standing in the doorway.

Emma laughed nervously. If only it could have gone on a little longer. "On my deathbed, Cliffy, then, and only then, will I scream out, 'Taxi!' But I promise to die before one comes."

"We're going to be late."

"Listen, I have got the name of one terrific place for us to have lunch!"

Claude's eyes narrowed. He was outraged at his own stupidity. But Clifford shook his head before Emma could betray him. "Not one of *your* places, kiddo." He pointed a finger at Claude. "I want to know where *he* eats."

Claude looked directly at Emma. "As I just told Madame, I eat here."

"No," Clifford said, "I mean when you're off duty. There must be some place you drop into on your way home."

"This is my home. I live here."

"You live here?" they asked at the same time.

"No kidding?" Clifford said. "That's terrific. I bet they don't even charge you rent."

"Cliffy!" Emma sensed that Claude was offended. "Why don't we go? You're right. We're going to be late." She looked at Claude and put away the notebook in which she had written *Café Zola*.

"Hold on a minute. If anybody has inside information, it's got to be him." He turned back to Claude. "Look, you don't have to worry. Our readers aren't the Hawaiian-shirt type of tourist. They're working-class people like you and me. You must have some pretty interesting places up your sleeve.

Claude smiled. As though preparing to share his innermost secrets, he leaned toward Clifford. "You are right. I do. For example, in the morning I sometimes walk over to Maxim's, where the chef prepares for me Oeufs en Cocotte with a dash of Madeira. Or I may have breakfast at the Plaza, the Crillon or the Bristol. They are all superb. All of them. Lunch?" He shrugged his shoulders. "If I do not grab a quick piece of quiche, or a slice of trout pâté here, I may wander over to Lasserre or the George V, depending on whether they are serving a billi-bi or a bouillabaisse."

Emma took Clifford by the arm. "I found a really easy way to get to the convent. All we do is walk to the rue du Louvre and wait for the number 21 bus to the Gare St.-Lazare. Then we transfer to the number 53. And voilà! That puts us only ten blocks away!" As she and Clifford left the room, Emma turned back. "Thank you," she said.

"No, Madame." Claude smiled. "Thank *you*."

Emma and Clifford walked silently through the drafty stone corridor as Sister Gabrielle led them to the Mother Superior's office. Emma put her arm through Clifford's and huddled close to him.

"It would be most importunate to complain of the cold," cautioned Sister Gabrielle, looking at Emma. "And you must not call her Mother Superior. She is still Sister Marcella." Clifford nodded. "In the event she offers you something warm to drink, please bear in mind that we have hardly enough to go around as it is."

107

Sister Gabrielle brought them to the door. She took one final look at Emma and Clifford. With a sigh of resignation, she knocked on the door and opened it.

Sister Marcella sat imperiously behind on old bridge table in the corner of an otherwise empty room. She was dressed in white. Her wire-framed glasses were tinted dark blue and lightened gently as they reached her very cold red nose. "You must not call me Mother Superior," she cautioned, rising. "I am still Sister Marcella, although we all know it is a year since I was appointed Acting Mother. No matter. It is part of the harassment which we have learned to bear."

"A pleasure to meet you, Sister Marcella," Clifford said.

"How do you do, Sister Marcella?" Emma echoed.

"Just call me Sister. Now that we're over the formalities, I suggest we go into the corridor, where there is a bench on which we may all sit." She led the way and pointed to a stone bench. "Make yourselves comfortable." As Emma and Clifford sat down, the cold raced through their clothes. "Would you like something warm to drink?"

"Oh, no," Emma said quickly. "We're fine."

Sister Marcella smiled and raised an eyebrow. "Sister Gabrielle, I gather, has told you of our plight. She did not mean to be ungracious. Merely protective of those who are left." She smiled. "Actually, she has a heart as big as the Ritz."

"In your letter . . ." Clifford began eagerly.

"The problem we have here, young man, is the very same problem faced by the major film studios. We have been caught in the midst of a spiraling inflation. We are unable to meet our overhead. Else why do you think in the year since Mother passed on, the Bishop has not seen fit to make my appointment formal? You see," she said, as Emma huddled closer to Clifford, "they are trying to freeze us out."

108

"But why?" Emma asked.

"It has been almost four years since we had a new applicant. And our number has dwindled through attrition. There are only a handful of us left." She sat up straight. "The Bishop has been advised to shut the convent and sell the land to cover losses in other areas of the Archdiocese."

"That's awful."

"It's such a beautiful building," Clifford said.

"Our Lady of the Apparition is one of the finest neo-Gothic examples in the quarter. It is the responsibility of those who remain to stop them from turning our order into chaos."

Emma stifled a smile. "Is there really a nun shortage?"

"When I was a novice the halls were filled with young girls eager to serve."

"What happened?" Clifford asked.

Sister Marcella shrugged. "Times have changed. In my day, a good percentage of girls from respectable families grew up knowing they would someday enter the sisterhood. Today," she said with a sigh, "everyone wants to be a stewardess!"

"And so you plan to cover the deficit by offering accommodations for tourists?" Clifford said. "It's a brilliant idea!"

"Oh, I knew you were the right people to talk to as soon as I read your chapter on Rome! You really *can* do the Vatican on next to nothing."

"Sister, what is it you're offering here?" Emma asked, taking out her notebook.

"Single rooms furnished with the traditional simplicity of the finest in clerical accommodations."

"Which means?"

"A bed and a Bible."

"That's it?" she asked.

"Several rooms have a stool and a coat hook. Naturally, I would expect to charge more for those."

Emma sat back. She put her pad in her lap and looked at Clifford. He was pursing his lips, searching for an angle.

"What about food?" he asked.

"With all due modesty, before we fell upon hard times, it was to our convent that all the priests came to eat." She smiled broadly. "Oh, I just know if we are but mentioned in your book, our halls will be filled once again with the bustle of silent pilgrims."

"How much are you planning to charge?" Clifford asked.

"Well, considering the competition, very little. I needn't tell you what an appalling tourist trap Lourdes has become. An absolute disgrace. We wish to appeal to the more discerning pilgrim. The pity is that we did not put the plan into operation sooner. But blessed Mother Minvielle had a rather laissez-faire attitude toward the leisure industries. Otherwise, we would have a piece of the action by now. Be on the map, as it were. However, we are a hearty group, and we are prepared to pull ourselves up by our Oxfords."

"How much are you planning to charge?" Clifford repeated.

"You must consider the following. One, we are tucked safely away from the hubbub and hawkers of sordid Parisian night life. Two, we are in a particularly attractive setting for quiet contemplation. And three, the weary traveler need not cope with the burdensome problem of dressing for dinner."

"Why not?" Emma asked.

Sister Marcella's face brightened. "We each eat alone in our rooms. Of course, if a guest chooses to dine out, we never lock the gates until five."

"A.M. or P.M.?" Emma asked.

110

"Such witty people. Be sure to note that guests may read in their rooms until seven."

"P.M.," Emma muttered.

"Sister, will it be American or European plan?"

"It is neither American plan nor European plan." Sister Marcella raised both hands to the heavens. "It is His plan!"

Emma's eyes widened as she watched the sleeves of Sister Marcella's white habit fall back to reveal a red quilted ski jacket. She poked Clifford and motioned toward the door.

"How many rooms do you have, Sister?" Clifford asked, making a point of ignoring Emma.

"With or without windows?" she asked.

"Both."

"We have twenty-four rooms with windows and twenty-two without. Of the twenty-two without, there are seven with no doors."

"No doors?" Clifford asked.

"Just a minute, Cliffy!" Emma said, as she wrote down the specifications. "Now, just how many is that with hooks and stools?"

"Nineteen. Of which twelve have windows and two have no doors. Now, you mustn't forget that every room, from the most modest to the deluxe—"

"The ones with hooks and stools," Emma clarified for Clifford.

"Every single room," Sister Marcella continued, "will have a matching color-coordinated sheet, blanket and hand towel by Yves Saint Laurent."

"Saint Laurent?" Emma asked.

"I have a nephew in the business. Morning porridge will be served in Limoges seconds, courtesy of my niece. I see no reason why Christianity and good taste cannot go hand in hand."

111

"Well," Emma said, taking a deep breath, "here's what it boils down to. Let me read this back to you, Clifford dearest darling, so you get the full picture." She cleared her throat. "They have twelve rooms with windows and doors and hooks and stools, twelve rooms with windows and doors but no hooks and stools, five rooms with doors and hooks and stools but no windows, ten rooms with doors but no hooks and stools and no windows, two rooms with hooks and stools but no windows and no doors, and five rooms with no windows, no doors, no hooks and no stools."

"You know, I think you just might have something here, Sister," he said with great conviction for Emma's benefit. "But the question is still How much?"

Sister Marcella leaned over and spoke with great intensity. "I know we're not the Inter-Continental, where they get four hundred francs a night."

Emma shrugged. "Well, they've got a snack bar, a newspaper stand. Running water. Heat. That builds up the overhead."

"Exactly," Sister Marcella said. "I certainly wouldn't expect to charge four hundred francs a night."

"What about baths? Showers?" Emma asked.

"Well, now," she said, playfully shaking a finger at her, "you're slipping back into that four-hundred-franc philosophy again."

"Sister, you *still* haven't told me the rates," Clifford said.

"For one of our deluxe rooms . . ."

"Window, door, hook and stool," Emma clarified.

". . . which comes with two meals plus a daily blessing, I think we could bring it in somewhat under a hundred francs."

"Twenty bucks a night?" Clifford asked in horror.

"With meals!" Sister Marcella reminded him.

"And hooks and stools!" Emma added.

"That's impossible, Sister! It's too much money!"

Sister Marcella raised an eyebrow. "For Heaven's sake, we're offering atmosphere, religion and Saint Laurent!" She paused. "Ninety francs!" Clifford shook his head. Sister Marcella sighed. "It could be done for seventy-five, I suppose. That is, if we get the PR we need. Not least of which is a rave in your guide."

Clifford said firmly, "Our book is called *The Penny Pincher's Guide.*"

"Obviously you intend to pinch all of those pennies out of *me!*" She narrowed her eyes. "Seventy! I'm preparing a multimedia presentation for the Bishop. Sister Henriette is taking before and after pictures. It was Sister Berthe's idea to add a sound track. Something from *The Sound of Music.*"

"Sister, we have literally millions of readers who depend on us for low-budget accommodations and meals."

"Sixty!" She waited and then said sharply, "We have to charge *something*, Mr. Benjamin! This is not a kibbutz!"

"Suppose you didn't include meals?" he asked. "How low could you go?"

"No meals? But Sister Mathilde has already planned Coquille St. Francis, Boeuf Bernadette, Apple Pius—"

"How low?"

"And still include Saint Laurent?"

"No. Bare bones. No frills."

Sister Marcella sighed. "No meals. No Saint Laurent. No Limoges. No scented candles." She pursed her lips. "No fun. Twenty!"

Clifford beamed. "Sister, you've got yourself a deal! We'll have to work fast from here on. We've only got tonight. But if everything checks out by morning, you'll be in the spring edition."

"Tonight?" Emma stared at Clifford.

"I insist you dine with us." Sister Marcella got up.

113

"It would be a pleasure," Clifford said.

"I know we'll get the money from somewhere to feed you. Don't move, you two—I'll be right back." She hurried down the corridor."What a terrific find!" Clifford said, taking out his notebook.

Emma shrugged. "If you have Catholic tastes."

"Emma," he said, taking her by the shoulders, "this could be even bigger than the gondoliers' cafeteria!"

"Cliffy, you're not seriously considering spending tonight under the same roof as Attila the Nun?"

"This is a scoop, Em! It's cheap, it's clean, it's honest. It would be an incredible experience for any kid—"

"Like us?"

"Don't worry. I'll get you the cell next door." He smiled and kissed her on the nose. "I'll even spring for one with a hook and a stool." He took his forefinger and began tapping on her nose. "We could send messages to each other."

"What did you just say?" she asked.

"I said let's meet in the herb garden and do it." Emma tapped the tip of his nose. "What did *you* say?"

"I said Not tonight, Clifford. I have a headache."

"C'mon, Em. It's our last night in Paris!"

"That's the whole point. I don't want to spend it here at the Celibate Hilton."

"Then what *do* you want, Emma?"

"It seems we stood and talked like this before." She got up. "I'm not staying here, Clifford. I'll do my job from nine to five. And I'll do it good. But I won't sleep here. What's more, I won't even pretend I like any of this. Any fool who had enough money would never stay here."

"And you're any fool?" he asked.

"I guess so."

He stood up and put his arms around her. She pulled

back. Almost involuntarily. "Em, what's happening? Why did you pull away?"

"I don't know."

"In all the years, Emma, you never before told me you had a headache."

She shrugged. "What an ingrate I am. To have a headache when Diamond Jim wants to get me a room with a hook and a stool!" Emma's eyes filled with tears. She pressed her lips together, fighting back the rage that was replacing the sadness. She began to breathe heavily, almost uncontrollably. Emma raised her hand and, staring directly into Clifford's eyes, slapped him hard. She was even more stunned than he. "Oh, Cliffy," she gasped.

Clifford's eyes searched her face for an explanation. But Emma turned and ran down the corridor. He watched until she was out of sight and then sat down on the stone bench. It was very, very cold.

THE office of the Louis Q's chef de cuisine was furnished as a room in a hunting lodge. The pebbly walls were crisscrossed with wood beams. Surrounding the stone fireplace was a collection of mounted animal heads. Xavier Ronay leaned across his writing desk, narrowed his eyes, pointed a finger and said fervently, "It must be tarragon!"

Dwight raised his arms in despair. He leaned back in the stuffed leather chair. "Never!" he proclaimed, refusing the Greeks entry to Troy.

"But what is wrong with tarragon?"

Dwight leaned forward and spoke in earnest to his old friend. "It's not me! That's what's wrong. It simply is not me!"

Xavier banged his fist on the table. "What are you saying, it is not you? When·God looked in at the Sistine

Chapel even He did not say that! I have spent weeks creating this dish and you tell me you are not tarragon!"

"Dear boy, you know how much I appreciate the honor. I have always said in print you are one of the world's greatest chefs. To have you create a dish for me guarantees my immortality in the esteemed company of Pèche Melba, Chicken Tetrazzini and the Napoleon!"

"So? That is not so bad as a bullet in the head."

"You have known me long enough, Xavier. My integrity is impeccable! I cannot in all honesty lend my name to a dish I do not like. Perhaps, if instead of the tarragon you considered using sorrel—"

"No! No! No! There is already a Saumon à l'Oseille! I am proposing a culinary breakthrough with my Saumon Simon."

"I suppose dill is rather passé."

"Dill?" he repeated with horror. He shook his head. "It is very sad what has happened to dill. Tragique. They are using it everywhere. Every fool in Paris is snipping fresh dill as carelessly as if he were circumcising his wife's lover. No! No! No! I am afraid, my dear friend, the good old days of dill are finished. Which is why I have proposed to begin a new era with my Saumon Simon."

"Then you refuse to substitute something for the tarragon?"

"Aha! You, my dear friend, think you are the only one with integrity, eh? Ha! The tarragon stays! The *name* will go!"

"So be it, dear boy. If there is no other way. Flattered as I am to be immortalized by a talent such as yours."

Xavier pointed to the heads on the wall. "But you are obviously not as flattered as the moose was. I am lucky the moose did not speak English."

"You're running out of wall space, you know. I presume these are rather special."

117

"No. In the dawn they are all the same."

"I've never understood that side of your character. Killing for sport."

"Would you prefer me to hand the head of a chicken over the mantel? I tell you, Dwight, it has been a very strange part of my life. It began while I was still in cooking school. A trout. A lobster. A pigeon. Then as we learned about carving meat, I became possessed. Cooking was not enough." He looked at Dwight and paused. "But I do not think you have come here today to talk of hunting."

"Au contraire, mon ami. That's precisely why I am here. Lily and I are doing the Louis from top to bottom."

"A full tour of inspection?" he asked in horror.

"I'm afraid so."

Xavier leaned back in his chair. "Ah, but not the kitchen?" Dwight nodded Yes. "Mon Dieu, I have not been in the kitchen since . . . since . . . I cannot remember. Oh, my dear friend, you bring back such bad memories. The heat. Always the incroyable heat. And the noise. The sweating." His eyes narrowed as he changed his tone. "Of course, the kitchens of the Louis are above reproach."

"I can leave no stove unturned, mon ami."

"This is even more depressing than the tarragon. Is there not some way, some more civilized way in which to handle your inspection?"

"I fear we are again facing that old demon, integrity." He avoided Xavier's eyes. "You know," he said, opening the bidding, "it is quite painful for me to lose my rightful place in the gastronomic hall of fame."

"The kitchen is fine. Trust me," Xavier said, beginning to show his hand. "You have known me long enough. I give you my word. Do not make me go in there!"

Dwight smiled. "Are you suggesting I compromise my principles because of our long and valued friendship?"

118

"I would never do such a thing!" Xavier turned up his last card. "I would no sooner do that than you would suggest I substitute for tarragon finely chopped bulb of fennel." He rose from the chair, his hands suddenly expressive and graceful as he swept in the winner's chips. "And on top of the fennel, to crown Le Saumon Simon, a single perfect lacy leaf!"

LILY strode down the second-floor corridor of the Louis Q. She wore an apricot velvet tunic over her lemon silk dress. Around her neck was a lemon chiffon scarf. In her hand was an apricot leather clipboard. In her heart was righteousness.

All the forces of evil had conspired against her— l'affaire de la marmalade, l'affaire de Murphy and worst of all, l'affaire de Dwight. Lily was at last ready to play St. Joan. If she only had understood what it meant to be a savior twenty years ago! The reviews would have been spectacular.

Without knocking, she opened the door behind which lay the target of her sneak attack. She stepped into a world of beige suede walls and Barcelona chairs. A thoroughly modern mademoiselle looked across the reception desk through her lavender eye shadow. "Bonjour, Madame."

"I wish to see the Gouvernante Générale."

"Do you have an appointment?"

"I am Lily Simon," she announced with an authority that negated the need for an appointment to see the Pope.

"One moment, please." She buzzed the inner office. "Madame Simon est ici à vous voir. . . . Oui." She smiled and signaled for Lily to enter.

The Gouvernante Générale stood behind a chrome-and-glass desk. A very chic white flower was nestled in her

119

very blond hair. She wore a pale gray pinstripe pantsuit with an ivory satin blouse. By no means your everyday chambermaid, Lily thought.

"Madame," Marie-Thérèse began with a smile. "What can I say?"

Lily stared for a long moment. "How about 'ouch'?" She laughed and sat back. "Relax, Mademoiselle. I'm here this morning to discuss your role as housekeeper, not as femme fatale. Bit players have never interested me. You see, darling, I have a rather unfair advantage over you."

"Aside from being older and wiser?"

Lily smiled. "Yes. I've been there before. Often. For all the years Dwight and I were on the stage, we each quite believed the roles we had. I've been his wife *and* his mistress. We've had hundreds of glorious affairs set in Padua, Philadelphia, Berlin, Vienna, London—everywhere! I know just how convincing he can be."

Marie-Thérèse acknowledged Lily with an icy smile. "How may the Gouvernante be of help to you?"

"I wish to be reassured that the opinion my husband and I had of the Louis Q is still valid."

"I see. You wish an inspection tour."

"Yes."

"You wish to observe the staff." The phone rang.

"Yes."

Marie-Thérèse continued without taking her eyes from Lily. Seemingly, she had no intention of answering the phone. "But most of all you wish to observe me."

"Yes." Brring. Brring. "Do feel free, Mademoiselle, to go about your business as though I were a mere speck on the wall."

"With pleasure." Brring. Brring.

Lily shrugged and finally took her eyes from Marie-Thérèse to glance at the phone. "Someone might be out of Kleenex." Lily leaned back in her chair. Brring. Brring.

"Mmm. Perhaps an overflowing commode. I'm just dying to find out."

Marie-Thérèse reached for the phone. "Well, Madame, as long as you are dying." She brought the receiver to her ear. "Oui?"

If only she weren't so young. So clever. The others had all been pretty, but they had lacked the sophistication of this supersonic Mrs. Bridges. Lily smiled as Marie-Thérèse put down the receiver. "You look unhappy."

"An early arrival. They are so bothersome. The room is not yet ready, but the guest is impatient." She stood up. "I am pleased for you, Madame. You will be able to judge us in a crisis situation," she said sarcastically.

Lily stood up. "Bombs away, darling!"

"FIRED?" Dwight asked in horror. "Marcel Oriole was fired?"

Fernand Duprat, the newly promoted Premier Maître d'Hôtel, sighed. "I could not believe it either. He was like a father to me."

"Good heavens." Dwight pulled a chair away from the table and sat down. L'Alouette Ancienne, the main dining salon of the Louis Q, was not yet open to the public. "I've known Marcel for years. He was a superb maître."

Fernand sat down. "Would you like some coffee?"

Dwight shook his head. "Marcel knew I don't drink coffee."

"Mon Dieu."

"Marcel knew," he said sadly.

Fernand leaned over to Dwight. "I am only forty years old. I am not yet ready to be Premier Maître. I told them that."

"But why was he fired?"

Fernand stiffened. "Perhaps you would care for some-

121

thing from the bar?" He knew from Dwight's look that he had again made the wrong suggestion. "Just to help you get over the shock?" Dwight shook his head. "You see," Fernand confided, "there is no chance for me in this job. As a maître, I was fine. My tartare, my crêpes"—he put his fingers to his lips and kissed them—"were superb. The best. I can filet a fish like a surgeon."

"Yes, Fernand. You have always served us beautifully."

"But I am not ready for the big step to Premier Maître. Mon Dieu, do you know that Marcel was forty-four when he took over? And that was only because Roger Abadie had a massive coronary while boning a squab for a Swedish prince. Marcel, like the great maître he was, picked up the knife almost before it had fallen to the floor. He snapped his fingers. They removed Roger's body, and the carving continued without missing a beat. The squab was saved, and Marcel became the youngest Premier Maître in the history of the Louis!"

"An extraordinary tale!"

"Someday they will make a film of Marcel's life. *Le Maître des Maîtres.* A fighter in the Résistance. A hero at the carving board. For such a man to have fallen! To have fallen because of the . . ." Fernand took a deep breath.

"Because of the what?" Dwight asked.

"Because of the man who fired him," Fernand said nervously.

Dwight took a long look at the pubescent Premier Maître. He narrowed his eyes and lowered his voice. "I am here today for a surprise inspection."

"Mon Dieu!"

"Surprise!"

"But it is my first day!"

Dwight reached across and held Fernand by the shoulder. "You may have come on duty as a maître d'hôtel de rang, but you're coming back a Premier Maître d'Hôtel!"

122

"Do you think I can do it?"

Dwight stood up. "The entire restaurant is depending on you. They who must chop and stir but cannot serve."

Fernand stood up. "So be it."

Dwight walked to the door as though he were just entering the restaurant. "Bitte, Herr Ober," Dwight began in his most arrogant German accent. "Haben sie einen Tisch am Fenster?"

"If you were German, I would instead seat you near the radiators in the corner. The British go between the radiators and the windows. The window tables are reserved for the Italians. The French—we do get one or two a week—are of course given the best tables up front, as are movie stars or anyone who is beautiful."

"And the Americans?"

Fernand shrugged. "Anywhere. Either they do not complain or no matter where you seat them it is wrong. Of course, we try always to seat them next to their own kind."

"In the 'pigpen,' " Dwight said.

"Marcel told you? Well, I too believe a restaurant is like an art gallery. It is the maître's art to arrange the patrons as though they were paintings. That is why you always put the little gray people in the back. They do not add to the élégance parisienne of the room."

"May I ask you something, Fernand?" Dwight looked deep into his eyes. "Am I not the leading expert in this field?"

"Oui. To be recognized by you is an honor for anyone."

"Fernand, I am beginning to recognize *you.*"

"But Monsieur, I have only just begun."

"That is what makes me an expert. Any fool can tell how the dinner was after he's eaten it. I sense a unique talent for one so young." He held Fernand's arm. "Consider for a moment the first time Mozart's teacher heard him play."

"Monsieur."

123

"What happened to Marcel will never happen to you."

"It will not?"

"Never. You would never do anything as foolish." Dwight looked at Fernand and waited. It took only a moment.

"You are right. I would never have served the Mandarin Orange!"

"My God!"

"Mon Dieu!"

"So that's what we did to dear Marcel!"

"What will happen to me?"

"All because of the marmalade!"

"It is the end for me!" Fernand whimpered.

"And for me too, goddamn it!"

THE chambermaid was smoothing the bed pillows. The valet stood on a ladder in front of the marble fireplace cleaning the mirror. "Bonjour, Annette. Bonjour, Georges." Marie-Thérèse stepped across the vacuum-cleaner cord and entered Room 355.

"Mademoiselle la Gouvernante," Annette said, smiling nervously. She looked at Lily. "We have not finished."

"Bonjour, bonjour," Lily said brightly. "Please don't concern yourselves about me. Just go right on with whatever it is you're doing to those pillows." Lily's voice changed dramatically. "I'm sure you have your reasons for slapping instead of plumping. I don't want to disturb you either," she said cheerily as Georges looked down from his ladder. "Else you'll forget to clean the absolutely evil streak on your left. See it, there, darling? A vôtre gauche? Oui! Bravo!" She turned back to Marie-Thérèse. "As long as they're in here, why don't we girls go to the bathroom?"

Lily walked into the pale blue tile room. She inhaled

deeply and began nodding her head. "Pleasant. Very fresh. Bon!" Marie-Thérèse folded her arms and leaned against the door frame. Lily smiled with the good cheer one reserves for greeting terminal patients. "Now on to the waterworks! After all, isn't water what the bathroom's all about?" Lily turned on the faucet in the sink. She counted aloud as she waited for the water to warm. "One peccadillo, two peccadillos, three peccadillos . . . fine, just fine. You know," she said, turning off the hot water and switching on the cold, "nothing upsets Dwight more than having to wait for the hot water." She walked to the tub and turned the hot-water faucet. "One meaningless fling, two meaningless flings, three . . . there! We were in Ravenna, having an absolutely glorious time. Dwight had pinched the chambermaid a few times, and so the service was extraordinarily good." Lily raised her voice to be heard above the water running into the sink and tub. "Of course, once she began changing the linens twice a day, I suspected it had gone a bit further than usual." She laughed. "Then one morning Dwight got orange water when he turned on the faucet. Well, that was the end of poor what's-her-name." Lily walked over to the toilet and flushed it. She nodded approvingly at the pressure. "Still, he always sends lovely things to them once we get home." Lily turned off the tub faucet and then the sink. "You'll see." She unfolded the towels and sniffed them. "Did I say Ravenna? What could I be thinking of? The orange water was in Rapallo." Lily was examining the hems on each towel for rips. "You must forgive me, it's so hard keeping track. Ravenna was the chambermaid Dwight promised to marry." Having finished water and linen, she moved on to paper. First, she took a facial tissue and rubbed it between her fingers. Then she snapped off a piece of toilet tissue. "Poor dear. Pity is, he believes what he says at the time." She crumpled the tissues and dropped them onto the floor. "Ah, the curse of Thespis!" She opened the medicine chest and began unwrapping the bathroom glasses. "I suppose I should be furious with him." She ran her finger around the rim for chips. "But he really suffers more than they do." She unfolded the shower cap to make certain there were no holes. She felt the hot towel rack. "You'll see." Lily turned on the lights around the makeup mirror. She turned on the infrared heat lamp in the ceiling and the ultraviolet sun lamp. "Goody," she said, walking out of the room. "Now everything can be seen for exactly what it is."

Marie-Thérèse stared at the chaos. The sink and tub had puddles of water around them. Towels lay crumpled on the floor. Shredded tissues littered the bath mat. Glasses were overturned on the shelf and their wrappers strewn on the counter. Bars of soap lay melting in the sink. An open shower cap was tossed over a makeup light. That was exactly the way it was.

An abstract painting titled *Céleri et Laitue* hung on the wall behind the rosewood-and-chrome desk at which Alphonse Menard, the Louis Q's distinguished Directeur de Restauration, sat eating an Egg McMuffin. Dwight sipped a glass of champagne as the dapper Alphonse brushed a crumb from his waxed moustache. "What a fool Ponce de León was!"

"What?"

"It is true." He pointed to the greasy waxed paper. "*This* is the fountain of youth. Learning to accept change. Learning each day to be moderne." He leaned across the desk. "I tell you, Dwight, as we were brought up on Carême and Escoffier, and today they worship Bocuse and Point, tomorrow it will be McDonald!"

"Dear boy, that thing has gone to your head."

126

"As it should. It is food for thought. I eat one of these dreadful things every day to remind me. Food, like couture, changes with the times. Those who do not change with it become old very quickly. Outmoded. Passé. The replaceable parts of society."

"Would you, then, discard the great masters? Close the Louvre?"

"Jamais! The great masters are where they belong. But the sweet young girls in miniskirts who visit them will think nostalgically about their Big Macs as Proust thought about his Madeleines."

"You're really serious about this."

"Mon ami, did you ever think you would see women without brassieres walking down the Champs-Elysées? Mais, non. Did you ever think we would go to the cinema to laugh at comedies about the war?" Alphonse shook his finger at Dwight. "If we have no inhibitions about tits or Nazis, why fight against margarine?"

Dwight walked around the pedestal on which sat an enormous bronze green pea. He peeled back the movable metal stem. "Then what must you think of me? On an expedition to ensure that the Philistines have not invaded the kitchens of the Louis?"

Alphonse shrugged. "I think, dear Dwight, if I were a rich American I would be very fortunate to have someone like you en garde for me." Alphonse cleared his throat. "Of course, that presumes I would be obsessed with the quality of the toilet paper and whether the ashtrays were emptied at sufficiently frequent intervals."

Dwight turned angrily. "Or whether I preferred the Dark Seville to the Mandarin Orange?"

He looked up. "That too."

"How could you have fired Marcel?"

"I could not. I did not. It was Pierre." He smiled. "Le Directeur has never eaten an Egg McMuffin."

"I feel dreadful about it. There have been hundreds of waiters and clerks we've insisted be fired."

"And now you are so famous, they fire maîtres and chefs. Congratulations."

"You know, dear boy, there are times you're quite dislikable."

"Oui. It is one of my saving graces. But stepping out of character for just one moment, let me assure you not to worry about Marcel. He has found an even higher-paying position."

"It's not Marcel I'm worried about."

"Then at least both of us have not stepped out of character."

Dwight absently fingered the plastic petals of the cauliflower sculpture that stood in the corner. "I've known you a long time, Alphonse."

"Be careful," he said warily, "I am not yet ordained." Alphonse smiled. He anticipated what Dwight wanted to say. "She is very lovely. I envy you Marie-Thérèse."

"You know?"

"A hotel is like a circus. Everyone watches the bareback rider. You must give us credit for being at least as interested in your sex life as in your marmalade preference. How dull you must think we are."

"I am in love with her."

Alphonse raised his eyebrows. "Then you have indeed found your own Egg McMuffin."

"Yes."

"But you find it too rich a diet."

"Clearly I'm not as sophisticated as I thought."

"Certainly not, if you are considering giving up the entrée for the hors d'oeuvre."

"You think I'm insane."

"No, of course not. It is merely the upbringing. Americans have never known how to eat properly. I do not mean which knife to use. You have never understood the composition of a meal."

"Alphonse, I do not like my work anymore."

"That is clear from what Xavier and Fernand tell me."

"You have spoken to them?"

"We sometimes discuss things other than the price of artichokes."

"I still love Lily."

"But your book has become *Mrs. Simon Says*."

"It doesn't seem important anymore."

"You do not trust your old values."

"*You* seem to have a grip on the realities of life, Alphonse. What do you advise?"

Alphonse sat back in his chair. "I think you do not have the correct perspective. It is like the joke, Dwight. A man goes to his doctor and says, 'Doctor, I have a terrible problem. For breakfast, I eat fraises de bois, croissant and coffee. After breakfast, when I go to the toilet, out come fraises de bois, croissant and coffee. For lunch, I have salade niçoise. I go to the bathroom and out comes salade niçoise. For dinner, I have caviar, rack of lamb and a soufflé. When I go, out come caviar, rack of lamb and a soufflé. Doctor, what should I do?' The doctor looks at the patient, he thinks for a moment and he says, 'Eat shit'!"

LILY stood in front of the open closet. Annette was remaking the bed after Lily's devastation. Georges was putting back the papers that lined the drawers. Marie-Thérèse sat on the sofa, almost not hearing the steady patter coming from the closet.

"You know, darling, if truth be told, I love it when there aren't enough hangers, as there aren't nearly enough now.

129

It gives me an immediate opportunity to call the chamber-maid and let her know precisely what my requirements are."

Pierre stormed into the room. He looked at Annette and Georges and, to his horror, saw Marie-Thérèse sitting on the sofa, one leg swinging languidly back and forth. "What is going on here? Why isn't this room ready? I have the Baroness Frieda Krupp von Wittenberg downstairs getting drunk in the lobby, compliments of me."

"Fat Fritzi?" Lily called out. "Here?" Pierre's mouth dropped open as she stepped from the closet. "Well, what a hoot that is!" She looked at Marie-Thérèse. "Darling, why in the world didn't you include her name on the list?"

Marie-Thérèse watched Pierre's eyes bulge. She looked at Lily, smiled and nodded. "Madame, you are very good at this game."

"Gouvernante!" Pierre shouted. "You were the one?"

"Pshaw," Lily said, pronouncing the "p." "There I go again. Now listen to me, Pierre." She took him by the arm. "I must have your oath, on Chevalier's grave, that you will do nothing nasty to our little Marie."

"I cannot believe she was the informer!"

"A little harmless collaboration. You French are so paranoid over that concept it's a wonder Moët and Chandon ever made it!"

Marie-Thérèse stood up. "Madame, will you at least allow me to defend myself?"

"Oh, you poor, sweet thing," Lily oozed. "If only you could!" She walked to Marie-Thérèse with outstretched arms and grabbed her firmly. "Don't you think I know what you're going through?" She turned to Pierre. "I tell you this in the utmost confidence." She looked back at Annette and Georges. "Do you hear, everybody? In the utmost confidence!" Lily smiled benevolently into Marie-Thérèse's blazing eyes. "She was forced to do it! The poor

130

girl has the hots for my husband. *He* persuaded her to be a traitor. Ah, that naughty puss. He could have convinced Gertrude Stein a rose wasn't a rose!" Marie-Thérèse pulled away. Lily walked toward the terrace. The lighting was better there. "I suppose," she sighed, standing in the doorway so that the sun would catch fire in her hair, "if I weren't so accustomed to it, I'd be terribly embarrassed. But what am I do do? The man is a sexual kleptomaniac."

There was a pause as Pierre looked from Lily to Marie-Thérèse. "I do not know what to say," he said.

"I do." It was Dwight.

Annette opened her mouth and sat down on the bed. Georges, who was already kneeling at the bottom drawer, sat back on his heels. Pierre took out a handkerchief and mopped his brow. Marie-Thérèse turned to Dwight with tears in her eyes. And Lily wished the clock had stopped five minutes ago. "Darling," she said without looking at him. Then, referring as much to her indiscretion as to his, "What ever shall we do?"

"I would have played the scene differently, Lily. Much more intimately. But since you've assembled a cast of thousands, they might as well be in on the finale."

"You must pardon me." Pierre turned to leave.

"Don't!" Dwight shouted. "I want you and you and you," he said looking at Annette and Georges, "to hear what I am about to say."

"I suppose I do deserve your being miffed at me."

"Lily, what you did was unspeakable!"

"Oh, don't I ever know it, Dwight! I never meant to get the little tyke in so much trouble. But you know me. Put a nickel in my mouth . . ."

"I have reached a decision."

"Good. Then we can buy her something in Paris and save the postage."

"I'm not getting any younger, Lily."

131

"I know. Who is? These little episodes must be absolute hell on your nerves. I know they are on mine."

"Lily! Don't you hear what I'm saying? I am leaving you." Marie-Thérèse looked up in astonishment. She put her hands to her face and began to sob. "After the tour, when this commitment is over, I am leaving you and going away with Marie-Thérèse."

Lily took a deep breath. She sat down. "Exit. Curtain. End of Act One. Get your red-hots here."

Dwight put his arms around Marie-Thérèse. "I'm sorry for what you've been put through."

"It doesn't matter now," she cried. "No one can hurt me now."

Lily sat staring at the wall. Pierre walked quickly to the door. He motioned for Annette and Georges to leave with him. Dwight led Marie-Thérèse out. He never looked back. Lily ran a hand across her forehead as though she could brush away the fears. But there were too many. There was the fear of losing Dwight. The fear of growing old. The fear of being alone. And, as she looked around the room, the overwhelming fear that Georges had forgotten to refill the stationery folder for Baroness Frieda Krupp von Wittenberg.

ETIT Meurice was not in Paris on Saturday, August 26, 1944. He was not there as Le Général stood beneath the Arc de Triomphe and relit the flame at the Tomb of the Unknown Soldier. He did not cheer at two o'clock that sunny, cloudless day as Le Général began his victory march down the Champs-Elysées. He was, instead, pacing outside a schoolroom in Epernay while the American doctors worked to save Claude's leg.

It was a sunny, cloudless morning nearly thirty-five years later when Petit Meurice finally stood beneath the Arc de Triomphe to begin his liberation march. He appeared every inch the boulevardier in his cream-colored suit with widely spaced brown stripes, tan shoes, white shirt, brown tie and best brown cap. As though planning a wonderful surprise for himself, the wish that comes true when one has blown out the birthday candles, he closed his eyes while still staring at the flame. Petit Meurice turned about face, his eyes tight shut. He smiled and opened them. There it was! As it had been that August 26! The very heart of the city! The Champs-Elysées!

> *The last time I saw Paris*
> *Her heart was warm and gay,*
> *I heard the laughter of her heart*
> *In ev'ry street café.*

Petit Meurice dodged the traffic rounding the Etoile as if stepping across a pond from stone to stone. He was startled as someone bumped into him. People did not bump into one another in Epernay.

He peered in at Le Drugstore. What was it? Un restaurant? Un tabac? Une pharmacie? Une librairie? Une boutique? Une boulangerie? All of them. All in one. It was a breathtaking sight. What a number Fred could have done in such a place! He looked closely at the plates of those in the café. Even the food was exotic. He would come back later for lunch and order something he had never eaten. A hamburger! He began to laugh, saying the word over and over in his mind. Hamburger! Hamburger! Hamburger!

> *The last time I saw Paris,*
> *Her trees were dressed for spring,*
> *And lovers walked beneath those trees,*
> *And birds found songs to sing.*

Farther down the Champs was the Bureau de Tourisme de Paris. Such beautiful pictures. He pushed the glass door and walked inside. The young man behind the counter did not look up.

"Bonjour," Petit Meurice said.

". . . jour," he sighed.

"I am going to walk down the Champs-Elysées. I will stop to visit with someone. Then I would like to know how to walk to Notre Dame."

"Walk? Not even Quasimodo walked. It is endless. So boring." He sighed again and took out a map. "However, on this route," he said, carelessly marking a thick yellow line, "you are least likely to be run over, or die of carbon monoxide poisoning."

"Merci." Petit Meurice picked up the map and hesitated. It could not be the right way. De Gaulle could not have been afraid of carbon monoxide. He looked at the young man, who had returned to his book. He held up the map. "Monsieur, is this the route of the liberation march of Général Charles de Gaulle?"

The man raised his eyes without moving his head. He tightened the corners of his mouth and reached out for the map. He tore it up. As he penciled a new line on a new map, he said, "You should have told me you wanted the De Gaulle waltz. One, two, three," he mumbled as he drew the line. "One, two, three."

"Merci." Petit Meurice smiled. "I have been considering a holiday in Epernay," he began in his most elegant tone. "Perhaps you have some information on Epernay?"

"Epernaaaaaay?" he asked, giving the last syllable the full range of his disbelief. "For how long?"

Petit Meurice shrugged. "For the season."

"I wouldn't give it more than a morning." He reached behind the counter for a brochure. "Here. This is all we have on Epernay."

"Have you ever been there? It is where they make champagne." The man nodded. "Do you not like champagne?"

"I like champagne. I also like caviar, but I do not take my holiday in a sturgeon's stomach."

"Did you know Epernay was very important during the war?"

"Which war?"

Petit Meurice stood frozen.

I dodged the same old taxicabs
That I had dodged for years;
The chorus of their squeaky horns
Was music to my ears.

He continued walking along the Champs. All the women were so beautiful. They moved past him like an assortment of finely wrapped candies on a conveyor belt. Hard candies. He stopped at the Air France office.

"Monsieur?"

"Bonjour," he said, leaning on the counter. "I have been thinking for a number of years about a trip."

"I would be happy to help you, Monsieur. Where do you wish to go?"

He leaned closer to her. "Lisbon," he whispered. "But I have heard it is impossible to get to Lisbon."

"Not on our *Lisbon for Lovers* package. Three days and two nights, including two lunches, one dinner, a bullfight, Estoril and a book of discount coupons for shops and restaurants. What day would you like to leave?"

If only Ingrid Bergman and Paul Henreid had gone directly to Air France! "Tell me," he began quietly. "What about . . . Berlin?"

She smiled. "You will have a wonderful time on our *Moonlight in Berlin* package. Everything worth seeing, starting at the bombed-out church, the site of the Reichstag and all that sort of thing if you're a history buff. Then,

136

after dark, we take you to the six top night spots at no additional cost, including gratuities and champagne."

"Champagne?"

"May I make a reservation for you?"

> *The last time I saw Paris*
> *Her heart was warm and gay.*
> *No matter how they change her*
> *I'll remember her that way.*

The office of *Paris-Watch* was at 47, avenue des Champs-Elysées. Louise Vigran worked in the subscription department. She was in charge of address changes.

"Joseph sent you?" she whispered, looking up from her worn copy of *Le Code Postal et Vous.* She put a nail-bitten finger to her lips to signal him to keep quiet. A very plump woman in her late thirties, Louise Vigran had three pencils lodged in the curls of her unruly brown hair. She wore an oversize heavy knit sweater whose weave spread noticeably as it covered her enormous breasts. Her harlequin-shaped glasses were attached to a string around her neck.

"I have a message from Joseph."

"Shhhhh!" she said. "Sit down," she whispered. "Just push those envelopes onto the floor. They're No Forwarding Address Given, and to hell with them." Petit Meurice was careful to arrange the envelopes neatly. "Either they give you no address or they are like R. Villeneuve, who changes his/her address every month. No sooner do I get R. Villeneuve's address plate settled in the right tray than he/she moves again. Always lovely little notes from him/her. But that and one franc fifty will get you on the Métro."

"The plan has been changed."

"What plan?"

"The plan you and Joseph had."

137

"Which plan?" She became frightened.

"You know."

She narrowed her eyes. "You mean, The Plan?"

"Yes."

"He told you?" she gasped.

"There was no choice."

"My God. He said they would kill him if they found out." She waited for Petit Meurice to tell her.

"We did not kill him."

Louise Vigran stood up. A pile of envelopes with address changes fell from her lap. She put her hand to her mouth and pointed to him in horror. "You are one of them!"

"Enchanté, Mademoiselle!"

"You have come to kill me!"

"I have come to speak with you."

She began to cry. "It was all his idea," she pleaded as she sat down, crushing a pile of envelopes. "What do I know of such things? I have no imagination. The most exciting thing that happens to me is when R. Villeneuve changes his/her address."

"I have come to speak with you."

"He told me this was to be my ticket out of Address Change and into Editorial." Tears began to fall. "I did not think when he told me I would be out of Circulation that I would be out of circulation." She sniffed deeply and wiped her eyes with her wrists. "So, this is how my subscription gets cancelled." She sat back in the chair and took a deep breath. "What have you done with Joseph?"

"We have done nothing with Joseph. He is one of us."

"Aha! So there is a branch of the Old Boys Club even in the Maquis. Joseph saves his skin while Louise the drudge becomes Addressee Deceased." She grabbed the telephone, but before she could dial, Petit Meurice pulled the cord from the wall.

"Mademoiselle, when I leave this office I shall continue my walk down the Champs-Elysées, across the river Seine and to the Cathedral of Notre-Dame. I shall enjoy my walk, Mademoiselle, because I am confident you will never at any time in your life mention anything about this plan to anyone. I know I need not worry about such a thing ever happening."

"You do not have to worry, Monsieur. Trust me!" she pleaded. "Even the new postal codes terrify me. Do you think I am the type who would make trouble for you?"

He paused and took a breath. "Mademoiselle, I have a cousin who works for Sabatier. He has given me a small four-inch blade that is thinner than a razor."

"My God! You are planning to stab me to death!"

"No, Mademoiselle. I will take you from this office to the basement of a café where we will not be disturbed. There is a single bare light bulb over a long table. I will tie you to the table very securely. Then I will very carefully remove all your clothes."

"My God! You are planning to rape me!"

"No, Mademoiselle. I will take my special knife and begin to slice your nose." Her eyes widened. She put her hand to her mouth. Then to her nose. "I will first slice off all of the skin on one side, and then I will slice off all of the skin on the other side. As though trimming the meat from each breast of a chicken, I will slice away your nose."

"Oh, my God!"

He continued in his most polite manner. He leaned over toward her. She froze against the back of her chair as his forefinger gently traced the outline of her mouth. "Then I shall take my special knife and slice away your lips in a single circular cut. They will fall from your face in one piece."

She slumped in her chair. "I swear. I will never say anything."

139

"Then, while you are lying there, bleeding from your nose and mouth, and trying not to swallow your own blood, I will take a very small mouse and carefully insert him into your vagina."

Petit Meurice moved back as Louise Vigran threw up on her envelopes. He heard her retching as he walked to the elevator. Once downstairs, he walked to the parked car in which Emile sat waiting. "You can take her to the airport now," he said. Petit Meurice left 47, avenue des Champs-Elysées confident he would never have to worry about Louise Vigran.

No matter how they change her
I'll remember her that way.

THERE were always unfamiliar faces at the Café Zola for lunch. Few of the evening regulars worked in the area. The Zola offered Claude a welcome anonymity. There were no polite nods to be acknowledged, no friendly faces reassuring him they knew who he was. Except for Emma Benjamin.

Claude glanced behind the bar. Emile turned away. Even the waiter avoided Claude's eyes. What were they thinking as she sat copying the menu?

"I'm so glad I came," Emma whispered as she saw him. "This place is a super find!"

"Madame."

"What a coup! Only fifteen francs for a three-course lunch. No wonder you tried to keep it to yourself."

She had bested him. He had been incredibly stupid to

think she would consider the Zola off limits. "How incredibly stupid of me."

Emma was shocked by the anger in his voice. She had made her cover too convincing. "Please," she said. "Sit down. I'm here alone."

"Monsieur Benjamin?"

"He doesn't even know I'm here," she said, hoping to exonerate herself.

Claude stood stiffly over her, his hand atop a chair as though to steady his rage. "Ah, then let me help you with your research. First, you must remember to tell him about the bistro chairs. They are prewar and not mere reproductions. You and your readers will also be interested in the bullet hole in the mirror over the bar. One night Madame Lacroix tried to kill a waiter for serving her an overdone omelette. It will add to the local color."

Emma turned away from the loathing in his eyes. "I hate overdone omelettes too," she said softly.

Claude leaned toward her. "The perky little yellow ashtrays add a charming Gallic touch, don't you agree? You should really be taking notes, Madame. These are all details that could make this the find of the year. By the way, the cassoulet on Tuesday is better than the lamb stew on Thursday. An inside tip. Exclusive to you. However, the most guarded secret of all, Madame, is that the basement of the Zola is said to have been used by members of the Résistance during the occupation of their country."

Emma stood up. "I'm sorry," she said flatly. "I didn't realize what time it was." She looked down at her wrist— but she had given Claude her watch. "I'm late." She turned away, unable to bear the hatred in his eyes.

"Why have you come here?" he asked.

I thought I would be meeting a friend. I was wrong."

Claude had seen the enemy many times before. But there was something in Emma's face he did not recognize.

He grabbed her by the elbow as she started to leave. He spoke softly. "Your friend was delayed at the jeweler's. Mickey's little hand has been repaired."

"Thanks." She was still afraid to look at him. "Will it glow in the dark?"

Claude turned her toward him. He put his hand under her chin and raised her head until their eyes met. "We shall see."

Without a word, they sat down at the table. He snapped his fingers for the waiter. He took her hand and fastened her watch as though symbolically uniting them. There was no need to speak.

"Are we really going to have an affair?" she asked in a rush.

The concept was dizzying. Erotic. Unexpected and totally irresistible. To make love to Emma Benjamin on the eve of battle. Literally, to bare himself before the enemy. "Yes."

"I know this nifty little hotel on the rue de Dragon. For under fifty francs, including Continental breakfast, we can get a room on the top floor overlooking a lovely garden." She saw the displeasure on his face. "Well, then I know a cheaper hotel. There's a color TV in the lobby, but it's still very Old World. You'll adore it. I think it's in the fourteenth."

"Madame, you must not plan the tour for this affair."

She sat back in her chair and laughed. "I've done everything wrong so far." And then, before he could agree, she added, "Maybe I could relax if you stopped calling me 'Madame.' "

"Emma."

She shrugged her shoulders helplessly. "I'm afraid 'Concierge' is all I know."

"Claude. Claude Picard."

"Bonjour, Claude."

143

"Hello, Emma."

"Mon Dieu," she said, with a deep sigh. "What a jour! Who would have thought? Although I guess I knew I was headed for Something Big the moment I left Clifford."

"How did you know?" He reached for her hand.

She leaned forward as though recounting an ancient folktale. "I stood there. Outside the convent. It was cold. I was alone. Crying. Frightened. And then, as though it were the most natural thing in the world to do, as though I had done it hundreds of times before, I just raised my hand and hailed a taxi."

"Monsieur?" It was the waiter, careful to avoid eye contact with Claude.

"Have you eaten lunch?" he asked.

"I'm too nervous."

He smiled. "You are a very dangerous woman."

"Me?"

"Yes. The most dangerous people are those who do not hide their feelings. They are not afraid to take risks."

"Are you a risk?"

"You know nothing about me. I could be your worst enemy."

"You? Do you think I give my Mickey to every man I meet? I know who to trust."

"And does your husband also know who to trust?"

"Of course."

"Does he trust you?"

"You bet your brioche! What kind of marriage do you think I have?"

The waiter cleared his throat. "Monsieur? Votre plaisir?"

"Perhaps something to drink?" Claude asked her.

"Yes."

"What would you like?"

"You decide."

Claude looked at the waiter. "Une verre de champagne pour Madame."

"Et pour Monsieur?"

"L'usuel. Naturellement."

"Naturellement," the waiter muttered, and walked away.

Emma looked down at her hands. "I wish I smoked. Or at least bit my nails."

Claude caressed her hand. "You have never done this before?"

"Are you kidding?" She stared at him in horror. "Clifford would kill me if he knew I took a taxi!"

CLAUDE opened the door to his room. Emma hesitated as though entering an alien atmosphere. Without a word she walked across the Aubusson and ran a finger over the lacquered top of the harpsichord. She turned and stared at the ebony writing table whose curved lines were decorated with the finest of Boulle marquetry. She touched the Baccarat decanters and tapped her fingers on the Hache desk. On her way to the window she stopped to look up at the Saint-Louis chandelier. Then, pushing aside the white silk curtains, she stared out at the Eiffel Tower. She turned back to Claude, who was leaning against the locked door.

"How dumb do you think I am?" she asked.

"I don't understand."

"You think I don't know you can get the key to any room you want? Why are you trying to palm this museum off as yours?"

Claude smiled. He walked to her and put his hands on her shoulders. "This is where I live."

145

"Like hell it is!" She walked to the door. "I may not know much about having affairs, but I do know that members of the oppressed working class don't live like this!"

Claude put his hand on the door and stopped her. "This room is mine," he said quietly. "Everything in it is mine." He walked past her, pointing to each object as he spoke. "The paintings, the first editions, the furniture—all by the greatest artisans of France. I bought them myself. In this room you see my savings, my house in the country, my car, my vacations, my family." Claude stood in the center of the room and pointed to the window. "And outside, my horizon. This is the part of me I wanted you to see. The most intimate part of my life. It is very important that you see all of this."

Emma took her hand from the doorknob. She walked back into the room, circling her way around the furniture. It was an extraordinary collection, even to her unprofessional eye. "Okay," she said, sitting down in an ornately carved armchair. "But you better have receipts!"

Claude hung his jacket in the closet. "The chair in which you are sitting is carved in the Rococo style typical of furniture made for the court of Louis XV." He turned to her as he took off his tie and unbuttoned his shirt.

"Oh, really?" she whispered nervously.

"The word 'Rococo' is a combination of the words 'rocaille' and 'coquille.' It means a type of rock-and-shell work which was a very popular motif during the period." He took off his shirt.

"I didn't know that." She watched as he walked past her to the window. He drew the draperies, coaxing the room into a gentle twilight. "But then, I've never known very much about Louis XV furniture."

Claude walked to the bed and pulled back the cover. He folded it neatly as he spoke. "Classic French design is delineated most easily by the three kings Louis XIV, Louis

146

XV and Louis XVI. The first period, known as the Baroque, was imported from Italy." Claude untied his shoes and took off his socks. "It was known for its gravity, pomp and heroic proportions." He unzipped his trousers and hung them over a chair. "I personally prefer the influence of Louis XV, in which Rococo developed as a more playful, decorative and witty style." He took off his shorts.

Emma stared at him and took a deep breath. "Oh, I don't know. You look pretty Baroque to me."

Claude walked to her and held out his hand. "Emma."

"Mommie!" she whimpered, standing up. "This is really going to happen, isn't it?"

"I will not tell you I love you," he said, putting his arm around her.

"That's some line you've got!" She felt him unbutton her blouse. "Maybe when you turn to me later and ask—"

"You will tell me what I want to hear." She wore no brassiere. He put his hands gently to her breasts and kiss her. After a moment, she dropped her clothes. He pressed himself close to her. "Emma, you are very special to me." Stretching to feel every inch of her body, he whispered, "But I cannot be gentle with you." He carried her to the bed.

Emma looked around the room as she lay in his arms. "What's so terrific about gentle?"

He put Emma down on the bed and kissed her again. Their mouths open, teeth pressed firmly against teeth, they began to roll from side to side. His hands crushed hers. He pressed his body against her as tightly as he could. Emma felt she could not tolerate any closer contact. Only a moment ago she had felt like a leaf in his arms, and now she feared he would shatter her. She gasped as he entered savagely.

"Look around the room!"

"This incredible room. I'll never forget it."

147

"Remember this room, Emma. Remember the chandelier."

"Yes."

"Remember the harpsichord."

"Yes."

"Remember the desk."

"Yes. And the chair."

He thrust forward angrily. "And the paintings."

"The beautiful paintings." Her fingers dug into his shoulders.

"And out the window?"

"The Eiffel Tower."

Claude reached under her and pressed himself as deep as he could. "It is not outside the window, Emma."

Amid the credentials of the heritage he guarded, Claude held the enemy in his arms. It was the threat of Emma Benjamin that made the room even more alive. It was as though the artists themselves, in the presence of danger, had come back to cry out, "Vive la France!"

Claude did not have an orgasm. He remained hard inside her as he whispered, "The room, Emma Benjamin. You must always remember it."

"You can call me Emma," she said, gasping for air.

ONCE they separated, neither spoke. They lay on the bed without touching for a very long time. Emma felt confused. Cheated. It had been so violent. So unsatisfying. She turned her head to look at Claude. "What the hell was that we just did?" She reached out to touch him, but drew her hand back.

Claude propped himself up on his elbow. "Emma . . ." It was difficult to say her name. "Emma, why did you come to the Zola?"

148

Instinctively, she reached for the sheet and covered herself. "I had a fight with Clifford. I needed a friend."

"You think your husband is not your friend?"

"He needs me. He has no choice. Poor Cliffy."

"You are not happy with him." She turned away. "I am sorry. Why do you wear that watch?"

"My Mickey? What's wrong with my Mickey?"

"You are not the person you pretend to be."

"Are you?" she asked.

"I am always the person I pretend to be."

"Just an ordinary, everyday concierge who spends a few million francs collecting the history of France."

"You find that difficult to understand."

"No. As long as you realize we both wear Mickey Mouse watches."

He reached out and gently caressed the curve of one breast then the other. "They are perfect," he said.

"They're not the pointy kind."

His finger traced the outlines of her nipples until they hardened. "The rounded breast is more elegant, I think."

"Me too," she whispered. He buried his face in her breasts and sucked gently on the nipples.

"I don't understand you," she said softly.

"I am just an ordinary, everyday concierge." He lay back on the bed. "I make dinner reservations. I cancel flights. I book seats at the theater."

"I know," Emma said. "But what do you do in real life?"

He laughed. "In real life?"

"Yes. I know what kind of job you have. But jobs are different from real life."

"Is your job different from your real life?"

She sat up. "You want to know what my real life is?"

Claude began tracing the outline of her mouth. "No, you must never tell me."

"I just wanted to be honest with you." She reached toward him, but withdrew her hand. She laughed. "You're afraid of being honest, and I'm afraid of touching you."

"Touch me."

Emma put her open palm on his shoulder. She moved her hand down his chest, across his stomach, and gripped gently at his thick pubic hair. Then she cupped her hand under his testicles. "They're uneven," she said.

"I know."

"Clifford's are pretty even. But yours aren't." She took hold of his penis. "You know, you start out quite Baroque, but I'm afraid you have Rococo balls."

He laughed. "They are the one part of the male anatomy that is truly Rococo in concept."

"I like them."

"Then I am fortunate indeed not to be Chinese." They both laughed.

"I wouldn't want them without the rest of you," she said.

Claude took her face in his hands. "You are a beautiful woman."

"If you go for neo-Gothic noses."

"I mean what I say."

She paused. "Then you are very dangerous too."

"Yes." He leaned toward her. "What would it be like to kiss you very gently?" Their lips touched for a moment.

"How was it?" she asked.

"Fatal." He kissed her again, opening his mouth slowly, allowing their tongues to meet, circle once and part. "I am very dangerous for you, Emma."

She put her head on his shoulder. "How dangerous can you be? I'm leaving tomorrow."

"Yes."

"Checking out of your life. Heh heh."

Claude raised himself above her and entered slowly.

150

"There are very many things I cannot tell you." He pushed carefully inside her.

"Dark, terrible things?"

"Yes."

Emma put her arms around his neck. "Then how can I trust you?"

"You cannot trust me."

She held on to him tightly. "Should I be afraid?"

"Yes."

They lay perfectly still, concentrating on the tender pressures they exerted on each other. Emma squeezed gently as he flexed deep within her. They began to breathe in unison. Motionless, except for the throbbing of muscle around muscle, they drifted into intimacy.

Her lips touched his ear as she whispered, "I am afraid of you."

"And I," he said breathlessly, "I am afraid of you."

ETIENNE Duvert sat behind the Comfortilt steering wheel of his day-old bright red Chevy Impala Landau Coupe. The electric sliding steel sun roof was open, and the in-dash 40-channel CB with AM/FM stereo radio and stereo tape system was blaring the theme from *La Guerre des Etoiles*. He sped along the avenue de New York, making a left turn against the light onto the Pont d'Iéna. Once across the Seine, he made a sharp right without slowing down and then an impromptu left amid the shouts and honking horns of those around him. He raced down the avenue de Suffren, past the parked tour buses, and stopped with a screech in a No Parking zone on the avenue Gustave Eiffel.

It was an absurd place, he thought, for Murphy to want to meet. He glanced nervously at the electronic digital clock and pulled down the visor to which he had affixed his OFFICIAL BUSINESS parking permit. He was upset at being late. He was upset at not being able to unhook his seat belt. But he was most upset at never having been to the top of the Eiffel Tower.

The Secretary of Tourism threaded his way through the crowd. He found himself in the center of a group of undulating clusters delineated by clothing, language and height. It was as though he had just stepped into an interplanetary waiting room filled with representatives from distant solar systems. There were shouts of "Wo ist meine Mutter?," "Quando fu costruito?," "Jak sie tamto nazywa?" and "¿Donde está el lavabo?" He walked quickly to the front of the line at the ticket window.

"I've jolly well had it with you Germans," a woman shouted. "Why the hell don't you queue up like everyone else?"

"I am not German, Madame. I am a member of the French Government here on official business."

"And I am Queen Elizabeth and I'm about to save five francs by walking up instead of taking the lift." She turned from him and slid her money under the window.

Etienne realized it would be faster to pay than to explain who he was to the ticket clerk. "To the top!" he said, reaching into his pocket for some small change.

"Twenty-seven francs."

Etienne looked up. "Twenty-seven francs? I do not want to buy it. I just want to see it."

"Twenty-seven francs, Monsieur."

"You charge twenty-seven francs just to go to the top of the Eiffel Tower?"

"Oui, Monsieur."

"For one person?"

"It is only twenty-two francs if you walk up the first two stages."

"It is an outrage!" He took his wallet and opened it,

showing his identification to the clerk. "I do not understand how you expect to do any business here at all with such prices!"

The clerk shrugged as he handed Etienne a pass. "Over three million every year."

Etienne narrowed his eyes. "Well, you people are very lucky! If you had to build this thing today, you would never make back your money!" He grabbed the pass and walked angrily toward the ascenseur. He marched to the front of the line.

"Bonjour, Monsieur," the old guard said, allowing him to enter the half-filled elevator.

Etienne nodded and tapped his foot as he waited for the car to fill. "Pardon," he said, turning to the man next to him, "have you the correct time?"

The man smiled. "Ich spreche kein Französisch."

Etienne shook his head and suddenly felt himself being shoved against the metal side of the car amid squeals and cries in Japanese. "Ito! Ito! Gomen nasai! Ippai desu ka? Isoide Kudasai! Iezusu Kirisutosu!"

"Mon Dieu!" Etienne muttered, sticking his elbow into someone's back.

A tall blond man turned quickly and yelled at him, "Ett ögonblick! Vad heter det där?"

"Oooooooh!" As the elevator began to rise, the crowd suddenly shifted its focus from the discomfort of being jammed together. "Blast off, Artoo-Detoo!" someone yelled.

"La Forza! La Forza!"

"Ito? Goran nasai!"

Etienne closed his eyes. Twenty-seven francs! As they jostled to a stop, he followed the crowd and walked toward the elevator that would take them to the second level. Somehow he got mixed into the center of the Japanese group. He tried to smile pleasantly as he towered over the

154

sea of Oriental faces. Tourists, he thought disdainfully. Nothing but tourists. He turned to an older man standing next to him. "It looks like the ascent to the top of Mt. Fuji," Etienne whispered.

The man smiled. He nodded his head and said, "Przepraszam. Nie rozumiem."

"Haaaaaaaaaaa," the crowd moaned as they reached the second level and began sorting out. Not everyone was going to the top, and Etienne quickened his step to ensure a place in the smaller elevator to the final stage. The Japanese group, sensing they were closer to their destination, began opening their camera cases, screwing special filters onto their lenses and checking film supplies. As a joke, one of them began taking pictures of the others as they prepared to take pictures. Etienne estimated that by the time they reached the top, over fifty percent of the people in the elevator had taken his picture. Some as a single-subject portrait.

The moment the elevator doors opened, cameras were being raised to eye level, and the sound of shutters snapping wafted onto the late-afternoon sky as though a swarm of crickets had been unleashed. He waited for them all to file out and then began searching the figures along the edge for Murphy's silhouette. He stopped suddenly. Something in his peripheral vision. Below him, away from the snapping of shutters and cries for Ito, was the incredible confection called Paris. He stood motionless. His eyes cautiously followed the meanderings of the Seine as though fearful of finding warts on the face of a beautiful woman. He identified landmarks and found himself mentally pointing a finger with such joyful recognition one would have thought he had never seen them before. Despite the jostling from the man next to him, he felt suprisingly benevolent. The Secretary of Tourism realized, for the first time, that he was standing where the action was.

155

The man next to him had just stepped on his foot. "Monsieur, s'il vous plaît!" Etienne said angrily.

"Gotcha!" Murphy said with a wink. He put his arm around Etienne and turned him back toward the view. "That's one helluva town you got down there, old buddy."

"I come here often."

"I bet it gets you every time."

"The perspective is necessary for one in my position."

"Here." Murphy handed him a brand-new case with a pair of binoculars any U-boat captain would have been proud to own. "I want you to have these."

Etienne took them. "But Murphy, you are so generous."

"Yes, I am. I want you to be able to see things for what they really are. I learned long ago you've got to take a close look at everything yourself. Few things are ever what they appear to be." Etienne was focusing the binoculars. Murphy leaned close to him and spoke softly. "You know, when it was time for me to learn what life was all about, I didn't pick it up on the street. When I was old enough, and my time had come, my father showed me."

Etienne put down his binoculars. "He showed you?"

"That's the kind of guy he was. Dad knew he was the best, and he wanted his son to see him in action."

"A truly extraordinary man!"

"Don't think I wasn't nervous when he said I could watch. I tell you, I was pretty damn scared at the thought of seeing him perform."

"Of course."

"He had the chauffeur drive us downtown. I can still remember how I felt when the driver helped me out of the car."

"You were very nervous."

Murphy shrugged. "How do you describe the moment

you become a man? I stood there with him on the street, looking up at the Stock Exchange. There was no turning back."

"The Stock Exchange?"

"Jesus. It could have been yesterday, it's so clear in my mind. We walked onto the balcony. They cleared a place for him right at the railing. For me too. He didn't say a word and no one spoke to him. We just stood there, looking down at the action on the floor. Then I saw my dad take out a pair of binoculars. He looked down at the faces. He watched the expressions. He found his man. He watched what his man was doing. He saw his man raise three fingers and look up. My dad shook his head No. He only had to shake his head once. Then he tapped me on the shoulder and we left. And that's how I found out what my dad did for a living."

"What did he do?"

"He shook his head."

"Well, perhaps in America . . ."

Murphy grabbed Etienne's arm. "It's the same anywhere, me bucko! You've got to know when to shake your head. And then you have to know when to buy a pair of binoculars."

"I am afraid I do not understand what you are trying to tell me."

"I've been thinking. It's time my dirty half-dozen became the magnificent seven. I want you on my team. You're my kind of guy."

Etienne took a deep breath. To leave behind the bureaucracy of the government! To be away from prying eyes! To be able to accept bribes in peace! "But what would I do? What are you offering me?"

Murphy smiled. He made a broad gesture with one hand and swept across the horizon. "That's what I'm offering you." He took a small box of newly printed business cards from his pocket. "This!"

Etienne took the box and opened it.

ETIENNE DUVERT
Executive in Charge of Paris

"Mon Dieu," he whispered.

"The way I see it, you're gonna be my French connection. I'm a pretty damn good judge of character, and I need somebody here I can trust. I'm giving you the nod. Just like my dad did."

"But what do you want me to do?"

Murphy patted the binoculars. "I want you to keep an eye out for me. I want to be sure the Château Norwalk gets built without any problems from the building inspectors, the fire inspectors, the zoning inspectors . . ."

"Of course. That is simple. But what will I do once the hotel is built?"

"That's when your job will just begin. I want you on the board of directors of my hotel. And then what I really want is for you to work with my other guys. I'm smart enough to know there's not another son of a bitch in all of France who has his finger up the ass of tourism the way you do. I gotta keep my hotel filled. And you and I know that can't be done with the wine-tour stiffs alone. You gotta find me more tourists. I want them coming out of the woodwork! Round them up! You can do that better than anyone else. This is your town!"

The newly appointed Executive in Charge of Paris stared down at his territory. His Paris. To love and to cherish. To have and to hold. From this day forth.

CLAUDE walked quickly down the corridor. He knocked on the door. "Madame!" he called. "Are you all right?"

Lily stood poised on the other side. She brushed a wisp of hair from her face as she awaited her cue.

"Madame Simon! Can you hear me?"

Lily held on to the doorknob as though it were a smoking gun. If only The Theatre Guild could have seen her.

"Madame, you must open the door. Otherwise, I will be forced to break it down!"

And upstage her entrance?

"Madame!"

Enter Lily. She opened the door, stood frozen for a moment and then pressed the back of her hand to a fevered brow. Claude took one step and she fell limp against him. Overwhelmed by déjà vu, he carried Lily back into

159

the room. Only a few hours earlier he had held Emma Benjamin in his arms. How ironic. How ecological. How different she felt from Emma.

As he put Lily on the sofa, she turned to him and whispered, "Champagne!"

Claude smiled. He leaned over and said, "I would suggest '71."

She opened her eyes for a moment to flutter approval and then pointed to a bucket of chilled champagne and two glasses. As he filled her glass, it occurred to him that perhaps NAA had put Claude Picard on the itinerary. He sat down and carefully brought the glass to her lips. "This will help, Madame."

Lily puckered and, purposely making the loudest noise she could, sucked in all the champagne in the glass. "Dear Claude. How good of you to rescue me."

He refilled her glass. "You must tell me, Madame. What happened?"

Lily looked directly at him. She leaned forward and spoke slowly, precisely, to be certain he understood. "The sun was in my eyes."

He understood. Without hesitation, Claude picked up the challenge. "What did you do, Madame?" he parried. "When it happened?"

"I shut my eyes."

"Show me how." She closed her eyes. "Exactly right, Madame. Then what did you do?"

Lily's eyes were still shut as she groped in the air. "I couldn't see a thing. I stumbled to the telephone. I called you."

"Tell me what you said to me."

Lily opened one eye for a moment. She had not expected him to be so adept a player. "Claude!" she called, re-creating the moment. "I need you! Come to me!"

He framed her face in his hands. He watched her eyes

160

widen as he leaned closer and kissed her gently on the lips. He felt her shudder as he put his arms around her. "Madame, my darling. Do you trust me?"

Lily nodded breathlessly. "Did Piper trust Heidsieck?"

"Then we must leave this room at once."

"Why?" she asked, pulling back from him.

He leaned forward and brought his lips to her ear. First he kissed her, and then he whispered, "It will return."

"It will?" she asked intently.

"Yes, Madame."

"What will?"

He put his hands over her eyes. "The sun."

"WHERE are you taking me?" Lily asked as they walked down the service stairs.

"Are you having second thoughts?"

"About what?" she stopped.

"About going to bed with me." He looked up at her on the staircase. He was having second thoughts. But why? Not even Zorro, or Pimpernel or Rassendyl had the chance to sleep with the enemy. Why was Le Dom hesitating?

"Darling, don't be ridiculous. I haven't finished my first thoughts yet." He smiled. "I like your smile."

"Do you say that to all the concierges?"

Lily turned away. "My God, is that what you think?"

He walked up the stairs and put his arms around her. "Madame . . ." He was hesitating because of Emma. The closer he got to Lily, the more he wanted Emma. And the more he wanted Emma, the more threatened he was.

She faced him. "I've never done this before. Ever."

He paused. "Then you have given me a grave responsibility."

161

She smiled and put her hand through his hair. "Dear Claude Picard. The man who thrives on the impossible."

"But not, until now, the improbable." Claude took her hand and kissed it. He needed Lily for symmetry. He needed her to restore perspective. It was safer to sleep with *all* of his enemies. "Madame, you will never know how much I want to go to bed with you."

"Concierge, I am a woman whose life is devoted to experiencing the best."

"I have never disappointed you, Madame."

"Never." He pulled her close and put his tongue into her mouth even before their lips met. They stood on the service stairs holding one kiss for a very long time. They might have kissed a hundred times before she rested her head on his shoulder. She paused to catch her breath. "Concierge?"

"Oui, Madame?"

"That was an excellent kiss."

LILY walked from the harpsichord to the window. There was the same Eiffel Tower she and Dwight had stared at yesterday. Or was it a different one? Of course! There must be hundreds. She'd put that in the next edition. 'Beware, Dear Reader, the latest racket in Paris is fake Eiffel Towers. They've sprung up everywhere you look!' Lily turned to Claude with a sigh. "It was not necessary to lie to me, Concierge."

"Lie?"

"Whose room is this?" Lily rubbed her hand across the velvet on the Pathier chair. "Does Pierre know what you do with his best suite?"

"This is my room."

"Rented for quick liaisons with mature ladies? Come now, Concierge. Neither of us is that desperate."

162

Claude leaned against the door. He was just that desperate. He could not let her escape. He had to have both Lily Simon and Emma Benjamin before they left for Champagne. And in the same bed. He smiled. "Ah, yes, you wish to see my receipts?"

Lily laughed. "Receipts? I don't need receipts, Concierge." He watched her every move, comparing every step with those taken by her predecessor. But Lily was truly incomparable. Her veneer was more exotic than that on the Hache desk. Her polish was brighter than the sparkle from the Saint-Louis chandelier. She walked to Claude and put her hand on his cheek. "La vérité will do."

Claude put his hand to her breast. She gasped. He felt her body tense. "Did I not secure the window table at Chez Gustave?"

"Oui."

Both breasts. "A box at the Opéra?"

"Oui. But—"

"A runway chair at Balenciaga?"

She put her arms around his neck. "Mais oui. Mais oui."

"And still you do not believe me?" He kissed her neck and began opening the buttons on her kimono. Lily shook her head No. "Then this is how Dreyfus felt." They sat on the edge of the bed.

She turned toward him and touched the tip of his nose with her finger. "J'accuse, darling."

Claude brought her face to his. "How can I convince you, Madame?"

Lily lay back and let her arms fall gracefully. "Je ne sais pas, Concierge. Surely there must be some way for you to convince me you are telling me the truth."

Claude began to unbutton her kimono. He paused to caress her bare shoulders. "As though polished by Rodin," he whispered.

"Bravo, Concierge. At last, la vérité!"

He lifted her gently and slipped off her kimono. "Never have I seen such elegant breasts, Madame."

She moaned as he kissed her nipples. "How wonderful it feels to hear the truth!" Lily opened her eyes as he stood up. His back was to her. "What are you doing, Concierge?"

"I am undressing, Madame. I am taking off my uniform."

"How will I know you without your uniform, Concierge?" She watched as Claude took off his shirt. "How splendid, Concierge."

He turned to her as he unzipped his trousers. "You must not call me 'Concierge,' Madame."

"Aha! There is to be a French Revolution after all! Citizen, what shall I call you?" she asked, staring as he took off his shorts.

"My name. Claude Picard."

Lily touched his penis. "You must be lying again, darling. See how it gets longer when you do?" He lay down next to her. "My Pinocchio. My dearest Citizen Pinocchio."

"I am a Citizen of France," he said, kissing her thigh.

"C'est bon," she whispered.

He lay close to Lily, his hand between her legs. The moment she was moist, Claude moved on top of her. "France must belong only to us. It is the birthright of the French."

Lily moaned. "Of course, darling. And the birthplace of the French fry."

"We have the greatest artists in the world."

She took hold of Claude's penis and began to ease him inside her. "And the best French toast."

He entered in a single thrust. "French is the language of literature."

"And of French pastry."

He began rocking. "French justice has served as a model for the world."

164

"So have French cuffs."

"The great French composers."

"French doors."

"The great French philosophers."

"French bread." Lily held tightly to Claude. They were both breathing heavily.

"French architects." He pushed harder and harder.

"Ooh. And French postcards!"

"French wine."

"The French Foreign Legion." Lily began to moan. Her fingers dug into Claude's back as she tensed. "Oh my God, darling! We almost forgot the French horn!"

Claude buried his head on her shoulder and lay motionless except for the spasms. He was, at the height of his pleasure, thinking only of Emma. After a few moments, he whispered, as though to reassure himself, "Yes, Madame. You are right. There is to be a French Revolution after all."

IT was six o'clock. Clifford was tired and hungry and angry. His afternoon with Sister Marcella seemed interminable as she took every opportunity to re-open negotiations on price. Normally, he would never fight to save an entry, but if the convent was not a dramatic "stop press" recommendation, he couldn't face Emma. He realized, as he stood in the chill twilight, that even with the "stop press" entry he didn't want to face Emma. Clifford turned up his collar and walked to the corner.

One lone taxi sat waiting at the taxi stand. He walked slowly toward it. The driver sat reading the paper while his dog slept in the seat next to him. The man did not look up as Clifford got in. The dog opened one eye and went back to sleep. "Monsieur?" the driver asked.

"Bonjour."

"Bonjour, Monsieur," the driver said, turning the page.

And then, after a moment, he repeated, as though not to appear impolite, "Monsieur?"

"Bonjour." Clifford hesitated and then said, "Je voudrais diner."

The driver glanced at his watch. He shook his head. He shrugged his shoulders. "C'est un taxi, Monsieur. Non pas un restaurant. N'est-ce pas, Simone?"

Simone barked. The driver turned to Clifford and pointed to Simone, the bark of reason. He repeated the judgment. "C'est un taxi."

Clifford rubbed his hand nervously across the fabric on the seat. He looked around. "C'est un bon taxi."

The driver nodded. Clifford nodded. Simone barked. The driver picked up his paper and continued reading. After a moment, without looking up, the driver said, "J'aime mon taxi."

Clifford patted the fabric on the empty seat next to him. "C'est un bon taxi," he repeated. The driver folded his paper very slowly and very carefully. He turned around to look squarely at Clifford. Simone sat up and turned around to look squarely at Clifford. As he patted her head, Clifford leaned forward and said to Simone, "Je voudrais le 'best' restaurant de Paris."

Simone turned to look at the driver, who asked, "Le 'best'?"

"Oui," Clifford said. "Le plus très beau grand bon!" He was searching for the restaurant that would save his marriage.

Mimicking the intensity in his voice, Simone raised her head and began to howl. The driver accelerated with such force that Clifford was thrown against the back of the seat. Simone did not stop howling until they reached Chez Gustave.

"BONJOUR, Monsieur. May I have your name?"

"My name is Clifford Benjamin."

The impeccably dressed young man in the dimly lit downstairs vestibule consulted his book. He shook his head as his finger followed the list of names. "Your name is not here, Monsieur."

"What book is that you're looking in?"

"It is our book of reservations."

"Oh, well, you won't find my name in there. I have no reservation."

The impeccably dressed young man looked up. "You have no reservation?"

"Of course not," Clifford said. "I never make reservations."

"But why?"

Clifford shrugged. "I am too rich."

A pause. "I see."

"Too damn rich," Clifford said, suddenly angry. He reached into his pocket and took out a one-franc coin. "This is for you, young man."

"Merci, Monsieur Benjamin," said the impeccably dressed young man. "I will have your table ready in a moment. Please follow me. The elevator is this way. I shall call upstairs."

Clifford sat on a small white-and-gold brocade settee in the mirrored elevator. The car moved with a slow, deliberate motion. Clifford felt as though he were entering another dimension. The only way back to Emma was an uncharted course. He knew he must first embrace the good life before he could again embrace Emma.

"Monsieur Benjamin. Bonjour, and welcome to Chez Gustave." The tall man with a silver streak in his black hair opened the door. He extended a hand toward Clifford.

Chez Gustave was red. The walls, carpet, linen and flowers were bright crimson. On each table was a small illuminated replica of the Eiffel Tower in deference to the restaurant's namesake, Gustave Eiffel. The large picture window had an unobstructed view of the Tower. The room was empty.

"Hi," Clifford said.

"Monsieur, how may we help you?"

"Well, I was on my way back to the hotel when I realized I hadn't eaten lunch."

"I see. But it is very late for lunch and it is very early for dinner."

"I know. But I am very hungry."

"Pardon, Monsieur. I am not certain I understand. Are you telling me you are hungry and that is why you have come to Chez Gustave?"

"You got it!"

The maître shrugged. It was though someone had told him deux and deux equal cinq. "You have come to Chez Gustave because you are hungry?" he repeated incredulously.

"I'm starving! I really need something to eat."

"You must pardon me, Monsieur, but if you need something to eat there are many bistros and cafés that are in business to feed the hungry."

"But that's what I came here for. I want you to sell me some cooked food that I can sit down here and eat."

"I am afraid that is impossible."

"I want to speak to the manager," Clifford said.

"So do I!" The maître signaled in back of him. In a moment, Jacques Mertens walked briskly toward Clifford. Jacques was a large, gregarious man who greeted him as though he were a long-lost friend.

"Monsieur," Jacques offered. "How may I help you?"

"How do you do?" Clifford said, shaking hands with him. "I am a very rich hungry man. I have spent the afternoon pricing a convent."

169

Jacques nodded to the maître. "Then you must wish some refreshment."

"Boy, do I! But I am afraid I do not have a reservation."

"I believe I can find you a table, Monsieur. We are not yet at capacity. The hour is early."

"Terrific," Clifford said, following Jacques down the steps to the empty dining room. "Except there is one thing you must remember."

"Monsieur?"

"I want only the best. Money is no object. What do you think such a dinner would cost?"

"Monsieur, it will depend. The wine. The entrée. Mon Dieu, the cognac alone could cost five hundred francs."

Clifford reached into his pocket and took out three hundred dollars in traveler's checks. He signed them and handed them to Jacques. "I don't want to discuss cost anymore. I am hungry and thirsty and I want to have the best dinner my money can buy."

"Of course, Monsieur. But there is one final question of a monetary nature."

"Very well," Clifford said testily. "What is it?"

"Do you wish the amount you have given me to include service?"

"Jesus." Clifford took a deep breath. "Yes. I want the three hundred dollars to include tips. I will not under any circumstances give you one penny more, and I expect you will provide me with value to the penny."

Jacques smiled. "Please do not be upset, Monsieur. It is always best in these matters to understand the limitations under which we work."

Clifford gritted his teeth and followed as Jacques led the way to a table in the corner. Once settled in, Jacques opened a napkin and offered it. Clifford nodded. He looked up and smiled. "So, what's cooking?"

170

Jacques drew himself up. "First, may I suggest an apéritif?"

"Yes, you may."

Jacques sighed. "Perhaps Lillet. Or Kir. Or even Kir au Champagne."

"Champagne?"

"Yes. Of course, the cassis ruins the champagne, but if you prefer bubbles, then that is more important than the taste of the champagne."

"Which would you suggest?"

"For myself, I would have white wine with a twist of orange peel."

"That sounds terrific."

"You will have that?"

"Absolutely."

"Très bien."

Clifford reached up and grabbed his arm. "How much does it cost?"

"How must does it cost?" Jacques asked in horror.

"Listen, I just want to make sure you don't stick me with a two-hundred-and-fifty-dollar drink."

Jacques was speechless. "The apéritif will be, as you say, on the house."

"Nice." Clifford nodded his head in approval.

"For your hors d'oeuvre, I might suggest a Tourte Quercynoise—a tart of minced morels, sliced truffles and poached foie gras of duck baked in a silken custard. Or perhaps one of our famous truffle dishes, Truffes à la Serviette, in which whole truffles are served on toast with a Port wine sauce, all wrapped in a napkin."

"Sounds good, but very messy for the napkin."

"Then, there is Truffes en Feuilletage, in which the fresh truffle is covered with a foie gras mousse and wrapped in ham before being baked in a puff-pastry en-

171

velope. And of course, we are privileged to offer Truffes Fraîches sous la Cendre, in which very large truffles are cooked in Port, rolled in foie gras, wrapped in a half puff pastry and cooked under the ashes of a wood fire."

"I see."

Jacques cleared his throat and sighed. "Naturally, if you do not like truffles, you might prefer our Mousse de Grives au Genièvre."

"Now, that sounds good!"

"It is a mousse of grape-fed thrushes mixed with juniper berries and goose fat." He waited and then continued. "Pâté de Merles is made with one hundred boned Corsican blackbirds and lard." Clifford raised his hand to signal he'd heard enough. "Of course, if you prefer, there is always tomato juice."

"Aha!" Clifford said, smiling for the first time. "I knew you were saving the good stuff for last. I'll have a nice glass of tomato juice with a quarter of a Sunkist lemon."

"Do you wish a large glass, Monsieur?" he asked haughtily.

"Better not," Clifford said confidentially. "I don't want to spend it all on the hors d'oeuvre."

"To follow, I would suggest our Brochet a l'Ardennaise—slices of poached pike covered with matchstick slices of ham and coated with a cream-and-butter sauce enriched with champagne. Or you might prefer our Marinière de Brochet Charolaise, which is a matelote of pike in a superb sauce of cream, cognac and Worcestershire sauce."

"That's what I want," Clifford said. Jacques sighed with relief. "I want some Worcestershire sauce with my tomato juice."

"Of course."

"And I don't expect to be charged extra for that!"

"Our Quenelles de Brochet are served with a sauce Nan-

172

tua. The dumplings of pike are poached—" Clifford shook his head No. "Perhaps a Mousselines de Brochet Florentine, in which individual molded pike mousses are put on a bed of spinach—"

"Spinach? Ugh!"

"We have today a Matelote d'Anguilles à la Lyonnaise."

"I think I had that yesterday."

"It is stew in which eel is cooked in both red and white wine."

"No, I must be thinking of something else." Clifford picked up the menu and opened it. "God, I'm hungry! What's this?" he asked pointing to Poularde Dauphinoise.

"It is one of the house specialties. We force truffle slices under the skin of a chicken . . ."

"Not bad."

". . . stuff it with foie gras . . ."

"Getting better."

". . . and then carefully fit the chicken into a pig's bladder—"

"Next!"

Jacques sighed, trying not to lose his patience. "We received a special award from the Académie Culinaire de Paris for our casserole of kidneys cooked with vegetables and anchovies. The Tournedos Curnonsky are topped with a thick slice of poached beef marrow." Clifford shook his head. "You might prefer our Lapere aux Sautés au Romarin et aux Girolles, which is a superb fricassee of rabbit—"

"Rabbit?"

"Rabbit," Jacques, said, curling his lip.

"You mean bunny?" Clifford sat back in his chair. "You people eat bunnies here?"

"Monsieur, perhaps Chez Gustave is not the place for—"

"I'm sorry. Please. Go ahead."

173

"You would most likely, then, not enjoy Lièvre?"

"What is it?"

"Hare."

"As in Tortoise and the . . .?" Jacques nodded Yes. "No. That whole family is out. I also do not like rat. I never have. Try as I may to develop a taste for it."

"Tripe?" Clifford shook his head No. "Beef tongue?" Clifford shook his head No. "A sirloin steak in wine sauce?"

"Now, tell me about that one."

"We cook the steak in renderings of pork belly and coat it with a sauce of garlic, shallots, thyme, bay leaf, parsley stalks and wine." Clifford signaled thumbs up. "And then, this delicious sauce is thickened with fresh chicken blood."

Clifford held up his hand again. He looked around the room in order to find the entrance to the kitchen. He took a deep breath and yelled toward the swinging doors, "Hold the T.J.!" He stood up and threw the napkin on his plate.

Jacques knew there was trouble ahead. "Chez Gustave is a three-star restaurant frequented by royalty and gourmets from throughout the world."

"Well, you're sure as hell right about one thing."

"Monsieur?"

"Nobody comes here when they're hungry."

"Our guests come here to dine, not to eat."

"Well, not this guest, pal. Give me back my three hundred bucks."

"With pleasure, Monsieur," Jacques said bitterly. "Perhaps you would find the food at Pam-Pam or Pizza Pino's more to your liking."

"I would find the food at the Paris Zoo more to my liking! So this is the big number, eh? This is what Emma says I've been missing? This is what growing up is all about?"

174

"I am sorry Monsieur did not find anything to his pleasure here," Jacques said snidely.

Clifford snatched back his traveler's checks. "Well, this is one thing I'm gonna find to my pleasure," he said, carefully putting them back into his wallet. "And here's *another!*" Clifford swung around and punched him in the mouth. "This is from me and the rest of the kids in Never-Never Land!"

Jacques fell to the floor and was immediately surrounded by a crowd of waiters. Clifford, his heart beating wildly, ran down the stairs and onto the street. He kept running for blocks, bumping into people. He ignored the lights and dodged car after car. His chest ached as he ran on and on, nearly unable to catch his breath. Clifford never thought he would make it, but there it was. The number 57 bus back to the hotel.

$\mathcal{T}$HE mighty pots and pans of Le Petit Pigeon hung down over the stainless steel counters looking like the weapons of a medieval army. Deserted since receiving its nightly hosing, the kitchen of the Louis Q's three-star luncheon restaurant was illuminated by a single light that reflected itself in flashes of aluminum, copper and white tile. It was almost midnight. The baker would not arrive until six.

Claude sat alone at the small table used by the head chef. A cup of coffee had long since gone cold.

He wondered how the Louis's, the Henri's, and the Charles's had felt before the day of battle. Had they waited in their tents consumed with fear or with lust? For certain, they had not been preoccupied with whether Mickey Mouse was Baroque or Rococo.

176

Did men of war ever consider an alternative other than victory or death? Was that why Claude was afraid? There was little chance he would die, but the alternative to victory could be worse than death. Rococo. Mickey was definitely . . . Damn! The truth was, everything that would happen tomorrow in Epernay, even victory, frightened him. Emma was too much on his mind.

"Such deep thoughts," Marie-Thérèse said.

"What are you doing here at this hour?" He reached out for her hand.

"What are *you* doing here at this hour?" She leaned over to kiss his ear. "Surely this was not the only place the great Claude Picard could get a reservation?"

"It is the only place to be. The most exclusive table in all of Paris."

"Is it?"

He nodded. "There is only one chair."

"Then you are here alone?"

"You sound disappointed."

"Yes." She walked to the large glass-door refrigerators. "I was looking for Le Dom." He got up and followed her. "Suprême de volaille again?" she complained, absently pushing the dishes aside.

"He is not here."

She turned to face him through the other side of the glass door. She reached for his hand. "You can make him come. Tell him I need him." And then, looking back at the shelves, "I thought they had turbot today."

"He will not come."

Marie-Thérèse sniffed a terrine and put it back. "Why?" She handed Claude a bowl of raspberries.

"He is angry with me."

She took a pitcher of crème fraîche and closed the door. "Why?"

Claude followed her back to the table. He held the chair

as she sat down. "Perhaps I can help?" He brought over a stool and sat opposite her.

"You?" She shook her head. "A mere concierge?" She poured the entire pitcher of crème fraîche into the bowl of raspberries. "There is something I must tell him." She leaned across the table and fed him a spoonful of berries. "I must tell him goodbye."

"What are you saying, Marie?"

"I am saying goodbye. I shall remember you both always."

He sat back. "What has happened?"

"Something for which I was not prepared. I have not fallen in love."

He smiled. "With whom have you have not fallen in love?"

"You. It is the final injustice of all."

"Marie . . ."

"No. It must be said. I thought the worst thing that happened to me was being born into incredible wealth. Although at first, I never suspected anything was wrong. I assumed everyone had a house on the Seine. And on the Loire. And on the Côte d'Azur. It was inconceivable to me that all the little girls who played in the Bois did not have monogrammed underwear. My family tried to hide the truth from me. But I outsmarted them."

"You escaped to the Louis."

"It was the most demeaning job I could find. It brought me into contact with reality."

Claude opened his arms to her. "Welcome to Reality."

"So I thought. But you, you were my precious fantasy. By day I mopped and scrubbed. By night, I fought at your side, crying with fear as I shared your memories."

He laughed. "I do not see what more any girl could want."

"I was truly happy. You gave me a very wonderful gift,

178

something my parents had denied me—World War Two. But then came promotion after promotion. My paradise became a living hell."

"Until you met Dwight Simon."

"You know about him?"

"As le Directeur has told us many times, it is our job to know the pleasures of our guests. Of course, I did not think you would personally be one of them. What is he offering you?"

"Poverty. Scandal. Few prospects, if any. The scorn of his former friends."

"How will you live?"

"Shamefully, of course. On my inheritance."

"He would do that?"

"Yes," she said proudly. "Isn't it wonderful? Just when I thought nothing was going wrong, he will show me a side of life I had never hoped to experience. Indolence. Sloth. Pretense. And boredom."

"It sounds ideal."

Marie-Thérèse stood up angrily. "Don't look as if I had betrayed you." She spoke bitterly. "They bombed Mailly. They killed the Nazis. You had your war. I have at last found my own."

"You are not fighting for anything, Marie. You are surrendering. You have betrayed yourself," he said quietly.

"I have written my resignation."

Poor Marie-Thérèse. He put his arms around her. He held her tight as they rocked gently back and forth. They kissed. Claude took her hand and very slowly they began to waltz. Tears ran down her cheeks as they danced past the stoves. They turned circles in front of the sinks.

"I shall miss you," he whispered. "I shall always remember what we had." He smiled. "Even though it was not the best of times."

179

Marie-Thérèse leaned her head on his shoulder. "It was not the worst of times."

They danced into the service area and through the pantry. Around and around and around and around. And then, as he was afraid he might, he betrayed himself. He wished she were Emma. But he knew he would never again hold Emma in his arms. There was no turning back.

Wednesday

AT sunrise precisely, Claude left his room. He walked down the empty corridor. Two folded French flags were cradled in his arms. The flags were brand new. They had never been flown.

He unlocked the door to the Louis Q's elegant ballroom, Le Salon de Printemps. The sharp sound of his footsteps on the polished wood floor echoed through the room. He walked in cadence to the beating of his heart. Neither his heart nor his walk disturbed the sleeping cherubs on the ceiling fresco.

The windows at the far end of the ballroom opened on to a small balcony directly over the main entrance. Two white flagpoles stood at forty-five-degree angles to the iron railing. As he untied the ropes, Claude began to recite Chapter One of The Constitution of the Fifth Republic.

"France shall be a Republic, indivisible, secular, democratic and social. It shall ensure the equality of all citizens before the law, without distinction of origin, race or religion. It shall respect all beliefs.

"The national emblem shall be the tricolor flag, blue, white and red.

"The national anthem shall be the 'Marseillaise.'

"The motto of the Republic shall be 'Liberty, Equality, Fraternity.'

"Its principle shall be government of the people, by the people and for the people."

Claude stood on the balcony between the flags as they snapped noisily in the breeze. Each hand held on to a flagpole as though he were on the prow of a great warship. "For the people," he repeated as the flags whipped around him. "For the people of France!"

few minutes before eight, Murphy strode into the lobby carrying two enormous bunches of red roses. Etienne struggled to keep pace with him as Murphy turned around and said, "Bullshit!"

"It is true, Murphy. It is a fact."

Murphy stopped. "Listen, you want to know what a fact is? A fact is that I did it for the first time when I was ten. You got that? Ten years old." Etienne sighed as Murphy's voice became softer and more confidential. "And you know who I did it to?" Etienne did not know. "The sommelier at Le Pavillon." Murphy's eyes glazed over as the recollection made him smile. "You should have seen that big, fat son of a bitch. You know, real snotty, the way the French are." Etienne nodded. "My dad had taken me out for lunch before the chauffeur drove up to Yankee Stadium. I ordered a '34 Haut Brion to have with my hamburger. When we were all finished, my dad hands me three bucks and says, 'Go get him.' You should have seen it. Two bucks turned that punk into putty."

"You said your father gave you three dollars."

"I pocketed a buck. Truth is, dad was a sap." Murphy turned and looked across the lobby at Claude. "Is that him?"

"Yes."

Murphy shrugged his shoulders and winked. "Haut Brion '34!" Etienne walked quickly ahead, leading Murphy across the lobby.

Claude watched them approach. Murphy was smiling, and Etienne rolled his eyes. "Bonjour, Monsieur le Secrétaire," Claude said, stepping out from behind the desk.

Etienne shook hands with him and came right to the point. "I would like to introduce Mr. Murphy Norwalk."

Claude nodded. "Of course. The gentlemen with North American Airlines."

Murphy smiled. "And you, I hear, are the man who can do anything."

"I fear the Secretary has exaggerated somewhat."

"I hope not," Murphy said, handing the bouquets to Claude. "I could sure as hell use some water for these."

"Of course," Claude said coldly. He snapped his fingers for a page and instructed him about the flowers.

"You're too modest," Murphy said, reaching into his pocket. "You *can* do anything." Etienne shrugged, trying to exonerate himself from what was about to happen. "Seriously, I want you to know how much I appreciate the fine service you've given my dear friends, the Simons and the Benjamins." Murphy reached across the desk and shook Claude's hand.

As Claude withdrew his hand, he allowed the folded five-hundred-franc note to drop onto the desk. Murphy

186

watched with surprise, Etienne with terror. Claude carefully unfolded the note and then held it out in his palm. He looked at Murphy and asked, "What is this for, Monsieur?"

"For taking care of the Simons and the Benjamins."

"I see." Claude looked down at the note and then at Murphy. "I am afraid it is not enough for taking care of the Simons and the Benjamins."

Murphy glanced nervously at Etienne. He narrowed his eyes as his hand went back into his pocket. "A man after my own heart," Murphy said with forced good spirits.

"Yes."

"Suppose you tell me how much. Another five hundred?"

"No. That is still not enough for taking care of the Simons and the Benjamins."

"You're a pretty pricey guy." Murphy's voice became tense. "I like that. How much?"

"How much do you have?" Claude asked.

Murphy laughed nervously. "A lot."

"A lot is not enough, Monsieur."

As though preparing to arm-wrestle, Murphy leaned on the desk. "What is enough?" He took out a money clip holding thousands of francs. "Is everything enough?"

"Everything is merely the beginning."

Murphy glared at Claude, while Etienne put a hand to his forehead. Gratefully, they all turned as they heard Lily's voice.

"Mon Dieu! If it isn't The Three Musketeers. Athos, Morose and Grandiose." Her laughter filled the lobby.

Pierre followed behind, snapping at the bellboy to be careful with her bags. He rushed over to shake hands with Etienne and Murphy. "Monsieur le Secrétaire, Monsieur Norwalk, what a pleasure!"

187

Lily's eyes were on Claude. They stared at one another until he turned away. "Claude," she called, challenging him.

"Madame." He looked back at her, afraid she was about to make a scene.

"Lily, my love," Murphy said, coming to her with open arms. "Lovely, lovely Lily."

She was indeed about to make a scene. Lily held up her arm and stopped Murphy from coming closer. "Claude!"

"Madame?"

"Get me an eleven-foot pole!"

Murphy scowled and took a step back. "I was hoping we could let bygones be bygones."

"You are not yet a bygone, Murphy. You are a here and a now. Unless you've come to fire me or pay me, I have nothing more to say to you."

"Lily, let's have truce. All I'm trying to do is make this experience as pleasant for you as possible. That's the truth of it."

She stared at Murphy for a long moment and then said, "Veritas Vos Vomitabit, darling. The truth shall make us vomit."

Murphy turned to Etienne in a rage. "Where the hell are the Benjamins?" he asked, as though Etienne were responsible.

Lily turned to Pierre. "I suspect they are still filling their pockets with free Kleenex."

Pierre cleared his throat. "Madame, I hope your stay was a pleasant one."

"I know you do, darling. It was, at least, terribly clean. That girl of yours is an absolute gem of a housekeeper. You must swear to me you'll never let her go."

"But of course. It is good to know you were pleased with your accommodation."

188

"Who ever said that, darling? I said it was clean. I most assuredly was not pleased with my accommodation."

"I do not understand," Pierre stammered.

"You gave us an intolerable location."

"But what was wrong?"

"The sun, Pierre." Lily looked over at Claude and spoke directly to him. "The sunset nearly blinded me."

"The sunset?" Pierre repeated blankly.

"I don't know what I would have done without Claude. Mon Dieu, if he had not been there to help me . . ."

"What happened?" Pierre asked.

"I was blinded," Lily said dramatically. She then added, "For the moment."

Claude smiled at her daring. "And now, Madame?"

She turned to him and spoke with great warmth. "And now, Concierge, I see things quite clearly."

Pierre stepped forward. He looked at Lily and said with great intensity, "Madame, I apologize for the sunlight."

No one noticed that Dwight had walked down from the second-floor offices. He stood behind Lily. "I must speak to you," he said urgently.

Lily sighed coquettishly as she put her arm in Dwight's and began leading him away. "Of course, my love," she said for all to hear. "Have you forgotten to pack your jammies again?"

Dwight spoke softly. "Lily, I meant every word."

"Darling, you've simply no sense of timing. Never had."

"Lily! You don't understand."

"Oh, Dwight," she pouted. "Of course I understand." She began to enumerate as matter-of-factly as reading a shopping list. "You've had it with me and you've had it with *Simon Says*. You are in love with the cleaning lady and will run off with her to Wash-and-Wax Heaven as soon as we return from our farewell performance of Goodbye Mr. Trips."

"I swear it!"

She leaned over and kissed him on the cheek. "I know. But darling, I've a thousand other things on my mind right now. Most of all, I want to get out of this hellhole. Darling," she said, putting her hand on his arm, "the faster we get out of here, the faster you can come back to Our Lady of the Laundry."

Dwight took a deep breath. He and Lily walked directly to Murphy. "Is the car here?" Dwight demanded. "Are we ready to leave?"

"The car is here," Murphy said.

"Good!" Dwight snapped. "Then we are ready to leave!"

"Have a wonderful time!" Murphy shouted angrily as he watched them walk out the front door. He turned back to Etienne, shaking his head as he saw the elevator doors open and Clifford come out carrying his duffel bag. An empty-handed bellboy shrugged his shoulders at Pierre.

Clifford strode over to Murphy and asked brusquely, "Is the damn bus here?"

"Yeah!" Clifford walked past him, hardly missing a beat. Murphy called out, "Where the hell is Emma?"

"Emma who?" Clifford muttered as he left the lobby.

Murphy turned to Pierre. "What is wrong with these people? What kind of a way is this to start off? I know they're mad at me, but what the hell are they mad at each other for?"

Pierre cleared his throat and leaned toward Murphy. He spoke with great confidentiality. "The Benjamins did not leave their rooms at all last night. Mrs. Benjamin called for room service at eight. Mr. Benjamin, who slept on the sofa, called for room service at nine. Mrs. Simon called for room service at nine-thirty. Mr. Simon was in the bar from

190

nine until one in the morning." He raised his eyebrows to underscore the significance of his report.

The elevator door opened and the bellboy walked out carrying a duffel bag. He held the door for Emma. She stood in the back of the elevator, leaning against the wall. Finally, the bellboy looked at her and asked, "Madame?"

Emma nodded. She walked slowly, her eyes fixed in Claude's direction. He saw her the moment she stepped out of the elevator and watched as she came directly to his desk. Her voice cracked and her eyes suddenly filled with tears. "I want my shoes back!" Claude reached beneath the desk and took out a package. He said nothing as he handed her the bag. "You might have called me. I was really waiting for a call . . . about my shoes. I didn't know if you'd even be on duty, and then what would I do . . . if I had to leave without seeing . . . if my shoes weren't here." She emptied the bag and, without looking at the shoes, put them on.

"I am sorry, Madame." He spoke softly. "I thought today you would be wearing another pair of shoes."

Emma sniffed and stood up straight. "No, I don't change shoes that easily. I told you these were my sensible shoes. I need them. Especially now. I want to leave here with exactly the same shoes I had when I came in."

"I expected that you would." Emma started to leave and then turned back. "Yes, Madame?"

Emma couldn't hold back the tears. "The shoes feel just great!" She walked to Murphy, sobbing loudly. "Where's the goddamn bus?"

Murphy swallowed hard and pointed outside. They all stood in stunned silence listening to her cry as she went through the revolving door. "Jesus." Murphy took Etienne by the arm and led him through the door.

A chauffeur walked into the lobby and came over to

191

Claude. "They are in the car. We are ready to leave." It was Nicolas Planchet. Vol. 4, G–I.

Antoine Baudin, Vol. 6, M–N, wore a short gray jacket and cap. He leaned over Claude's desk. "The bus is loaded. Everything is ready."

Claude reached for the flowers Murphy had forgotten. He removed the cards and handed one bouquet to Nicolas and one to Antoine. "Tell them these are from the concierge." He clasped their hands and whispered, "Vive la France!"

Nicolas and Antoine turned and left. The lobby was quiet. It was not yet eight-thirty, and the Simons and the Benjamins were his. It would be ten-thirty before their capture would be made public. Claude unlocked his drawer and took out the letter.

The letter was addressed to the President of France.

DWIGHT and Lily sat in the back seat of the limousine. Nicolas drove smoothly along the rue La Fayette and onto the avenue Jean Jaurès, which would lead into the N3 to Epernay. He glanced in the rearview mirror at his prey. They had been silent ever since leaving the hotel.

Lily made fastidious notes on her copy of the itinerary while Dwight merely stared blankly at his. Finally, he turned to her and said, "Lily, I want you to have the house in London."

Without taking her eyes from the page, or missing a stroke of her pencil, she informed him casually, "The house is already mine."

Dwight mumbled, "Yes." He looked out the window, unseeing. "What about the . . . no, that's yours too, I suppose."

193

"Yes."

"And . . ." he began haltingly.

"Mine." Lily put down her pencil and patted Dwight's arm. "It is so very comforting, my darling, to know that you don't not love me for my money."

He pulled away. "I suppose you think this is Düsseldorf all over again."

She smiled. "Good God, Düsseldorf! I'd forgotten all about Düsseldorf. No, actually I thought it more like Trieste. Or Geneva. Or even Madrid."

"Well, it's not. It's different this time."

"It's always different, darling."

Lily picked up the bouquet of roses. " 'From the concierge'! Dear Claude. Such elegant manners always. She inhaled deeply. "Have you noticed, darling, they're not making roses the way they used to."

"Really?"

"They're not. For one thing, they aren't nearly red enough."

Dwight smiled. "Dear Lily, for whom every cloud has a pewter lining."

"That sounds suspiciously like a eulogy."

"It's not. I expect you'll always search for redder roses."

Something in his voice frightened her. She turned and covered her eyes. "Then that, I take it, is the kiss-off."

Dwight reached into his pocket and took out a handkerchief. "Here."

She reached out, then hesitated. "Is this part of the settlement?"

"No."

Lily was crying. "Good. Then I'll take it." She blew her nose. "Here." She handed the handkerchief to him. "Give it to what's-her-name. Tell her to have it back in time for the final decree."

"Lily!"

Lily took a deep breath. "Mon Dieu," she said with forced gaiety, "will you just listen to me? I'm actually taking you seriously." She looked into his eyes and put her hand on his arm. "Do forgive me, darling. You know that's something I try never to do."

"Lily, I've put up the closing notice. This is our farewell tour."

She clutched his arm and leaned toward him. "Then by God, Dwight, by all that's deluxe and delightful, by all that's delicious and luxurious, let's go out in style!" He raised an eyebrow. "I know what you're thinking, but do trust me, darling. Let's go out with a bang! Oh, Dwight, let's make this a tour to remember!"

"Our tour de force!"

"Oh, yes, my witty darling." She held up the itinerary. "It's so perfect! We're starting out in Champagne!"

"Lily, how splendid of you to take it this way. I never dreamed you'd be such a sport."

"Dwight. Please! You're hurting my feelings. I admit I lost my head for a moment, but that's all behind us now." She put her arm in his and leaned on his shoulder. "Don't you see, my dearest? We're on the road to Epernay!"

Dwight sang out, "Where the flyin'-fishes play!"

ACCORDING to the plan, Antoine kept the bus a few hundred feet behind the limousine. Clifford had insisted they ride to Epernay in one of the buses NAA was to use for the tour. Emma sat in the first row. Clifford sat in the next-to-last row.

He had not spoken to Emma since she slapped him at the convent. She tried talking to him, but he wouldn't answer. He was angry. He was angry with her. He was angry with himself for having gone to Chez Gustave. He was angry at Murphy. He was angry at the Simons. But

195

most of all, Clifford was angry because he didn't know what to say to Emma.

'From the concierge,' Emma thought as she stared at the bouquet of red roses. How awful. Surely it was not her own vanity that convinced her the liaison with Claude had been more than casual. The man was not a casual man. He had a sweep, a certain epic grandeur about him. No. The message for which she had been waiting was not 'From the concierge.'

Emma walked up the aisle to Clifford. He pretended to be reading. She sat down in the seat across from him and held up the itinerary. "You know, Clifford, the Hôtel Hartenstein doesn't sound half bad." She flipped through the background notes. "Centrally located two hundred feet from the railway station. Two baths and two w.c.'s on each floor. Home cooking by Mama Hartenstein herself. And, a radio in the lobby!" She looked over at him, but he continued staring at the papers in his lap. "The Coeur d'Epernay sounds pretty good. They've got a sink in every room and, aha, they're right across the street from, of all places, Ma Mère Mathilde." She turned the page. "Which, luckily, is open every night during the harvest. Otherwise, only on weekends and Tuesdays."

"What are you up to, Emma?"

"Garbo talks!"

"Emma!"

"I am up to page one. And that's all I'm up to."

"You expect me to believe that?"

"Clifford, I tell you what. Why don't you take out a subpoena on my heart and make it talk? Or else just listen to what I'm saying."

"That's called lip service."

She sighed and held up the itinerary. "Cliffy, you kiwi! Here is where I'm gonna be for the next three weeks. Right next to you. Snug as a bug at the Hôtel Hartenstein.

196

Let's try. It could be like a first honeymoon." He turned away. "I promise I'll be good. No complaints. I swear I won't even read my bankbook until after you're asleep!" Emma got out of her seat and stood in the aisle. She leaned over to him and spoke softly. "I need you now, Cliffy. I need you to hold me. Even if you don't mean it. I need you."

He stared up at her for a moment and then put his papers down on the seat next to him. He held out his hands, helping her to sit in his lap. She nestled close, her head resting on his shoulder. He put his arm around her.

After a moment, she asked, "Do you mean it, Cliffy?"

He said, "No."

She shrugged. 'From the husband.'

"MUST be something wrong with the car," Dwight said as Nicolas pulled off the N3. He brought them to a short stop alongside a brown delivery van. Dwight rapped on the glass. "Driver, what's wrong?"

"Drat!" Lily humphed.

Nicolas got out of the car, put on a ski mask, leaned back in and pointed a gun at Lily's head.

"Mon Dieu," she whispered. "Highway robbery!"

"Good God!" Dwight reached for Lily's hand.

Not daring to move, Lily stared straight ahead. Her voice trembled as she said, "That is certainly not the proper way to hold a gun!"

"Quiet, Lily!"

"Get out of the car," Nicolas demanded.

Dwight opened his door. As Lily stepped out, she shouted nervously, "You'll never get anywhere in this world holding a gun like that!"

"Shut up, Lily!"

"Into the van!" The doors opened. Someone wearing a

ski mask extended an arm to help Lily up. There were long benches on either side. A third man, wearing an identical mask, hunched in the corner. He pointed a gun at them as Dwight sat down next to Lily. Nicolas jumped into the van. "Give me your bag, your jewelry, and empty your pockets."

"They're not going to kill us," Lily whispered as they took off their watches. "If they were, they would have killed us first and then taken everything."

"Well what *are* they doing?" Dwight's voice cracked.

"I think they're trying to upset us." Lily handed her watch and rings to Nicolas. She hesitated giving him her brooch. "This too?"

Nicolas grabbed it from her. "Everything."

"So much for my lucky pin," she hissed. "You might have been a gentleman about that. God knows you've taken enough money from us!"

He stuffed their things into a bag. "It's not your money we want."

Dwight and Lily looked at each other. They realized they were not merely being robbed. Nicolas jumped off the van and nodded to the other men. He raised his fist and shouted, "Vive la France!"

As the blindfolds were put over their eyes and they began to drive away, the driver shouted, "Vive la France!"

EMMA stared at Antoine's gun as she loosened her watchband. "And to think of all I went through to have this fixed."

"No," Antoine said from behind his ski mask. "Not *your* watch. Just his."

"But it works!" she said, suddenly defensive.

"Emma, he doesn't want it," Clifford snapped as he held out his watch. "Shut up!"

"Now your wallet!"

Emma gave him her bag. "Lucky for me nostalgia hasn't hit France," she muttered.

The brown van pulled off the N3 and stopped alongside the bus. "All right." He opened the bus door. "Get out."

"What for?" Emma asked.

"Move!"

Clifford stood up and grabbed Emma's arm. He led her off the bus. A man in an identical ski mask pointed a gun as he helped Emma inside the van. A third masked man seated her. As their eyes adjusted to the darkness, Emma and Clifford saw the Simons sitting across from them. Blindfolded.

"Jesus," Clifford muttered. Emma began to laugh.

"Oh, Dwight," Lily whispered. "That laugh! How terrifying!"

Clifford reached over to touch Lily's arm. She pulled back fearfully. "Lily, it's us! Clifford and Emma."

"What?" Dwight asked.

"Clifford?" Lily asked. Then her tone lowered a full octave. "You! You two? Of all the smarmy pranks! Aren't you ashamed of yourselves?"

"How could you do this to us?" Dwight demanded.

"We didn't!" Emma tried to explain, but she couldn't stop laughing. One of the men began blindfolding Clifford and Emma.

Lily held on to Dwight's arm. "They're taking us straight to hell."

Emma reached over, trying to find Clifford's knee. She patted it. "Too bad, Cliffy. Looks like this turned out to be a First Class kidnapping."

Antoine stood at the door while the others checked the blindfolds. Just before he shut the door, he called back, "Welcome to Epernay!"

The four of them sat still as they heard the driver yell, "Vive la France!" They lurched from side to side as the van moved back onto the highway.

"Did they hurt you?" Clifford asked.

"No," Emma said.

"I meant Dwight and Lily."

"Oh!"

"No, thank goodness," Dwight said. "Are you two all right?"

"Of course they are," Lily added quickly. "They must be accustomed to this type of thing."

"I thought you meant me," Emma said to Clifford.

"I knew you were all right."

"I don't understand why he didn't want my Mickey."

"Oh, dear," Lily said.

"What did she say?" Dwight asked.

"He didn't want her Mickey," Lily whispered. "It must be some type of street slang."

"My Mickey Mouse watch!"

"What fools they were," Lily said coolly. "To think they took my Piaget instead."

"Does anyone know why we're here?" Clifford asked.

"Or why they've taken all four of us?" Dwight said.

"Aside from lack of discrimination," Lily began, "I would assume it has something to do with NAA. God knows, I wouldn't put anything past Murphy."

"But why would he do a thing like this?" Emma asked.

"Maybe it's another airline trying to stop NAA."

"You mean TWA or Pan Am?" Dwight asked.

"No!" Lily said, solving the mystery. "It must be Air France. Remember how testy they became when I sent back the Brie?"

"My God!" Dwight gasped. "It might even be Aeroflot! That remark I made about the Mrs. Krushchev School for Stewardesses."

200

"Don't be ridiculous darling; if it's a joke that got us here, then the culprit is Polish Airlines."

"I'd almost forgotten," Dwight said fearfully. "The Orange à la Duck culinary award we gave them."

"Well *we* didn't make any of those remarks," Emma said.

"Why are we here?" Clifford asked.

"It's obvious," Lily said. "To torture us."

"Clifford's right. It's no coincidence they got all four of us," Dwight said. "It must have something to do with the NAA deal."

"Someone is trying to stop us from developing this tour."

"By kidnapping us," Dwight said.

"Or killing us," Emma said.

"Oh, who would take the trouble to kill *you*? It's us they want," Lily said. "And you two just happened to be there at the time."

"Why does everyone keep saying 'Vive la France'?"

"It really might be Murphy," Dwight said.

"God knows where they're taking us," Lily said.

"He said, 'Welcome to Epernay.' "

"Yes, he did." Dwight repeated, "He said, 'Welcome to Epernay.' "

"Perhaps he was being sarcastic," Emma said. "Or maybe that's where they want us to think we are."

"Murphy hates the four of us," Clifford said.

"Worse. He's afraid of us," Dwight added. "We could ruin his whole package."

Lily gasped. "What better insurance against our saying anything bad than to make certain we say nothing at all?"

They sat quietly for a few minutes, listening to the sounds of the van as it rolled along the road. Finally, Emma voiced what everyone was thinking. "We are all going to die."

201

WHEN the van came to a stop, Emma huddled close to Clifford. Lily cleared her throat nervously. They heard the doors open and someone whispered, "Mon Dieu!" upon seeing them. A hand reached out for Clifford. Then Emma and Dwight and Lily. Walking one behind another on a stone floor, they heard only their own footsteps. Through a door. Down some steps. Along a corridor. Another door. More steps. Along a corridor. Another door. More steps. Into a room. And then suddenly the sound of the door closing behind them. A key in the lock.

The four of them stood still. After a moment, Clifford raised his hand tentatively, as though reaching toward his blindfold. He expected to be stopped. They were the only ones in the room. "Take off the blindfolds," he said.

The room had four mattresses on the floor and no windows. It was painted white and was lit by a large ornate crystal chandelier. A door opened to a small bathroom with sink and toilet. The room was dominated by a large mahogany dining table and four matching red velvet chairs. The table was set with a cold buffet of at least a dozen elegantly prepared platters and as many bottles of chilled champagne.

"I don't believe it," Dwight said.

"I must be seeing things," Lily whispered. "Don't tell me that's really a Pâté de Caneton d'Amiens?"

"Is that all you can think of?" Dwight asked sharply. "For God's sake, who gives a damn about Pâté de Caneton d'Amiens? Don't you realize, Lily, you're standing right in front of a Tarte de Cambrai?"

"My God, what's wrong with me? I didn't even see it. You can tell my nerves are shot," Lily said, walking around the table. "Well, at least we know where we are."

"We do?" Clifford asked.

"Of course," Dwight said. "These are all regional specialties."

Lily sat in a chair at the dessert end of the table. "Pain d'Epices. Dragées. Gougère." She pointed directly to a platter of macaroons as though revealing the name of the murderer. "Biscuits de Reims!"

"We are in Champagne!" Dwight announced.

Emma pulled out a chair and sat down. "Am I the only one here who cares about dying? What is it with all of you? Is all you care about a delicious hereafter?"

"What a trying little pest you are, Emma darling." Lily leaned back in her chair. "Much as I hate to be the one to tell you, no one is going to kill you."

"How do you know?" Clifford asked.

"Biscuits de Reims, darling. Do you think anyone who's going to kill us would set up such a dazzling buffet? And mattresses? They might take our identification and bring us somewhere to murder us. But they wouldn't bring us somewhere to dine sumptuously and then murder us."

"What do you think they plan on doing?"

Lily stood up and took a plate. She walked to the Flamiche aux Poireaux, a Flemish leek pie, and cut into it. "Well, darlings, it looks to my baby blues like nothing more serious than a good old-fashioned kidnapping."

"But who did it?" Clifford asked.

Lily began to eat. "Someone with superb taste. Oh, this is glorious!"

"Why would they kidnap us?" Emma asked. "Who are they going to send the ransom note to?"

"Mmm," Lily said between bites. "For you, they will most likely contact Fagin. For us, there's not the slightest question. It's Murphy! Dear, dear Murphy."

"That's damned clever," Dwight said, sitting down. "And quite a relief!"

203

Clifford pulled up a chair. "It makes sense. Everyone knows how much this package is worth to NAA."

"Why else would they take all four of us?" Dwight asked.

Lily walked around the table. "Dwight, darling, you simply must have some of this divine Salade aux Moules à la Boulonnaise."

Dwight took a plate and looked back at Emma and Clifford. "It's only a matter of time until they get the money from NAA. Might as well make the best of it."

Clifford shrugged. "I guess so." He stood up. "Emma?"

She sat in her chair. "Before we turned this into a celebration dinner, we all thought Murphy had enough motive to want to kill us. Well, suppose he just never had the nerve?"

"So?"

"So, Cliffy. While you and the Gourmet Hittites are stuffing your gullets, Murphy might be stuffing his. I bet our ransom note would taste pretty delicious to him."

Clifford sat down. Dwight put his plate on the table. And Lily left her knife standing straight up in the Boudin Blanc.

THE Comte de Montaigne-Villiers walked up the steps from the cellar and closed the door behind him. He hurried along the corridor lined with portraits of his ancestors and opened the door to the Salon d'Est. Isabelle sat on a velvet settee. She put down her crocheting and took a sip from a glass of Montaigne-Villiers Extra Sec.

As Le Comte picked up the telephone and dialed, Isabelle noted, "I think someone peed in your '73."

He motioned to her to keep quiet as he completed his call.

"Concierge," the voice said.

"The harvest is in from the fields."

"The grapes have not been bruised?" Claude asked.

"Not at all."

Claude paused. "You are certain they are all right?"

"I do not bring damaged merchandise into the house of Montaigne-Villiers!"

"Vive la France, mon ami."

"Vive la France!" Le Comte hung up the phone.

Isabelle poured another glass of champagne. "I still think we should have killed the fuckers!"

CLAUDE kept his hand on the receiver. Every moment counted. Every moment, he thought as he hesitated. Then, while Judith Cornwell of Nyack, New York waited patiently in her room for the address of the Jeu de Paume, Claude picked up the phone and dialed the Café Zola.

"Bonjour."

"Emile, you may deliver the letter."

"Vive la France!"

"Vive la France!" Claude looked at his watch. It was not yet ten o'clock. Mickey's little hand would be on the ten, and his big hand very near the twelve.

THE President of France had a cold. His nose was red, his eyes were watery and his throat was sore. It was a condition of which he was particularly fond, because it gave his voice resonance. More important, under such conditions his pronunciation became even more impeccable. He remembered waking early, pleasantly surprised by the threat of congestion. It could have been a most enjoyable day had it not been for the letter.

Business as usual at the Wednesday Council of Ministers meeting in the Salon Murat of the Elysée Palace had been delayed indefinitely. The President of France put down his Rose Pompadour Sevrès porcelain coffee cup and sighed. The Prime Minister had passed the letter to the Minister of Foreign Affairs. Then it would have to go around the table, beneath the great Georges Bontemps crystal chandelier, to the Minister of Defense, the Minister of Cooperation, the Minister of the Quality of Life and the commanders-in-chief of the Army, Navy and Air Force.

"I shall read the letter aloud," said the President of France, holding his hand out toward the Minister of Foreign Affairs. "It will save time." He cleared his throat and prepared to explain to the Council of Ministers why there were four passports, three watches, two purses and two wallets in the center of the table. He was also about to perform what he regarded as one of his most solemn duties as head of state: to exemplify the correct pronunciation of the French Language.

TO THE PRESIDENT OF FRANCE,

We hereby demand that all foreign tourists leave the city by six o'clock tonight.

We demand a period for reawakening traditional French values before we are buried alive under fallout from the tourist explosion. They have invaded more than our privacy; they have invaded our national heritage.

We demand that the people of Paris be given room to stand at the top of the Eiffel Tower, to sit at the Opéra, to dine peacefully at the restaurant of their choice, to walk along the boulevards and once again hear their own language spoken.

Unless every foreign tourist has left Paris by six o'clock this evening, the four American travel writers we are holding will die.

The conditions for their release are:

1) by noon: announce the deportation of all foreign tour- ists

2) by six o'clock: Paris is to be cleared of all foreign tourists.

They must not be allowed back on French soil until sunset Friday.

Otherwise, the four will die.

We have taken this action because we are patriots.
We are not militant; we are dedicated. We did not allow
Paris to burn. We must not allow her to smother.
We who fought against, and survived, the occupation of
France in 1940 did not do so for Paris to be reoccupied by
an equally deadly army.
The Paris of Pasteur, Zola and Curie, of Lautrec, Cé-
zanne and Degas, of Proust, Balzac and Dumas must be
returned to the people of France.
Vive la France!

There was a stunned silence. The Minister of Defense glanced quickly at the Minister of the Quality of Life. The President of France drew a deep breath. Then the Prime Minister smiled. The other Ministers looked at him and nodded. To a man, the Ministers rose from their chairs and applauded.

MURPHY paced the Ambassador's anteroom, nervously folding and refolding his Hermès handkerchief. He had rushed to the American Embassy immediately after Etienne's call and had been waiting for nearly half an hour. Finally, the door opened and Channing Bannister Millman came out.

"Mr. Ambassador!"

"Terrible, terrible," Millman bellowed, patting Murphy on the shoulder. Two aides followed behind as he led Murphy quickly down the corridor. "I don't know what the hell's going to happen."

"Mr. Ambassador, they're American citizens!"

"Why the hell aren't you people satisfied with taking tourists to the Caribbean, where they get sunshine and pools and casinos? Don't you aces know by now that's all anybody really wants?"

"They're depending upon us to help them!"

208

Millman walked down the stairs that led to the garage. "I sure as hell don't feel I've had a proper vacation unless I've been swimming."

"Mr. Ambassador," Murphy pleaded.

Millman stopped. "I know. You want me to tell you the demands will be met and your people will be safe. Well, I can't. We've got over twenty nations involved in this mess. Not one of them has ever given in to terrorist demands. Now, I grant you, that was not your run-of-the-mill guerrilla love note, and the demands were pretty esoteric, but they might as well have asked for a pastrami sandwich. You can bet your ass the French won't budge an inch." Millman continued down the steps. "Listen to me, ace. It would cost the French Government millions to evacuate Paris. You really think they're gonna buy that?"

"Sweet Jesus," Murphy said, his voice catching. "What will happen to them?"

"I wouldn't hold the presses if I were you."

"I'll never forgive myself."

The aides led Millman to the limousine. "They're waiting for me now at the Elysée. I'll do the best I can." Millman got inside and slammed the door.

Murphy motioned for him to open the window and leaned over to speak softly. "I can remember the first time I read a Lily Simon restaurant review. She was ripping apart a chef who dared to make an espagnole demi-glace with arrowroot rather than flour. You know what that woman has done for our country?"

"Pull yourself together, ace. You may have to drop some names from your Christmas-card list."

THE Council sat waiting in the Salon Murat. The scene resembled a Dürer sketch in which every face expressed another point of view. Except for the President of

France, who sat expressionless as he inhaled a mentholated cigarette and sucked on a pineapple lozenge.

In the next room, the Prime Minister was conferring with the ambassadors from Australia, Belgium, Brazil, Canada, Germany, Italy, Japan, The Netherlands, Portugal, Denmark, Norway, Sweden, Spain, Switzerland, the United Kingdom, and the United States of America.

The Minister of Justice sighed as he glanced at the passports. "Empty. There is nothing in those faces."

The Minister of the Interior put down his calculator. "It is an impossible figure to estimate."

"To say nothing of the tourist dollars that would be lost during the period of withdrawal." The Minister of Economy and Finance shook his head. "Eurodollars, Petrodollars and now we have Tourodollars." He shrugged. "I suppose there is also a difference between widows and old maids, but by the time they have become what they are, they are all the same."

The Minister of Justice smiled. "We must take care not to embrace the empty symbolism of the café intellectuals. That is, if we are to survive the unfavorable publicity of our decision."

The Ministers nodded at one another and listened for some response from the next room. Finally, the long period of waiting ended as the door opened and the Prime Minister came in. All eyes were on him. "Of course, they were not pleased with our decision," he said defensively.

The President of France stood up. "I do not expect them to be pleased! We agreed there was no choice. The problem is not whether they are pleased. The problem is, how do we get them all out by six o'clock?"

"THEY can't be serious!" Murphy said. As Etienne drove rapidly along the rue Royale, he repeated

210

over and over again, "They can't be serious! The travel industry will never recover from this!"

"Mon Dieu! Would you prefer that the Simons and the Benjamins were killed?"

Murphy thought for a moment. "Watch out for that bus," he muttered.

Etienne slammed on the brakes as the Cityrama bus pulled out in front of him on the turn into the rue du Faubourg St.-Honoré. "Do you see what that fool is doing? He will make me late!" Etienne began honking his horn. "Late for the President!"

Murphy pointed to the bus. "It's your own fault, tiger, for doing such a good job."

Etienne nodded ruefully, and then a bitter smile crossed his lips. "It will be interesting to see the city without tourists." He stared out at the crowds on the most famous shopping street in Paris.

"Don't be ridiculous. They'll never do it. They'll find another way. Just as soon as somebody adds up what it would cost."

"There are some things, Murphy, that are worth doing no matter how excessive the cost may seem to be."

"Right you are," he said with a smile. "And you just happen to be driving one of them."

Etienne turned away. He put his hand full on the horn as though bleating out his response to Murphy. "Damn them!" he muttered. "Get moving!" he yelled out the window.

"Mind you," Murphy said with a shrug, "there's no sum of money too great to save my dear friends." He raised his eyebrows as though advising his ears they need not believe what his mouth just said. Etienne continued honking. "It's just that we're gonna have one sweet time regaining the tourists' confidence. You know, it's gonna make your life a helluva lot harder."

211

"I will not have a life unless that bus moves! I cannot keep the President of France waiting!"

"Tell him it's because you've done such a terrific job. He'll be very impressed. There are so many damn tourists in Paris the traffic can't move. Jesus. I can't wait to see a traffic jam like this in Epernay!"

"I have been Secretary of Tourism for six years and I have never met the President! I have never even been invited to the Elysée Palace! Now I am the most important man in an incredible international crisis and I cannot get there because of the traffic!" He honked and honked and honked. "They are right!" he cried out. "Everything they said was right! We should get every last one of them out of Paris!"

"So what kind of mileage you get on this baby?"

Etienne narrowed his eyes. "You think I do not mean that," he said softly.

"Maybe, old pal. But you'll never go through with it."

"You think we will never tell the tourists to get out."

Murphy nodded. "I know you will never tell the tourists to get out."

Etienne released the automatic door lock. He turned to Murphy. Without any expression on his face, he said, "Get out."

"It's a good thing you're only the Secretary of Tourism and not in charge of the panic button."

"I said, get out. Get out of the car."

Murphy rubbed his head. "You mean, as in Get out, this car ain't big enough for the two of us?"

"I mean, as in telling the tourists to get out of Paris. I mean, as in Paris is not big enough for the two of us!" Etienne waited. He leaned over to open the car door on Murphy's side. "Get out!"

Without saying a word, Murphy stepped from the car.

212

Etienne reached over and closed the door. He pressed a button to raise all the windows. He pressed a button to lock the doors. He pressed a button to turn on his headlights. And he kept his hand on the horn all the way to the Elysée Palace.

Murphy stood on the sidewalk. He heart was pounding. As in The prisoner was condemned to death.

WHILE the Ministers sat around the table, the Elysée Palace physician-in-residence looked down the throat of the President of France. He narrowed his gaze. "Say 'Chablis.' "

"Chablis," said the President of France.

The physician nodded approvingly. "Bon. Now say 'Bordeaux.' "

"Bordeaux."

The physician, careful to save the tongue depressor for a nephew, closed his bag. "There is no cause for alarm. The condition is sure to last for at least two more days."

The President smiled and, as the physician left, motioned for the Minister of the Quality of Life to continue.

"Monsieur Duvert," the Minister said nodding at Etienne, "has informed me there is an average for the month of October of somewhat under half a million tourists. If we divide this figure by thirty-one days, we have approximately sixteen thousand tourists per day."

"And they are all at Julien's when I want a table!" said the Minister of Cooperation.

The Chief of Staff of the Armed Forces pushed up his cuff and turned on his calculator watch. "I suggest, to be safe, we escalate the figure to twenty thousand."

"I agree," said the Minister of the Interior. "That will account for the overflow at La Coupole."

213

The Chief of Staff continued. "If we say twenty thousand, and then divide by an average of two hundred seats per plane, we need only one hundred planes."

"But to get them to the planes," said the Minister of Planning and Regional Development, "we would need some four hundred buses or trucks."

"Mon Dieu," muttered the Prime Minister. "Four hundred buses and trucks." He paused for a moment. "All filled with tourists." He brushed back a wisp of hair from his face. "All filled with tourists," he repeated slowly.

"Being taken away," said the Minister of Cooperation.

"Bus after bus after bus," mused the Minister of Justice.

"Far out of the city," sighed the Minister of Foreign Affairs.

There was a very long silence. The Minister of Planning and Regional Development took a deep breath and spoke softly. "It will be an unforgettable sight!"

After a moment, the Minister of Foreign Affairs asked, "I wonder what will be the best place to see it from?"

"We must keep the children up to watch until the very end," said the President of France.

"If only my son were older," said the Chief of Staff. "Still, I am sure there will be pictures."

"There will be more time for this later." The Minister of Foreign Affairs cleared his throat. "We must determine where the planes are to be sent."

"I have the ambassadors in the next room," said the Prime Minister. "I shall inform them now that we require their assistance."

"It is first and foremost a mission of mercy," said the Minister of Justice.

"Oh, no," laughed the Prime Minister. "I do not think we can expect them to understand that."

"No, no," said the Minister of Justice. "I do not mean for *us*. I am talking about saving the Americans."

"Of course," said the Prime Minister. "That is our only concern. Surely they will help."

The Minister of Economy and Finance shook his head as he came out of a huddle with his staff. "The cost will be enormous. What do you think the chances are they will share the expenses?"

The Minister of Foreign Affairs shrugged his shoulders. "The American Government should be most generous. What do you think?" he asked the Prime Minister. "Can we cover some of the costs? I am willing to contribute a modest amount. After all, it would be expensive to underwrite a rescue mission. That is, if we even knew where they are being held."

The Prime Minister took a deep breath. "Yes. I think the Minister of Economy and Finance has come up with a splendid idea. But even though we may be able to arrange such a subsidy, we must be prepared that the tourists will still be a very costly item for us to export."

"Mon Dieu!" Etienne jumped up. "Pardon! But that is the answer!"

The Minister of the Quality of Life scowled. "It is my pleasure to introduce the Secretary of Tourism."

Etienne began walking slowly around the table. "Monsieur le Président, the Prime Minister has solved the entire problem. The tourists should be viewed as a product we are exporting. A product like any other. A bottle of wine. A piece of cheese. A machine. Oui. A money machine. The tourists spend money wherever they go. Is the Republic of France to give away to other nations that which we have worked so many years to attract to our shores?" Every eye was on Etienne as he walked from chair to chair, moving closer to the President. "No! If I were the Secretary of Transport, would you ask me to give away our trains and planes? No, you would not! If I were Secretary of Housing, would you ask me to give away our homes? You would

215

not! If I were Secretary of Agriculture, would you ask me to give away our crops? No! No, you would not! With all due respect, Monsieur le Président, I am Secretary for a product as valuable as any other. I beg you, let us not *send* the tourists away! I beg you, let us not *give* the tourists away! I beg you, Monsieur le Président, let us *sell* the tourists!"

For the second time that morning, the Ministers sat motionless as though in shock. Raised eyebrow met raised eyebrow. Inquiring glance met shrugged shoulders. And finally, Etienne met the President of France.

"What is your name, my son?"

"Etienne Duvert."

The President of France put his hands on Etienne's shoulders. "I cannot kiss you because I have a cold." He peered into Etienne's eyes. "Tell me," he asked, "how much do you think we can get for them?"

CLIFFORD stood in the corner with his ear pressed against the door. Emma paced the length of the room, rolling her head from shoulder to shoulder to relieve the tension. Dwight sat on a red velvet chair and stared into his plate of uneaten Salade aux Moules à la Boulonnaise. Lily was hunched over in her chair, staring intently from mattress to mattress, from corner to corner, from floor to ceiling. Her eyes darted around the room. She nodded as though approving some master plan.

Lily walked over to the mattresses. She bent down, grabbed one and began dragging it across the floor. Clifford and Dwight turned to watch. Lily pulled the mattress to the other side of the room and, after pinwheeling one end, rested it against the wall. She stood back and admired her chaise. While hauling a second mattress across the

217

room, Lily, groaned as Emma, still pacing nervously, nearly collided with her.

After manufacturing a second chaise, Lily positioned a red velvet chair as an end table. She took a vase of flowers from the buffet and put it on her table. Hands on hips, she admired her handiwork before turning to point an accusing finger directly at the two remaining mattresses. Eyes riveted to her every move, they watched Lily as though looking over the shoulder of a brilliant neuro-surgeon. She breathed heavily while piling one mattress on top of the other in order to construct a sofa.

Lily took a deep breath and removed her jacket. She rolled up her sleeves, narrowed her eyes and scrutinized the dishes on the table with the fervor of a mother hen searching for her chicks. Smiling, she reached for the Bet-teraves au Cumin, a chilled salad of beets in vinegar with caraway seeds. Lily then pinched each rosebud in the vase until she found one firm enough. She tucked a napkin into her blouse. With the Betteraves in one hand and her rosebud raised on high, she walked triumphantly to the blank wall between her Lily-the-First chaise and her Lily-the-First sofa.

As though tutored by Rivera, she dipped the rosebud into the beet juice and drew an enormous purple square on the white wall. Then she divided it into four equal parts by drawing a line vertically down the center and a line across the horizontal. Lily smiled broadly as her audience watched in astonished silence. She dipped and redipped the rosebud. With the greatest of flourishes, she drew cur-tains on either side of her window.

Dwight began to smile. Emma stopped pacing and looked over at Clifford. As all heads turned to watch, Lily selected a fresh rosebud. She picked up a dish of mustard and walked back to her window. She drew a large yellow circle peeking out from behind the curtains. Using the mustard with the assurance of Van Gogh, she painted a bright sun. As a final touch, she drew cheerful little rays.

Dwight applauded. He stood up and shouted, "Brava! Brava, Lily!"

Emma ran across the room and put her arms around Clifford. Lily's performance terrified her. "All the world is *not* a stage!" Emma yelled.

"Wouldn't you know she'd get that line wrong?" Lily said to Dwight. "See here, Raggedy Ann, I am merely trying to brighten things up a bit, to help us survive this ordeal more pleasantly."

"What makes you so certain we'll survive?" Emma asked.

Lily ignored the question and spoke to Dwight. "There's still one thing missing." She dipped her rosebud into the mustard and put a little yellow circle on the wall. "A present for you, my darling. Room Service!"

"Lily," Emma began.

"I know!" Lily interrupted. "The play's *not* the thing!"

"Don't you realize the danger we're in?" Emma asked.

"Would you really feel better, darling, if I beat my fists on the door and screamed?"

"It might convince me you were human. My God, Lily, aren't you worried at all?"

"Good news at last, Emma," she said sarcastically. "Yes, I am worried."

"Dearest." Dwight held her close.

She took a deep breath. "If you must know, I'm terrified the sons of bitches haven't asked for enough money."

"What?" Emma asked.

"See here, you don't think I want to be ransomed off like forgotten railway baggage!" She turned to Dwight. "I'll never be able to face anyone if this turns out to be some sort of penny-ante abduction."

219

Dwight tried to comfort her. "Lily, all you have to do is look at the table to know this plot was thickened with great care and style."

"Yes, yes," she said, brushing a wisp of hair from her face. "I know it's been beautifully catered. But you can't expect me to overlook these depressing summer-stock mattresses. Darling, they do give one pause."

"Jesus," Clifford muttered.

"I don't know. Maybe I'm the one who's wrong," Emma said. "Maybe I'm crazy."

"Perhaps it's merely that the Princess and the Pauper don't realize they've been in worse danger before," Lily said.

"Indeed," Dwight said. "I don't know how you two survived some of the restaurants you've reviewed. Seems to me you're safer right now than you've been in years."

Suddenly, Emma turned to Clifford. "Cliffy, is this the jacket you wore the day you got your hair cut at the barber school?"

"Yeah."

"Take it off!"

"Why?"

"Take it off. Please!" Clifford removed his jacket and handed it to her. Emma felt the inside breast pocket. She smiled. "It's still there!"

"What is?" he asked.

"The pencil." Emma was examining the lining. "You complained about the hole in your pocket. Oh, Cliffy," she said excitedly, "it's still there!"

"Splendid!" Lily gushed. "Now you can draw in little roaches on your side of the room and feel right at home."

"Let's all have a drink," Dwight said, trying to change the subject.

"My hero," Lily cooed.

Dwight walked to the wall and pressed the yellow button. "A bottle of bubbly coming up!"

"I've got it!" Emma shouted.

Lily sat down and sighed. "I can hardly wait to see what the Queen of the Vile has in store for us."

Emma pulled up a chair and cleared a space at the table. She smoothed out the cloth. "It's very simple, Diamond Lily. It's time one of us coped with the reality of being captured, imprisoned and in danger of being killed. I am going to write my will."

"Oh, Dwight!" Lily called out. "Do hurry with the champagne. At last, there's something to celebrate!"

Clifford sat down on the floor and kept his ear at the keyhole. Dwight began filling their glasses.

Emma hunched over the table as she began to write. "I, Emma Benjamin, being of sound mind and body, do hereby bequeath one-half of my vast fortune to American Express and the other half of my vast fortune to the Diners Club, provided they grant Honorary Member status to the Pizzeria Nunzio in Florence." Emma looked up at Clifford. Her eyes were moist. "Do you remember?"

"Of course I do."

Emma turned back to the tablecloth. "I hereby establish the Emma Benjamin Memorial Pizza Fund for starving lovers." She looked back at Clifford. "It was great pizza, wasn't it, Cliffy?"

"The best."

Tears began to stream down her cheeks. "I wonder if . . ."

Clifford's voice cracked. "Rudy."

"Yes, Rudy!" she sobbed. "I wonder if Rudy is still there."

Clifford began to cry. Emma laid her head down on the table.

221

Lily whispered. "Good God, Dwight, they made love in a pizzeria!"

They drank in silence. No one moved except Clifford, who, after emptying his glass in one gulp, stood up slowly. He reached for a chair, raised it over his head and smashed it against the door. Emma ran to put her arms around him.

Lily shook her head. "You oaf, that's usually done with the glass."

"Dear boy, that chair was worth more than you are," Dwight said. "You're sure to anger them."

"Anger them?" Clifford asked incredulously. "Are you afraid they might kidnap us?"

"On second thought," Lily mused, "they might put you in solitary." There was a noise at the door. A key in the lock. "Now you've done it," she said.

All eyes were on the door as it opened. They drew back as they saw an enormous man wearing a brown leather aviator's cap with the flaps hanging down on either side of his face. He put a finger to his lips cautioning them to keep quiet.

"Good morning," Petit Meurice whispered. "I am here to save you. Claude Picard sent me."

"Claude?"

"The concierge?"

"But how did he—"

"There is no time now. Do not speak. Follow behind me. Do not make a sound. They will kill us if they catch me taking you out of here."

Petit Meurice looked out into the corridor. He motioned for them to follow. As Emma stepped through the doorway, she gasped at the sight of Antoine sprawled on the floor. "Is he . . .?"

"Shhhhhh!"

IT was eleven o'clock. In one hour, the President of France would announce that his nation, in view of its close ties to the United States of America, was prepared to yield. All tourists were to be evacuated from Paris in order to save the lives of the four Americans held hostage.

In the basement of the Elysée Palace, the Emergency Preparedness Room had been activated. The noise was overpowering as personnel set about the administrative machinery required to move some twenty thousand people within a few hours. The room had already become thick with smoke.

Etienne, in front of a wall map of the city, was speaking to the Mayor of Paris and the Chief of Police. He slapped the tip of his pointer against the map. "The infestations are greatest in the first and second arrondissements, the eighth, the ninth, the tenth, fourteenth and fifteenth."

The Chief of Police sipped cognac from a crystal snifter. "They have really ruined the fifteenth. I once lived there. It was at that time a very pleasant neighborhood. But today"—he held up his hand in despair—"you cannot walk safely at night for fear someone will grab you and ask 'How do I get here?' or 'How do I get there?' "

The Mayor of Paris sighed deeply. "I had no idea it was that bad in the fifteenth."

Etienne's walkie-talkie signaled. "Yes?" he asked, pressing the button.

"Telephone, Monsieur le Secrétaire. Line eleven. Murphy Norwalk."

Etienne pursed his lips. "I am too busy." He switched off the unit.

"Attention, s'il vous plaît," boomed the voice on the public-address system. "The President has declared that all offices and schools will close today at noon."

The Director of Public Transportation ran over to the Mayor. "They are taking all my buses away from me!"

"It is worse than the war," the Mayor said.

"It *is* war!" Etienne corrected.

The Mayor smiled. "It will be a sight."

Etienne nodded. His pocket unit signaled. "Yes?"

"Telephone. Line fourteen. Aldo Manello. Commercial Attaché. Italian Embassy."

Etienne shrugged. "Merci." He picked up the phone. "Line fourteen, please. . . . Hello? Aldo?"

"Attention, s'il vous plaît," the voice came over the loudspeakers. "The President has ordered three reviewing stands. One at the Porte de la Chapelle to watch the tourists being taken to Le Bourget . . ."

"Etienne, this is Aldo. I have come up with two more 747's."

"But Aldo, the units are all allocated."

"Please, Etienne. It has not been a good season in Milan. The weather is terrible. The hotels are complaining! The restaurants are complaining! The merchants are complaining! They have *even* started being polite at Gucci! Two more planeloads is all I want."

". . . another at the Porte d'Italie to watch those leaving via Orly . . ."

"Aldo, I suggested you increase your order earlier. You could have had them before Luxembourg snapped them up."

"I didn't know then. Etienne, I must have another shipment! They will spend enough during the forty-eight hours to keep everyone off my back. I'll tell you what. I'll give you ten percent above. Anyway, what the hell will they do with themselves in Luxembourg?"

"Is ten your limit?"

"Why?"

". . . and the third reviewing stand at the Porte de Bagnolet for those leaving from De Gaulle."

"I may be able to get you one 747 if you agree to pay Denmark a penalty of five percent and pay me ten."

"Agreed. But Etienne . . ." He hesitated.

"Yes?"

"Is it possible to keep them longer than Friday night?"

"Aldo!"

"No, no, no. I meant only until the shops close on Saturday."

"Aldo, we have no control over the time period. We are merely following the demands."

There was a pause. "Of course you will let me know if there is a change."

Etienne hung up and then flashed the operator. "Get me the Danish Embassy."

The Chief of Police picked up a telephone and dialed Information. "At which stand will the President be?"

"The motorcade will visit each site prior to the Presidential Ball," the voice replied.

"Lars, this is Etienne. I may have to short-ship you. But I'm willing to pay a penalty."

The Danish Commercial Attaché laughed. "You spoke to Aldo, eh? He has been calling frantically. What is he prepared to offer?"

"Three percent."

"Is he crazy? Come now, Etienne. You know how much they will spend. I won't sell at three."

"Four?"

"How many does he want?"

"Two 747's."

"I'll give him one 747 at five. Take it or leave it."

"But he needs two!"

"To hell with him! We've already announced that Jensen will be open around the clock."

"All right, I'll take one at five." Etienne flashed for the operator. "Get me the German Embassy."

"Attention, s'il vous plaît," the voice said. "The President has authorized live coverage of the evacuation on closed-circuit television for all those in military and civilian hospitals."

"Etienne, old chum, what can I do for you?"

"Günter, I want some of the tourists back."

"You could have them all as far as I'm concerned. We are already having such a boom here we don't know where to put them all. Everybody loves a loser! Still, it would look like hell if we didn't take some. Especially after the whole World War Two thing."

Etienne consulted a list he took from his jacket. "I've

got you down for fifteen planeloads. I must have ten back."

"Take them, old chum. With my compliments."

"Also, you've got to pay an additional twenty percent for the five loads you have." There was a pause. "Otherwise you'll be low bid, and that will really look like hell." Another pause. "Especially after the World War Two thing."

"All right. But none of this thirty-day-payment schmutz."

"I'll give you sixty."

"What are you talking about? This is Germany, old chum, not Albania. I can afford to pay on delivery. And I will pay top price! The world must know we paid more than everyone else, and we paid faster then everyone else, because we are better than everyone else!" There was a loud thump as Günter banged on his desk.

Etienne held his breath for a moment and then asked nervously, "Günter, you do understand, don't you? You know you have to give them back on Friday?"

"I know, I know," Günter sighed. "Life is *not* a picnic, old chum."

"Wiedersehen." Etienne hung up. He walked to another desk, where one by one he picked up four phones. "Get me the Belgian Embassy. Get me the Dutch Embassy. Get me the Swiss Embassy. Get me the British Embassy." Holding two phones in each hand, Etienne turned his back on the dozens of people running into and out of the room. Once the commercial attachés were on the line, Etienne grouped the phones around his mouth and said precisely, "I have ten additional planeloads. The bidding will open at thirty percent above the previous figure. Gentlemen, you may begin."

AT twelve o'clock, they were in Pierre's office listening to the radio. Marie-Thérèse had a hand over her open mouth. Alphonse chewed noisily on a Life Saver. Pierre stared wide-eyed while Claude looked over the balcony into the lobby. Jean and the others from Reception were gathered around Sylvie's cage. Gaspar stood inside the revolving door, the bellboys gathered around him as they listened to his pocket radio.

" '. . . they have invaded our national heritage,' " pronounced the President of France. He paused as though to allow both Alphonse and Gaspar the time to nod in agreement. " 'Unless every foreign tourist has left Paris . . .' " The President continued reading the letter.

Le Dom had won. Yet Claude Picard had lost. A vulnerable piece of machinery, this Claude Picard, this wounded shell. It was not strange that he should wonder about her.

" 'Otherwise, the four will die,' " the President read.

How ironic to hide behind the wooden face of the concierge. Le Dom had won! The Republic had won! Where were the drums? Perhaps it was time to leave this Picard person. Surely, by now the defender of Champagne had earned his freedom.

" 'We did not allow Paris to burn. We must not allow her to smother,' " the President read with great feeling. " 'Vive la France!' " After a moment he cleared his throat. "Citizens of France, we cannot allow the Americans to die. However we despise this shameful threat, we cannot, in view of our long friendship and deep love for the American people, risk the safety of their countrymen."

Marie-Thérèse cried out. "Dwight! I know they will kill him!" She ran to Claude.

He put his arms around her. "They will not kill him."

The President continued. ". . . And so I ask the people of all nations to join with the citizens of France, their dear allies, not in a forced evacuation, but in a celebration. A celebration of humanity, to which the nations of the world have opened their doors."

Alphonse shook his head. "The pity is they are doing all of this for Dwight Simon."

Claude looked up with more anger than he wanted to show. "They are doing all of this *because of* Dwight Simon!"

"I suppose. But the Simons bring business. And they are more boring than harmful." Alphonse snickered. "And now, I think they will bring even more business than before. Money could not buy such publicity."

Pierre had not taken his eyes from Claude. "If that is true, and I believe it is, what do you think they will accomplish by all of this?"

"It has already been accomplished," Claude said.

"And if the demands had not been met?" Pierre asked.

"They were met," Claude said flatly. "I must go down

and help our guests to leave." Marie-Thérèse ran out crying.

Alphonse walked to the door. "A pity there will be no one to eat the prawns." He shrugged. "Perhaps a curry tomorrow."

"Concierge," Pierre said. "I would like you to remain." Once they were alone, Pierre offered him a cigarette. "I thought I recognized Antoine this morning. I think now the other driver was Nicolas. Yes?"

"I do not know what you are talking about."

"I suppose everyone was involved. Isabelle, Edouard, Le Comte, Joseph . . ."

"I must go. The guests will need my help."

Pierre slammed his fist on the desk. "Why did you not tell me what you were planning?"

"You are no longer one of us, Pierre." Claude smiled. "I am surprised you would take offense at not being included. But of course, how foolish of me. You could have taken Marcel's place."

"Mon Dieu, I should unmask all of you! Do you know how much this will cost me?"

"The cost to you, Pierre, is silence. Not money. Silence is the price you have to pay." Claude got up and walked to the door.

"Tell me, Concierge. Since we are so frank with each other, would you really have killed them?"

He held tightly to the doorknob. Claude refrained from answering as long as he could. "Yes." He slammed the door.

It was not until Claude was back in his room, with the door locked, that he dared unclench his teeth. "No," he said, leaning his head against the mantelpiece.

230

"No," he said, reaching up to touch the frame on the Fragonard. "No," he said, running his fingers across the leather bindings on the Proust. "No," he said, as his hand brushed the keys of the harpsichord.

Claude sat in the Pathier chair and picked up his Eiffel Tower. "Remember, Emma Benjamin." The words he had spoken to her echoed all around him. "Remember this room." He closed his eyes. He had not expected that this room, this incredible room as she had called it, could be so empty without her. "Tell me, Concierge, would you really have killed them?" He shook his head. No. It would have been impossible.

WHEN Claude walked down the flight of stairs to the lobby, he saw the British couple arguing at Reception.

"But we're not tourists!" the young man shouted.

Jean shrugged. "Then, of course, the orders do not apply to you. I shall have to notify the police, however. Can you tell me the nature of your business?"

Claude watched as the man reached into his wallet and then shook hands with Jean. "You see, we are here," he began haltingly, "to, uh, purchase samples of haute couture for a boutique we are opening in Kent. Our trip is totally business."

Jean smiled as he put the money into his jacket pocket. "Of course. I shall note that on my records."

As Claude walked over, Jean winked at him. Without saying a word, Claude put his hand on the flap of Jean's pocket and, in a single motion, ripped the pocket from his jacket. The British couple stood frozen as Claude methodically reached into the dismembered pocket and handed the money back to them. "You cannot be too careful in these dangerous times. There are spies everywhere."

231

Claude went back to his desk. Henri was shaking his head. "I have been deluged ever since the announcement!"

"I am sorry. I did not realize how late it was."

"The Baroness Settanni wishes a table at Lasserre," Henri said, rifling through his notes.

"Tell her it is impossible."

"Mr. Jackson wishes a table at Régine's."

"It is impossible."

Henri felt himself become nervous. "The Michaelsons wish to go to the Folies."

"It is impossible."

"The Colemans—"

"It is impossible."

Henri put down his notes. He stared at Claude, who sat expressionless. The telephone rang. "It is for you." Henri handed him the phone and left.

"Oui?"

"Le Dom?"

"Yes."

"They are gone," Isabelle said.

Claude was suddenly out of breath. "Gone?"

"Antoine is dead. The room is empty."

"Where is Meurice?"

"We cannot find him. Le Dom, I have not seen those finger marks on anyone's neck in thirty-five years."

"There is one chance. Go to the trunk room. You may still be able to stop him."

"Mon Dieu! I forgot!"

Claude held on to the receiver after she hung up. It was impossible.

HEY followed Petit Meurice without a word. He led them along a dim wainscoted corridor. They felt their way down dark, narrow stone steps. Unable to see, they shuffled slowly until they heard the angry squeal of rusted hinges. He led them into a very cold room. Once the door closed behind them, he lit a candle. Eight fearful eyes winced at the sudden light.

"Where the hell are we?" Clifford asked. They stared at the piles of old trunks, suitcases and cartons.

"And who are you, dear boy?"

"Oh, Dwight, I fear we're in the fire for sure."

"Did Claude say anything?" Emma began. "I mean, did he give you any messages?"

"How the hell did he know where we were?"

"Shhhhh!" Petit Meurice warned. "We have no time now. We are only halfway there."

"Halfway where?"

Petit Meurice did not acknowledge Clifford's question. Instead, he gave the candle to Lily while he began moving some of the cartons. "You will like the next part of our journey," he said, clearing a path toward an old walnut armoire. "Come." He opened the ornately carved door. "We must hurry."

Lily turned to Dwight. "Said the white rabbit to the sitting ducks."

"Hurry where?" Clifford asked. "Into a closet?"

Petit Meurice nodded. "It is an armoire. A very old one."

"You want us to go into a closet with you?"

Petit Meurice smiled. He took the candle from Lily and squeezed himself into the armoire. The four of them closed ranks as he removed the back panel to reveal a door. He pushed down the latch and leaned gently against it. They strained to see beyond the open door. There was nothing but blackness.

"Come," Petit Meurice urged. His voice echoed as though he were standing in a tunnel. Only his face, with those great bulging eyes, was visible in the candlelight.

Lily took a step back. "I think we should let the Benjamins go first." Everyone turned to look at Lily. "Well, fair is fair. We were kidnapped first!"

"I'm not going," Clifford said.

"Come," echoed Petit Meurice's voice.

"Where?" Clifford asked. "Where are you taking us?"

A pause. And then a great whisper resounded like the first wave in a sudden storm. "Somewhere over the rainbow!"

They stood in stunned silence. Lily shrugged her shoulders. "Well, what the hell!" She stepped into the armoire and looked back at Emma and Clifford. "Come, come, you two. You can ask the Wizard for a heart and a brain."

234

Dwight took Lily's hand. As he walked into the armoire, he leaned back to help Emma. She held on to him and dragged Clifford in behind her. After stepping through the false door, they suddenly found themselves struggling to maintain their balance on a floor that curved up around them. Petit Meurice cautioned them to be quiet as he searched the wooden wall of the giant tubular structure. He then sighed with relief, put his fingers to his lips and whispered, "Shhhh!" He blew out the candle.

They were in total darkness. There was a dim yellow light as Petit Meurice opened another door. It was some sort of a tunnel. He listened for a moment and then put his head out the door. He looked from side to side, stepped down and motioned for them to follow. They walked out of an enormous wooden cask into a seemingly endless arched brick tunnel. Lining the walls, as far as they could see, were other casks lying on their sides.

Lily looked around fearfully. "I knew it! A few hours with them and we're at the bottom of the barrel!"

Petit Meurice spoke in a barely audible whisper. "I have the pleasure to welcome you to the caves of Pommel et Bonnard."

"The champagne?" Clifford asked.

"Shhh! We are not out of danger yet. There are many people working down here. You must not speak one word," he cautioned them, "until it is safe." Then he smiled. "I will explain things as we go. I think you will enjoy it." He waited a moment. "Do you understand?"

The four of them looked at one another. As Clifford was about to say Yes, Lily put her hand over his mouth and nodded for him.

Petit Meurice turned back to the oak cask through which they had entered and closed the door. He smiled. "This was built for our most precious reserve. A reserve of old vintage wine is kept to blend with the pressing from the new harvest. It is the blending that gives the character unique to Pommel champagne. That is what all of these casks are filled with. The reserve. But this cask was built for an even more important mission." His eyes narrowed. "It was an escape route for the Maquis during the Occupation. Those of us who were hidden in the cellars could escape through the vineyards. And now"— he motioned for them to follow him—"I am taking you the same way we brought in Claude Picard over thirty-five years ago."

The four of them listened intently. "We carried him through here when he was wounded." Lily opened her mouth as though she had suddenly remembered something.

Unconsciously, Emma reached down toward her right knee. Then, with the sudden awareness of being watched, she turned. Lily was staring at Emma's hand.

They walked along the cold earthen floor, passing dozens and dozens of vats. "You see, unlike the fine wines of Bordeaux and Burgundy, the name on a bottle of champagne does not identify a single vineyard from which all of the grapes come. No, no. Champagne is a blend from a number of vineyards." He turned back and smiled. "As the Maquis was a blend of people from all walks of life." The smile left his lips as he said, "We were united in a common goal. To end the occupation." He stopped to look both ways as they came to a crossroads. There was a small blue-and-white enamel plaque on each corner that informed them they had been walking along Galerie B and were making a right turn into Galerie 16.

"Most people do not realize that champagne is a manufactured wine. It is not simply that you grow grapes, press them and put the juice into bottles like those simpletons in Bordeaux." They watched as Petit Meurice's breath fogged in front of him. Galerie 15. Galerie 14. Galerie 13.

"Then there is the decision of how much sugar to add."

236

He turned back to them. "During the occupation, the Nazis controlled it all. Poor Madame Pommel had to bargain with them for sugar. How terrible for her! To have to beg to continue the tradition of her fine family! You see, they too invaded more than our privacy. They also invaded our national heritage." Galerie 12. Galerie 11. "During the occupation they controlled everything. The sugar. The food. Even the films. Ah, the films they would not let us see! Such harmless films with pretty people singing and dancing."

The arched brick tunnel that was Galerie 11 led directly into a series of smaller, darker tunnels whose curved limestone ceilings were covered with mold. Lying flat on their sides, stacked eighteen rows high, were green bottles of champagne undergoing fermentation. The nearly six-foot-high stacks ran for miles along both sides of the tunnels.

Petit Meurice motioned for them to stop. He cocked his head, listening for a sound he could not hear. With a great huffing, he bent his enormous frame down onto the floor and stretched out a hand in front of him. Allowing just the tips of his fingers to touch the cold earth, he shut his eyes as though listening with his hand. He rose quickly, taking a deep breath, and pushed the four of them against the wall between two casks. His eyes ablaze, he lifted a finger to his mouth as his lips formed the sound "Shhhh!"

Emma leaned her head on Clifford's shoulder. Dwight embraced Lily. They heard nothing. But Petit Meurice stood still, barely breathing, as he nodded his head in anticipation. The hum had become a rumble, and then they heard a motor and the shaking of glass as a man on a front-load open truck hauled his cargo of bottles through the underground labyrinth. Once he could no longer be heard, Petit Meurice smiled and led them to where the bottles were stored.

"After the wine from the new harvest has fermented in vats, it is blended. So much from this vineyard, so much from that. And then the proper amount of reserve is added to bring the wine around. It has now become the special blend of the house called the cuvée. La cuvée. The specialty of the house." He turned to them and smiled proudly. "The characters of the champagne houses are as different as the musicals from MGM were from those of RKO and Paramount." He paused for a moment. "Can you imagine the Nazis not allowing us to see *Babes on Broadway?*"

As Galerie M led into Galerie N, Petit Meurice pointed to a dab of white paint on the bottom rim of each bottle. "The caviste marks each bottle. They are stored here for five years. Once each year every bottle is shaken to mix the sediment back into the wine. Then they are restacked."

Emma began to cry. She put her hands over her mouth and looked helplessly at the others. Clifford brushed away the tears. Lily turned, not wanting Emma to see that she too was terrified.

They were tired and cold as they walked mile after mile. Twice they stopped upon hearing the sound of an explosion. Excess gas produced by the sugar had caused some bottles to burst. "Of course, if the cuvée is composed solely of wine from a single harvest and no reserve is used, then a vintage is declared." Petit Meurice turned back to look at them. "Nineteen forty-two and nineteen forty-five were vintage years for us," he said defiantly.

There was light at the end of Galerie O. After over an hour of walking through dim, moldy tunnels, the mere promise of light, whatever the source, lifted their spirits. They walked quickly as though suddenly renewed.

Petit Meurice beamed with pride as they stepped into what appeared to be a lunar landscape. The smoothly arched ceilings of the tunnels gave way to the craggy, ir-

238

regular shapes of wedges cut from whitewashed lime-stone-and-clay walls. Echoing the almost triangular shape of the wedges were wooden, inverted-V racks in which thousands of bottles were placed neck down. "This is where I do my work!" he said excitedly. "You see, after the bottles have slept on their sides for five years, they are brought to me and put into these racks. Pupitres. It is my job to turn and angle the bottles so that the sediment will slide down into the neck and rest against the cork. It is a very delicate operation," he said, turning one bottle with each hand. "See?" He turned some sixty bottles in less than fifteen seconds. "All that is left for the others is to freeze the sediment onto the cork, remove it, add a little sugar syrup and recork it. But that part is very boring."

Suddenly, Petit Meurice had nothing more to say and, seemingly, no place to go. Clifford took his arm from around Emma. He did not whisper as he asked, "Why have we stopped?"

"Because we are here."

"Where?"

Petit Meurice reached up and loosened the screws that held marker number 9 to the wall. He pressed the latch, and a ten-inch-thick slab of limestone opened into a room. He motioned for the Simons and the Benjamins to enter.

The room was divided by floor-to-ceiling iron bars. Within the caged section were a table and four chairs. Petit Meurice held open the iron gate. With an overwhelming sense of doom, they walked to the table and read their names on the small white place cards. Silently, without being told, each sat in front of the correct card. They were not surprised to hear the cell door slam shut behind them.

IT was one o'clock. Or, as the voice in the War Room had just announced, "Bon Voyage minus five." Etienne stood across the table from the Minister of Economy and Finance, the Prime Minister and the Commander-in-Chief of the Armed Forces. He picked up his pointer and began moving markers across the map of Europe spread out before them.

"Our initial estimates were based upon a standard unit price for all Common Market members." Etienne smiled as he moved markers into Italy, Belgium and Luxembourg. "Our terms were full payment within thirty days." He moved markers into England and Ireland. "The Swiss were furious at our restricting the bidding to EEC nations and offered payment in only ten days. To their chagrin, the others followed suit. Germany, as usual, overreacted outrageously. They had already volunteered payment on delivery." Markers were pushed across the map into Denmark and The Netherlands. "All that was left, then, for the Swiss was to raise the price per unit. That was when everything got out of hand." He moved the last markers into Germany and Switzerland. "I am pleased to report to you that in addition to covering our projected expenses for the evacuation and return, we will have a twelve-to fourteen-percent profit above our costs."

The Prime Minister looked up and smiled. "Perhaps we should have such a sale every year."

The Minister of Economy and Finance put his hand on Etienne's shoulder. "You have done very well so far, Duvert. If your figures prove accurate, I am confident the President will be very pleased."

"Pleased?" the Prime Minister scoffed. "If his figures are what he claims, I would not be surprised to see Duvert replace Brezol on the Council next year."

Etienne felt his mouth grow dry. He did not know what to say for fear he would betray his excitement. He was grateful to hear himself being paged. "Excuse me, gentlemen," he said walking to the telephone. "This is Duvert. I have a call on line seven."

"Etienne?"

"Who is this?"

"Can you talk?"

"Who is this?"

"Durac. Pierre Durac. From the Louis."

"What do you want, Pierre?"

"I want to help you. I have information of interest to you."

"What information?"

"I know who is responsible for all of this. I can help you put a stop to it."

"A stop to what?" Etienne asked.

"To the evacuation! To this madness."

Etienne looked around, afraid someone might have overheard Pierre. "What are you saying? Is this a joke, Pierre?"

"A joke? Etienne, my life is at stake. I am calling on my private line, but I am not even sure that is safe. Listen to me, I can put an end to all of this!"

But it had all just begun for Etienne! By turning a national threat into a national profit, he had secured his entire future. And now Pierre was offering to put an end to it? "Listen to me, Pierre," he hissed. "If you ever mention this conversation to anyone, anyone at all, I personally guarantee the world will know you were the informer. Worse than that, I will see to it that you are audited annually! And I will arrange for monthly health and building inspectors who cannot be bribed! As far as I am concerned, you have not called to tell me anything other than how well the evacuation is proceeding at the Louis. Do you understand?" There was a long pause. Etienne looked around guiltily and spoke in a loud voice. "I am pleased to learn your guests are in the lobby awaiting transfer to the airport."

"And now you will listen to me, Etienne. If *you* ever mention this conversation to anyone, I personally guarantee that the Council will know you withheld vital information. You see, my friend, I have secretly been taping this entire conversation!"

Etienne put a hand to his head. "Why would you do a thing like that?" he whispered hoarsely.

Another pause. "Protection. In the event, as I feared, that you might be one of them. If you ever cause me any trouble, Etienne, I will release this recording more widely than a new song by Schubert! You will not dare to do anything to me. Do *you* understand?" Etienne smiled and sighed with relief. He would be safe now. Pierre was as frightened as he. "And so," Pierre continued, squeezing the last drop of venom out of the conversation, "you think my guests are sitting in the lobby? Ha! I am sorry to disappoint you. But there is no one sitting in my lobby except my doorman. Surely you realize that at one o'clock our guests are not still in their rooms. They are all out, Etienne. They are out having lunch, fittings or facials."

Etienne's voice grew tense. "How many units are sitting in your lobby?"

"How many *what?*"

"Tourists! How many?"

"One British couple."

"Where are the others?" he yelled.

"I told you. They are out. On the boulevards and in the boutiques. You will have to find them, my friend, if you wish to send them away."

"Mon Dieu," Etienne murmured as he hung up the receiver. He turned quickly to the Commander-in-Chief of the Armed Forces. "I must have a car and some trucks. At once!"

ETIENNE stood up in the front seat of the Jeep. A walkie-talkie was slung over his shoulder. He had Murphy's binoculars around his neck. And he carried a bullhorn in one hand. The driver looked up at him as they reached street level from the underground garage. Etienne nodded to the right. The driver turned back to the convoy of twelve open troop trucks and made a broad gesture to the right. They proceeded slowly along the avenue de Marigny toward Place Beauvau. Etienne could almost hear the steady beat of a sarabande. He switched on the walkie-talkie and brought the microphone to his

243

lips. Solemnly he announced, "We are about to take the St.-Honoré!"

As they turned the corner, Etienne gasped. Hundreds of shoppers were lined up in front of stores already filled to capacity. There were twenty in front of Lanvin. At least twice as many at Cardin. The chic butterflies who once had flown from flower to flower had been replaced by swarms of impatient locusts. Each line had its own energy as it spilled off the sidewalk and into the street. Some moved steadily; others pulsated as heads bobbed up and down and bodies shifted from foot to foot. Those who squeezed out of the shops laden with packages had but a brief moment of victory as they pushed past the crowd of envious onlookers merely to join the end of another line.

The most elegant shopping street in Paris had become an Arabian bazaar. Shopkeepers peddled armloads of handbags and sweaters to those standing in line. Young women swirled brightly colored designer-initialed scarves and yelled, "Cent francs! Cent francs!" Black men in caftans held up wallets and belts. Students showed freshly painted scenes of Montmartre, urging, "Buy direct from the artist!" Pastries and sandwiches were being hawked like hot dogs during the ninth inning.

Etienne leaned forward against the windshield. He reached for his binoculars to estimate how many units were lined up in front of Louis Feraud. In front of Castillo. Down the block toward Roger & Gallet. It was a thrilling sight! He began counting to himself. One 747! A thin smile stretched across his nervous lips. Two 747's! And that didn't include the mob in front of Saint Laurent! He signaled for Commandant Giffard.

"Monsieur le Secrétaire?"

"Commandant, we must get through."

"You don't mean through that?" he asked pointing down the St.-Honoré.

"Yes! I don't care how we do it. I don't care how many men we need. We must get behind their lines!"

"But—"

"It's not until we get them off the street that we can go in and clean out the boutiques!"

"But—"

"First we take the ones standing outside. Get them into the trucks quickly. We will need reinforcements. God knows how many of them are in Hermès!"

Commandant Giffard saluted. "A vôtre service, Monsieur le Secrétaire."

Etienne tapped his driver on the shoulder. "This is it. We are going in. Proceed slowly. Very slowly. But remember one thing: under no circumstances are you to stop until we cross the rue Royale!"

The driver took a deep breath and nodded. Etienne raised one hand to prepare those behind him. He lowered it, pointing straight at the heart of the St.-Honoré. He brought the bullhorn to his lips. "Mesdames et Messieurs. Distinguished visitors. Bonjour. As you know, it is imperative you return to your hotels at once."

The convoy, like a giant serpent, began pushing its way through the crowd. There were groans and angry cries as shoppers pushed closer together to make room for the hostile intruders. "We have provided free transportation and request your immediate cooperation. Merci beaucoup."

Women began raising their fists in protest. Others swung at the trucks with their handbags. Etienne was terrified. He held the binoculars against his eyes, which, no one but he knew, were shut tight. He consoled himself over and over again with the standing order from Lichten-

245

stein of sixty percent above retail for each hundred units. Daring to open his lids for a moment, he turned back and brought the walkie-talkie to his lips. "Truck Twelve to remain at Louis Feraud. Truck Eleven to remain at Castillo. Truck Ten at Helena Rubinstein."

Just after he passed Courrèges. a woman called out to him from a doorway. "What are you doing to us? Are you trying to put us out of business?" Obviously the owner of a shop, she raised her hands to plead with him. "For God's sake, let them spend in peace!"

"Je regrette, Madame," Etienne called out. "But the President has said—"

"To hell with the President!" she shouted. "Does he pay my rent?"

Etienne picked up the bullhorn. "Attention all tourists. The Government of France, in order to save the lives of the captured Americans, requires your immediate cooperation. Please come out of the stores. We will take you back to your hotels. This is an official order. Please get into the trucks in an orderly manner." They began throwing things at Etienne. A newspaper. Half a brioche.

Etienne put the binoculars in front of his eyes and closed them again. He turned on the walkie-talkie. "Truck Nine at Courrèges. Eight and Seven, get them at Saint Laurent. Six, get them all at Lancôme. Five, move every last one of them out of Laroche. Four, get Lapidus!"

The shoppers on the rue du Faubourg St.-Honoré had joined arms and formed a human chain diagonally across the street from Hermès to Givenchy. "Buy or Die!" they chanted. "Buy or Die!"

The Jeep came to a halt. Etienne stared down at the seething mob in front of him. They juggled packages, cameras and airline flight bags as they tried to hold their ground. The trucks in the rear could not get through to deliver their precious cargo. But ahead was the rue Royale, where there would be reinforcements. He had no choice. Survival meant that somehow he had to make it past Hermès, Carita, Jourdan and the stronghold at Givenchy. Etienne signaled the driver to keep honking. He picked up the bullhorn, and as though he were the first Frenchman to recite the words to "La Marseillaise," he sang out, "Marchons, marchons! Qu'un sang impur Abreuve nos sillons!"

The crowd began to melt. Assaulted by the honking of horns, the cries from Etienne and the fear that the trucks would run them over, they broke ranks and retreated. Cursing and weeping, they were loaded into the trucks. Etienne was still screaming "Marchons! marchons!" He kept his eyes shut until they reached the rue Royale.

The soldiers in the trucks behind him cheered. Etienne smiled and waved his hand. "We have broken through," he shouted happily. "But our mission is not yet over!"

"Vive la France!" Commandant Giffard called out.

"Vive la France!" everyone cheered.

Etienne pointed down the block. They proceeded slowly to the line in front of Lalique. "All tourists must leave immediately," he yelled into the bullhorn. "Foreigners are under orders to leave the premises now!" The women in line surrendered meekly and filed into the truck. But no one came out of the shop. "This is an emergency," he shouted. "All aliens must leave at once!"

A woman opened the door and stuck her head out. "You want me?" she screamed. "You're gonna have to come in and get me!" She slammed the door. The women in the truck applauded.

There was no choice. Etienne got out of the Jeep. Giffard ran to join him, but Etienne had decided to take Lalique on his own. As a precautionary measure, Giffard

247

posted two men on either side of the entrance. Etienne heard them cock their rifles as he opened the door.

Women were rummaging through the stock, pushing their way behind display counters and grabbing for goblets in the window. The noise level was deafening. Etienne reached for the bullhorn. "This store is now off limits to all aliens!" Something was wrong with the amplification. Although a few frightened shoppers left, others continued reaching for frosted-glass figurines, vases and ashtrays. Etienne kept flipping the switch as he shouted into the bullhorn. At the first sound of his voice, the electric megaphone shut off. Then, as he shook it angrily, it suddenly burst into an earsplitting squeal. Within seconds, the mirrors, the glass shelves, the crystal decanters, the cut-glass vases and the elegant goblets all shattered.

Everyone froze. The entire cristallerie had been reduced to rubble. Etienne was stunned. Propelled by fear, he marched to the doorway, crushing glass underfoot with every step. "Into the trucks!" he shouted. They followed behind him meekly. There was nothing left to buy.

As though in a daze, Etienne kept walking toward the rue de Rivoli. The Jeep kept pace with him. His heart was pounding and his hands were shaking. He needed something to drink. Fortunately, he was in front of Maxim's.

"Bonjour, Monsieur," the doorman said warily.

Etienne looked back onto the street and beckoned for Giffard, suddenly aware that without the Commandant his only form of identification was a credit card.

"Monsieur," the maître said. "Commandant. May I help you?"

"I must have a glass of Perrier," Etienne demanded, "and I must know how many tourists you have in here today."

The maître stiffened. "Mon Dieu! It is *you!* I am not afraid of you. This is not the St.-Honoré. This is Maxim's!"

Etienne narrowed his eyes. "The President has ordered—"

"I know precisely what the President has ordered! You may tell the President I have just filled the dining room and I shall not send them out hungry!"

"When will they be through?"

The maître sighed. "Well, by the time they ask what every dish is and how it is made, and by the time they make certain not to order the cheapest wine on the list, it will be at least two hours."

"That will be too late," Etienne warned.

"Monsieur, that is precisely how it will be. At least, as long as there is a breath left in my body. They will eat, then they will have their coffee, then they will have their little cookies and their candy. Then I will send them home to their hotels. Then you can chop them up for all I care. But you will do nothing to disturb their meal!"

Etienne took his Perrier from the waiter. "You have two hours. We will have a truck here to take them."

As Etienne and Giffard turned to leave, the maître was muttering, "It is not so much to ask. Two hours for The Last Lunch."

Once back on the street, Etienne turned to Giffard. "I have decided to give you full command here. The St.-Honoré is yours!"

"But I don't understand."

"You are to go back. Back to St. Laurent. Back to Courrèges, Castillo, Feraud. You must get them all. Commandant, you cannot stop until every last one of them is out of Harriet Hubbard Ayer!"

"But you have been our leader. Where are you going?"

"I will need the Jeep and two trucks." He lowered his eyes as he added, "Also your bravest men."

"Monsieur le Secrétaire, where are you going?"

"To the heart, Commandant. I must cross the Champs-Elysées!"

There was a sharp intake of breath from Giffard. "Mon Dieu!"

The Jeep, followed by a truck with the Commandant's best men, made a right turn and drove along the rue de Rivoli. Etienne stood up, leaning against the windshield as the fresh air blew in his face. His eyes were now wide open.

The glorious Place de la Concorde. The very spot on which Marie Antoinette had been beheaded. Perhaps exactly where the obelisk stood. He picked up his binoculars to focus on it. Suddenly he yelled, "To the obelisk!"

The Jeep screeched to a stop. The soldiers in the truck were thrown off balance as they came to a halt. There, sitting inside the railing, with his back against the obelisk, was Murphy. He had taken off his jacket and tie. In one hand he held a bottle of Lafite-Rothschild '45. There was a straw in it. At the sight of Etienne, he held up the bottle in a mock toast and took a sip through the straw.

Although they stood less than ten feet apart, Etienne picked up the bullhorn and adjusted it for maximum volume. "Are you a citizen of France?" he blasted.

"No."

"For what purpose are you in this country?" His voice reverberated across the open square.

Murphy smiled ironically. "Looks like I'm here just for the fun of it, Frenchie!"

Etienne put down the bullhorn. A thin smile parted his lips as he motioned to his men. "Take him away!"

"What the hell are you doing? Let go of me!" Murphy

screamed as he was lifted over the railing and into the truck.

Etienne was breathing hard. His fists clutched the rim of the windshield. The Arc de Triomphe was directly ahead. He raised his arm, pointing a very steady finger to the left of the Champs. For all the world to hear, Etienne shouted, "To Vuitton!"

THE huge bear of a man had promised escape. Instead they sat around a table, locked behind bars, staring at place cards.

"They're grave markers."

Dwight reached across the table and took Lily's hand. "Who said that?" he asked, looking into her eyes. "It couldn't have been my Lily. No." He patted her hand. "It must have been someone else."

She held tightly to him and began to cry. Clifford took out his handkerchief. Lily was surprised by his act of compassion. She took it, blew her nose and sighed. "I suppose it can't matter anymore about catching fleas." Clifford sat back in disbelief. "You're right, Clifford," she said quickly. "That was uncalled for." Lily put a hand to her brow. "Good God, it must really be the end if Lily Simon is apologizing to Clifford Benjamin."

"It is not the end." Emma stood up.

"Then of course I take it back."

"I believe Claude sent him to save us." Emma searched for an explanation. "Why would he use Claude's name if it weren't true?" She walked to the bars and pushed against them. "Why else would he do that?" The bars didn't yield. "He came to save us."

"Sure he came to save us," Clifford said sarcastically.

Dwight smiled. "How long do you think he intends to save us for?"

Clifford shrugged. "Dunno. A year. Maybe five. Hasn't it occurred to anyone that in order for Claude to send him for us, Claude would have had to know where we were?"

"And he couldn't possibly have known where we were," Dwight said with great finality. "That is, unless he knew where we were."

"You would have us believe, then, Inspector," Lily said, "that the concierge did it?"

"Guilty as charged!"

"He couldn't have!" Emma paced along the bars.

"Of course he could have," Clifford said. "He knew where we were going. He knew he'd get a good price from NAA."

"What I still don't understand," Dwight said, "is why he had us moved into the caves."

Emma spoke with great authority, as though her tone could ensure the truth of what she wanted to believe. "He had us moved here to protect us from the others. Claude could never go through with something like this."

"How do you know?" Clifford asked. "The guy fixes your shoes and he suddenly becomes your patron saint?"

Lily walked over to Emma. "Just what makes you so damn certain?"

Emma was grasping at straws. She pointed to the place

253

cards. "These! These are so like him. So very formal. So very elegant. So French."

"Darling, I'm afraid that kind of evidence won't stand up in this kangaroo court."

Emma turned angrily to Lily. "What will it take to make you believe these are his? Do you want to see receipts?"

Lily, who was rarely shocked, was shocked. She stared unbelievingly at Emma and chose her words carefully. "I suppose you envision him sitting at an ebony writing table." She dared Emma to respond.

Emma's eyes locked with Lily's. She took a deep breath. "Yes. Directly under a Saint-Louis chandelier."

Dwight fingered his place card. "He might have reserved a better table."

"What are you up to?" Emma asked.

Lily turned away. "Nothing, darling. I fear I'm not nearly up to it." Lily walked to the bars. She held on with both hands and began to laugh.

Emma leaned back in her chair. Claude must have been planning to kidnap her while they were making love. Claude must have been planning to sleep with Lily while they were making love. But worst of all, perhaps he'd slept with Lily *before* they made love. Perhaps she was merely part of some bizarre plan.

Lily held tight to the bars. How undermining to have her memory of Claude stolen! Having to seduce him was humiliating enough, but sharing him with Emma was devastating. Damn Emma! Damn Claude! She needed that memory. It had been so comforting. Not just the act of it, but the fact of it. She smiled. Yet if Claude had planned to kidnap her, wasn't it possible he had planned also to seduce her? It wasn't much, she thought with a sigh. But at least it was something to cling to.

"As usual, you have it all wrong, Emma darling." Lily stalked around the table. "The grown-ups seem to agree it

254

was Claude who done it. And who done it very carefully indeed. After all, he's an acknowledged master of such things. Obviously, the plan was already operative on Monday when we checked in. And," she said with a bitter smile, "As push came to shove, his plan reached its climaxes on Tuesday." She glared at Emma. "So you see, Gretel, everything he did was on the agenda. Planned in advance! Down to the minute!"

Emma stared down at her watch. She suddenly understood why they let her keep it.

"There are only two possibilities," Lily said. "Claude, who has been saving up for a tip the way Elizabeth saved up her virginity, decided to double-cross his gang for a larger cut . . ."

"Now, that I could believe," Clifford said.

"Or," she continued, "someone in the gang is double-crossing Claude."

"Which also makes sense," Dwight said.

"You're all wrong!" Emma shouted. "He couldn't go through with it! He changed his mind." She realized Claude had told them to let her keep the watch. It was a message from him. He had found a way to be honest with her. "Any minute now, that door is going to open . . ." There was a noise. They all turned as one.

The door opened. Petit Meurice carried a bucket filled with ice. "Good afternoon," he said.

The four of them rushed to the bars like puppies in the pound. "Where's Claude?" Emma asked.

"When do we get out of here?"

"Where were you?"

"What the hell is going on?"

Petit Meurice put the bucket down on the ledge. He turned to face them and smiled. "I made an excuse to see young Monsieur Pommel. I did not want him to suspect I was not working."

255

"Where is Claude?"

"It is not as it was with his father. But then, MGM is not the same without Louis B. Mayer either."

"Why are we being kept here?"

"It is time for some refreshment." He opened one of the cabinets.

"For God's sake," Emma screamed, "where is Claude?"

Petit Meurice winced. "I promise you, Madame, he is, by now, on his way."

"How soon will he—"

"But that is the last question I will answer. I have been waiting for you such a long time. There is so much I want to tell you."

"Oh, God," Lily muttered. She sat down at the table. The others, realizing they were powerless, began taking their seats.

Petit Meurice took out five trays of fluted champagne glasses. They watched with disbelief as he began lining up five dozen glasses and fourteen bottles of champagne.

"Perhaps he's with the Red Cross," Lily whispered.

"Not that young Monsieur Pommel does not have my complete loyalty. There is nothing I would not do for him. After having served Madame Pommel and her husband before her, there is nothing I would not do for the family. But the bottles can wait for one day." He smiled. "Do you know what I think about while I am turning my bottles?" He raised his hands and mimed the turning motion. "I think, This bottle will be for a birthday, and these are for a wedding. And these. And these. A very important wedding. At night. So many handsome people. An orchestra. Dancing. Pretty Japanese lanterns swinging in the breeze. What a good time they are all having! And this one is for a new baby, and this for a holiday, and this for a new house, and this for lovers on the beach. For a king. For an Academy Award!" He put his hands down and paused a moment. "It is such a wonderful job. I have such happy thoughts. Every bottle is a celebration. Every bottle brings happiness. I meet such lovely people." He glanced at the wall behind him. "Most of the time. Ja wohl, meinen Herren?" he shouted.

Lily grasped Dwight's hand. "My God, who is he talking to?" she whispered.

"I don't know."

"I am talking to the leaders of the other occupation." Petit Meurice raised his hand and pointed to the wall. "You must allow me to present Gruppenführer Rastenberg." He moved his hand along the wall. "Oberleutnant Koenig, and Unteroffizier Shtell."

The four of them looked at one another in horror. Why was he pointing to a blank wall?

Petit Meurice smiled. "Ah, there is so much to tell you. And so little time." He turned and put a bottle of champagne into the bucket. "We shall taste only the vintage years. But, of course, you know a vintage is not so important with champagne. It is Monsieur Pommel's blend that is important. André Bonnard knew that. It was in this room that Monsieur Pommel perfected his blend. He kept the samples behind bars, as you are now. It was in this cell that he mixed and tested and finally created the house blend that was to bear his name. This was his secret room, as it is now mine. Not even young Monsieur Pommel knows it still exists. He thinks it was destroyed during the other occupation. Bonnard was a disagreeable man, as are most dégorgeurs. Perhaps because it is such a noisy job to remove the corks. He had a violent temper." Petit Meurice turned the bottle gently and felt it. He nodded. "How unfortunate so many people overchill before serving. Well, it was here, in this room, that Bonnard stole the formula. He threatened to ruin poor Monsieur Pommel. And so the name was changed to Pommel et Bonnard."

257

He eased the cork out without a sound. "Fortunately, Bonnard had no family. When he died, all that remained of him was his name." He began filling four glasses. "I think that is what Bonnard wanted most anyway. To be part of history. Each harvest is part of history. The wine is France. Once cannot exist without the other."

Petit Meurice put the glasses on a tray. He walked to the bars. Lily shrugged, got up and took one. The others came over for theirs. "We shall begin with 1973."

"And where shall we end?" Lily asked nervously.

Petit Meurice smiled. "We will return to 1942." He pointed to the blank wall. "Until you have caught up to them."

EMILE drove the car while Claude stared ahead at the road. "I cannot believe he killed Antoine," Emile said.

"It is my fault."

"You cannot blame yourself because Meurice went crazy."

"He did not 'go' crazy. Meurice is the same as he has always been."

"Le Dom, this time he did not kill a Nazi. He killed one of his own!"

"This time, Emile, it is not so easy to know who is the enemy and who is not."

Emile did not respond immediately. Instead, he waited a few moments and asked with great care, "Le Dom, I have asked myself over and over, why did you bring her to the Zola?"

"I did not bring her!" he said sharply. "She knew I was taking her watch to the jeweler, that it was across the street from where I lunch."

258

"And so the mouse ran after the cat?"

"No," Claude said with a sad smile. "The mouse took a taxi."

Emile shook his head. "It is tragic. We have won. Yet we have suddenly lost. We have suddenly become terrorists instead of patriots." His hands clutched the wheel. "And if we are not in time, Meurice will make us murderers."

Claude watched the road. The chances of Emma still being alive were slight. Meurice had murdered Antoine as he had murdered the Nazis. He had twisted reality as easily as turning a bottle of champagne.

"Nineteen sixty-one already?" Lily reached through the bars and took the glass from Petit Meurice. "How time flies when you're having fun."

"I didn't like '61," Dwight said. "That was the year we toured Canada. Would you mind if I had another glass of '62?" Petit Meurice handed him the '61. Dwight frowned. "Now, see here, we have *some* rights under the Geneva Convention."

"You can't make him drink the '61 if he doesn't want to!" Clifford shouted.

Emma looked deep into Petit Meurice's eyes. "Remember Nuremberg," she warned.

"What a wretched little town," Lily said. "The Wurst!" she laughed.

"You must take it," Petit Meurice said to Dwight. "Please."

Dwight sighed. He sipped and shook his head. "Tastes just like Canada."

"I've never been to Canada," Emma said, reaching through the bars for her glass.

"You have so. We did a whole book on Canada!" Clifford frowned at Petit Meurice. He opened his mouth as though he were about to tell him off. But he couldn't think of anything to say.

"Was that Canada?" Emma asked.

"Six," Clifford said, making a sixth line in the table with his fingernail. "Six glasses."

"Did I like Canada?"

Clifford shrugged. "I don't know. I don't know what the hell you like anymore, Emma."

"Now, now, Clifford," Lily chided. "Now is not the time to become a crankypuss. You don't want to spoil our fun. I like '61. You know, darlings, it gets better the more back you go."

"There is absolutely nothing to eat there," Dwight said.

"Where?"

"Canada."

"Of course there is," Lily said. "There's a Trader Vic in Vancouver."

"You know," Dwight continued, "you get better French food in Mexico City than you get in Montreal."

"I've never been to Mexico," Emma said.

"You were. We did a book." Clifford began to laugh. "The *Peso Pincher's Guide!*"

Emma made two fists and raised them in the air. "Oh, is that the place," she asked, moving her wrists, "with those things you shake?"

Petit Meurice had uncorked the '59. He filled four fresh glasses. "Nineteen fifty-nine," he bellowed.

"And all's well," Lily yelled back.

"Now for the part I really like," Clifford said, getting up. He raised his glass and threw it forcefully into the bathroom alcove. It shattered amid the dozens of other broken glasses. They formed a line behind him—Dwight, then Lily, and then Emma, who was still drinking the last of her champagne.

"Say, how about some potato chips?" Clifford asked, taking a glass from Petit Meurice.

"Now, let's see," Lily said. "Where were we in '59?"

"Don't speak to me." Emma walked quickly past Clifford.

"Why not?" he asked. "What did I do now?"

"I didn't know you in '59."

"I will leave you for a few minutes," said Petit Meurice. "They must see me. They cannot become suspicious. It is time for my break."

"Three cheers for the Kidnappers' Union!" Lily waved.

Petit Meurice bent the bars open with his bare hands. "Here." He handed them the 1959 bottle. "In case I am a few minutes late."

"He just thinks of everything," Lily said, reaching for the bottle. "Don't worry. We'll wait right here." They watched Meurice open the door and leave. No one spoke. Then Lily said quietly, "I miss him already."

Dwight pointed to the door. "I have an idea! I think we should try to escape."

Clifford banged his fist on the table. "Goddamn it! You're right!" He stood up. "Let's get the hell out of here."

Lily emptied her glass and stood up slowly. She leaned across to help pull Emma up. "But he'll be mad at us," Emma said.

They walked to the bars and held on. "Okay, now let's get the hell out. All right? One, two, three, push!" They all pushed for a few seconds. Nothing happened. "Okay. Let's try again. One, two, three, push!" Despite their moans and grunts, all they accomplished was to push themselves back from the bars. "Wait a minute, we're doing it all wrong. One, two, three, *pull!*" They hugged the bars, pressing themselves against the metal.

"Are we out yet?" Emma asked.

"Sit down," Clifford said. "Everybody sit down."

"Good idea," Dwight said. "We'll try again later."

Clifford scratched another line into the table. "Seven."

"We're halfway there," Dwight said. "He had fourteen bottles."

"Halfway to where?" Clifford asked.

"Halfway to his killing us," Emma said.

Lily got up. "I will not go through that again! You absolutely ruined '66, '64 and '62 for me."

"I didn't mean to." Emma got up and followed behind Lily. "You were having such a good time planning your funeral. Services on the terrace of the Gritti. The gondola procession to St. Mark's. The outdoor luncheon. Purple tablecloths and napkins. Poached bass with a collar of black truffles."

"Squisita!" Lily cried out in her most enthusiastic Italian. "Although," she added quickly, "it should probably be sole."

"That Lily is going to cost you a fortune," Clifford whispered to Dwight. "Why don't you have spaghetti with black olives? You could save a bundle."

Lily shook her head in consternation. "No one I know eats spaghetti."

"What the hell else is there to eat in Italy?" he asked.

"Are you talking about Italy? Or are you talking merely about the squalid boardinghouses of Naples?"

"Italy, The boot. Italia," he yelled. "All of it!"

Lily poured another glass of champagne. "Firstly, there is nothing worth eating in Italy south of Florence."

"Nothing?" Emma asked.

"You've got to face it," Dwight said. "Southern Italy is even worse than Southern California. And everyone knows that Rome is merely another Chicago. All architecture. It's north of Rome that Italy really works."

"I only eat in Florence, Bologna, Milan and Venice," Lily said.

Clifford shrugged. "You know Fat Angelo's near the railway station in Milan?" He tried to refresh her memory. "He's got this counter with eight, maybe nine stools . . ."

"Was I ever there?" Emma asked.

"Don't you remember? He used to give you extra bread to fatten you up?"

Emma began to cry. "It's the curse of my life! I'm too thin and I'm too rich!"

Clifford turned away from Emma. "So what do *you* like, Dwight? Switzerland?" Clifford asked sarcastically. "Safe. Clean. Expensive."

"Antiseptic," Dwight said. "Besides, dear boy, you can't trust a country that's never gone to war."

"You can forget about Sweden, too," Lily added. "You have to be so careful lest you're hit by all those people jumping out of windows."

"When they're not committing suicide, they're taking baths," Dwight sighed.

"Of course, I know you two don't understand the difference."

"I don't like Holland," Clifford said.

"It's too flat."

"The streets are paved with herring."

"I, for one, can never relax in Germany," Lily said.

"I know I was in Germany," Emma recalled. "They tried to fatten me up there too."

"All those overstuffed people with their overstuffed beds," Dwight said.

"Still, darling, they're not half as annoying as the Austrians."

Clifford shook his head. "They think they're the French of Germany."

Emma sighed. "Such endless forced gaiety."

Lily made a sweeping gesture with her arm. "One enormous coffeehouse sinking in a sea of Schlag."

263

"It's the same with the Belgians. They think they're the French of Holland."

"Why do they all want to be the French?"

"The Czechs are the French of Poland."

"London isn't what it used to be," Dwight confessed, "now that it's become a suburb of Saudi Arabia."

Lily shook her head. "They'll soon be serving dates at teatime. No doubt St. Paul's will be demolished to raise a mosque."

Clifford frowned. "I've never understood the Irish. If they're not killed tragically by thirty, they're failures."

"Have you ever found a comfortable bed in Greece?" Lily asked Emma intently.

"You know, my problem is I can never keep awake long enough to have dinner in Spain. It's always past my bedtime."

Dwight rapped his knuckles on the table. "And something must be done about the Portuguese language. All those 'zh's' and 'ão's'!"

"Do you like Hungary?" Clifford asked Lily.

"Only if I've just come from Rumania."

"What's wrong with Rumania?" Emma demanded.

"Nothing. If I've just come from Bulgaria."

"Clifford loves Yugoslavia," Emma admitted. "I think he wants to retire there. All that scenic poverty. I hate it."

Lily shrugged. "But darling, surely you thrive on poverty. Good God, you're the only people in the world who managed to find the squalid side of Monte Carlo."

"I know a dirt-cheap casino two blocks from the Negresco," Clifford said.

"Was I there?" Emma asked.

"Sure. It's where the workers gamble."

Lily sighed. "There is simply no place left."

"Even Paris," Dwight said.

"Especially Paris!" Lily poured the last of the cham-

264

pagne into her glass. "One would think the United Nations could protect us against the Parisians."

Dwight smiled and shook his head. "You know, Lily, hard as it is to believe, the Parisians are probably saying the same thing about us."

"Not about me," Lily snapped.

"God knows, I'm not defending them," Dwight said. "But I suppose I can understand their resentment. If I lived there, *I* wouldn't want hundreds of thousands of foreigners clogging things up."

"There's no place left," Emma said.

"Nothing to discover." Lily sighed.

"The tourist shall inherit the earth," Dwight said.

"But not the moon!" Clifford proclaimed.

"Which moon, Cliffy?" Emma reached for his hand. "Was I ever there?"

"To the moon!" Dwight said, raising his glass. It was empty. "Where the hell is the waiter? Why are those people never around when you need them?" He turned the bottle upside down. Lily turned her glass upside down. Clifford shrugged.

"There's no champagne on the moon," Lily pouted.

"No matter," Dwight toasted. "The moon is the only place left to go." They raised their empty glasses.

Lily smiled. "Of course, you two should take the dark side. It's cheaper."

"We'll open the Luna Crescent," Dwight said. "Peacefully located on the Sea of Tranquillity. Moon-drenched private beaches."

Lily got up and continued the brochure. "Staffed by only the most elegantly striped Venusians selected for their slavish devotion to galactic housekeeping."

Clifford rose angrily. "Avoid astronomical prices! Cliff and Emma offer the moon on five dollars a day. Including an unlimited-mileage moon buggy."

265

Lily narrowed her eyes. "Don't dare miss our One Small Step for Man disco. Catch a falling star from the terrace as you dance a phase away to such lilting tunes as 'Miami Over Moon.' "

"Why not browse among the mooney-saving bargains in our gravity-free shopping center?"

Lily thrust an arm in the air. "The Luna Crescent has its own exclusive promenade deck from which our guests may watch the cow jump over."

Clifford banged his fist on the table. "Goddamn it! You've done it again! You've fucked up another planet!"

"The man is a lunatic!" Lily sat down and began tapping her foot. "What the hell kind of service is this? Where is that son of a bitch with the champagne?"

Dwight shrugged. "Perhaps if we tried again to open the bars. One of us could find him and bring him back."

"Well, for God's sake, let's not just sit here!" Lily got up. "C'mon, you two. Here's a chance to use your brains. Push!"

As the four of them leaned against the bars, the outer door opened. Lily yelled at Petit Meurice. "Where the hell have you been?"

"If you think we're going to recommend this place, you're crazy!" Dwight shouted.

"I don't care what it costs, I want my own table!" Clifford said. "And where are those goddamn potato chips I ordered?"

"Are we out yet?" Emma asked, still pushing against the bars.

Petit Meurice reached for a new bottle and four fresh glasses. "One of my very favorites. Nineteen fifty-five."

"It's about time," Clifford said, angrily hurling his glass into the alcove.

"I have friends at Michelin!" Dwight threw his glass down.

"All right," Emma said, tossing her glass, "one more for the moon."

"We might have died in here," Lily yelled, smashing her glass. "How incredibly thoughtless of you to leave your station! Next time, I damn well expect you back here before the bottle is finished!"

Petit Meurice smiled. "I will not be leaving you alone anymore."

JUST as they were about to arrive in Epernay, Emile pulled off the road next to an unmarked van. "Le Dom, I wish you would let me stay."

Claude grasped Emile's hand. "No. You must return at once." He got out of the car and, without looking back, opened the rear door of the van.

Edouard jumped up from the bench and helped Claude in. He banged twice on the partition to signal the driver. "What are we to do?" he asked nervously.

"Have you the envelope?"

Edouard opened it and began handing Claude its contents. "The used ticket from Paris. The conductor will say he remembers you because of the gold cigarette case. Actually, the conductor remembers you because his brother was Michel Limond, who helped us mislabel the Berlin shipments. The cab driver, René Cluny, sends his regards. He will say he left you near Pommel's storage building. One of the maintenance staff, a young boy named Claude Dupret, who says his father named him after you, will tell them he saw you enter the south entrance to the caves. And last, there is this." He handed Claude a gun.

"It will be traced to Meurice?"

"Yes. But I cannot believe we have come to this."

"Nor I." Claude checked that all the chambers were loaded and then put the gun in his pocket.

The van pulled into the covered garage that led directly to the Château Montaigne-Villiers. The inner corridor had a stone floor. Its white walls were lined with portraits of the Montaignes and the Villierses. Claude walked quickly toward the Salon d'Est. Without knocking, he threw open the door. Isabelle sat crocheting. Robert paced angrily. Le Comte stared out the window. They turned quickly. "There is no time to lose!" Claude shouted. They ran down the corridor after him.

"I will be ruined!" Robert said. "All these years of perfecting my recipes! My award from *Holiday!*"

"He is just worried about his stinking star!" Le Comte snarled as they went down a flight of stairs. "What about me? What am I to do if the police uncover my bedside manners? Epernay is not quite as liberal as San Francisco!"

"This should never have happened," Isabelle said breathlessly as she held on to Edouard's sleeve. "If only we had not been such fucking pussies. We should have planned to kill them ourselves!"

Claude stopped at the cellar room. "Clean it up. Get rid of everything."

Le Comte pointed to the body lying on a mattress. "What do I do with Antoine?"

"As soon as it is dark, take him into the vineyards and bury him deep. He must never be found."

"What do we tell his wife?"

"Nothing," Claude said, going down the dark flight of steps. "We have not seen Antoine. That is all. She knows nothing of this. A tragic disappearance. We will look after her."

He ran to the trunk room. Nicolas was sitting in front of the armoire. He held up a kerosene lamp. "There has not been a sound. I thought perhaps he might come back."

"Meurice will not come back," Claude said, stepping into

the armoire. "Seal this up immediately. Fill the cask with some of your reserve."

Le Comte was shocked. "You expect me to give that thief Pommel my reserve?"

"Fill it up!" Claude yelled. "You must seal this entrance!"

"But how will you get back?" Edouard asked.

"I will not be coming back this way. All of you must return home." Claude began searching for the latch. "Perhaps they are still alive."

"And if they are?" Isabelle asked.

Claude opened the door that led into the cask. "Then I shall be forced to be a hero."

EMMA was wearing Dwight's blazer. She had it on backward, as though it were a straitjacket. His arm was around her. They sat on the floor in one corner of the cell. Across the room, Lily wore Clifford's jacket as though it were a beltless greatcoat. She made cuffs on the sleeves, turned the collar up fashionably and wrapped it tight around her waist. Clifford's head was in her lap as he lay on the floor. Just outside the bars, Petit Meurice was digging into the limestone walls with a large shovel. He was carving out four graves.

As Emma and Dwight sipped the 1947 vintage, tears streamed down their cheeks. "But I could make you so happy," she pleaded.

"It's no use."

"I have so much money I just don't know what to do with it all."

"It's no use. I am destined for a life of penury."

Lily looked up as she stroked Clifford's hair. "Oh, Dwight. How dweary!" She took a sip of champagne and turned to Petit Meurice. "Can't you do that more quietly? What a racket! I can't hear myself drink!"

"Let's not come back here," Clifford said.

"Surely not until they finish renovating."

"What do you think it costs them?" he asked. "All these glasses. Has to cost. How much do you think the bill is gonna be?"

"Who cares? It's all on the expense account."

Emma looked up and began sobbing. "He never lets me cheat on the expense account."

Lily caressed Clifford's cheek. "How dweadful! I must take you in hand. There's so much I could teach you. Tipping. How to eat artichokes. How to buy fine leather. It would be wonderful! Like having a little boy of my own." Lily looked over at Emma. "You must let me adopt him."

"He'll make your life a misery," Emma warned. "Just like he did mine. Don't take a taxi! Eat the free hors d'oeuvre and we can skip dinner! You can see better from the balcony!" She began crying hysterically. "I'm thirty-six years old and I've never ordered à la carte!"

Lily pointed a finger at Emma. "Dwight, is she dwunk?"

Dwight took a handkerchief and dabbed at Emma's tearstained cheeks. "How could she be? The poor thing has only had a few." He pulled her close and with great tenderness asked, "My dear, are you dwunk?"

"Twelve," Clifford said. "So this is number twelve. Tastes just like eleven to me."

"Oh, Dwight," Lily laughed. "Isn't he dwoll?"

"You can't have both of them," Emma said. "You have to share."

"Share?" Lily said with disgust. "I hate sharing. It's a dwag."

"But you do share sometimes," Emma said meanly.

"Never!"

270

"Yesterday you did!" Emma accused. She was breathing hard as she got onto her knees and then, leaning on Dwight's shoulder, stood up. She pointed a shaky finger at Lily. "J'accuse!"

"Oh, dwat!" Lily put Clifford's head on the floor and slowly raised herself to her feet. "Hey, you," Lily called to Emma. "Come with me." Lily dragged Emma toward the small alcove with the toilet. "I'm gonna powder your nose."

"Save me," Emma whimpered.

They held on to each other as they turned the corner, careful to avoid stepping on the broken glass. Once inside the alcove, Lily grabbed Emma by the shoulders and pressed her against the wall. "Listen to me," she whispered. "If you tell, I'll throw *you* against the wall instead of my glass. I have never regarded you as anything other than a guttersnipe, Emma Penny Pincher."

"Lily, tell me! When did you and Claude . . ."

"What an ironic turn my life has taken." Lily began to cry. "Now, Emma, I know you do this sort of thing with delivery boys and garage mechanics . . ."

"Oh, please," Emma sobbed, "tell me what time?"

"Listen, you cheap floozie, I'll cut out your tongue if you say one word about yesterday."

"Oh, Lily," Emma pleaded. "I must know what time you and Claude—"

Lily grabbed Emma by the arm. "I thought I told you not to say one word—"

"But Lily, I would never say a word to Dwight about you."

"You dreary wretch, I'm not worried you'll tell Dwight about me. I'm worried you'll tell him about *you*."

"About me?"

"Don't you understand anything, you smarmy urchin? If Dwight knew Claude went to bed with you, the only

271

conclusion he'd draw is that Claude would go to bed with anyone!"

Emma began to smile. "Oh, I understand."

Lily began to cry for joy. "I knew I could count on you, you sleazy little tart."

Emma put an arm around Lily. "We might have been great friends if I'd been born dumb and heartless."

"It would have been an improvement."

"I'll promise if you tell me what time."

Lily sighed. "First, you must give me your most solemn oath."

Without breaking eye contact, Emma spat into the palm of her hand. Unable to suppress a smile, she turned the wet palm toward Lily, who closed her eyes in horror as she realized what had to be done. Lids at half mast, Lily spat into her hand. As though she were sucking a lemon, her face twitched while she bravely brought her palm to meet Emma's. Lily moaned as their wet palms touched. Emma shrugged. "After all, what's a foe for?"

They were startled by the sound of Petit Meurice announcing, "Nineteen forty-five!"

Lily turned and started walking back into the cell. "Oh, this is the one I've been waiting for!"

"Lily, you promised to tell me! Please! I'm feeling so sick."

"Darling, just as soon as I've had a drinkie. My throat is absolutely parched."

Clifford was sprawled on the floor staring at the ceiling. Dwight was sitting against the wall unable to focus. Lily shook her head as she bent down to pick up their glasses. She walked to the alcove. "You two had better get up. I have no intention of going to the bar unescorted." She began smashing their glasses. "This one is for you, Dwight. You dwip! And this is for The Vagabond King! And this

272

one, is pour moi." She made certain Emma was watching. "For Lily, who also rises with the sun."

"Before breakfast?" Emma gasped.

"Such a lovely way to begin the day."

Emma threw her glass angrily against the wall. "I don't remember the room!" she cried. "I don't remember the table! I don't remember the harpsichord! I don't remember the chandelier! And most of all, I don't remember the Eiffel Tower!"

Lily smiled smugly and put an arm around Emma. "What you need is a drink." She guided her over to Petit Meurice. "How about holding down the noise during this round?"

Petit Meurice smiled. "You must take a glass for Mr. Simon. He must taste every vintage!"

Lily took two glasses. "I can't promise. But why don't you try bringing the next bottle a bit sooner? The service here is really slipping. And just look at you. All sweaty."

"It is from the digging," he said. He held the tray for Emma.

"I don't feel good," she said. "I'm dizzy."

"Just two more glasses," he said. "This and then the '42."

"And then what?"

"And then you will not feel dizzy any longer."

Emma sat next to Clifford. Lily leaned back against the wall and slid down onto the floor near Dwight. She held out his glass. "Hey, beautiful dweamer."

He looked at her. "You're Lily." He took the glass and began to cry. "Can you forgive me?"

"No."

"I don't love that girl."

"Which one?" Lily asked.

"I don't remember her name."

273

"Marie-Thérèse," she said.

"Lily, can you forgive me?"

"There you go again."

"I love you, Lily. Can you forgive and forget?"

"I can forget."

"We'll never speak of it again," he said.

"Speak of what?" Lily clinked glasses with him. "I can forget."

Across the room, Emma held Clifford's head in her lap. "It's not that there's anyone else, Cliffy. I don't want you to think that. Even if there were someone else, I wouldn't be leaving you for someone else. I'm leaving you for myself." She drank her glass empty. "I say I'm leaving you, but that's not true. I've already left you. I just haven't said a proper goodbye." She leaned over to kiss him gently. "Proper goodbye," she whispered. She slipped her Mickey Mouse watch into his pocket.

Dwight and Lily were holding on to each other. Clifford was asleep, and Emma was crying. It was suddenly very quiet except for Petit Meurice's enormous sigh. He had finished the digging.

CLAUDE was lost. The indelible image he had carried for thirty-five years was unreliable. He could not navigate the reality of the caves on memory alone. He was panicked by not being able to recall his sense of direction. Now, even the caves were conspiring to make Claude doubt his every move.

In May of 1940, the Germans entered France via Champagne. He was seventeen. Isabelle was twenty and beautiful. They swore to defend each other, to defend France. Claude stayed in the caves in defiance of the French High Command's order to evacuate Epernay. Finally, in August of 1944, they cried with joy and vowed to defend France

274

forever. In August of 1944 they still knew their way around the caves.

The two hours he had been there seemed an even longer span than the years he had been away. Had the caves always been so cold? So dim? Surely the light was different when he and Meurice sneaked out to change the "a" in Hamburg to an "o" in order to misdirect the cases ready for shipment. O! Galerie O! It was from Galerie O that Meurice had taken him to Pommel's secret room. But which end of Galerie O?

Somehow the act of running, of reestablishing his role as hunter, made him feel less vulnerable. He would find the room, he knew that now. But would he find it in time? Claude was breathing hard. Number 6. Number 7. Number 8 and then number 9. He listened. Nothing. He reached up and loosened the screws that held marker number 9. He pushed the latch and a door opened from within the wall. He listened for a voice. He listened for Emma's voice. Claude stepped back as the door was pushed open. Petit Meurice appeared.

"Le Dom," he said, smiling. "Bonjour." He came out into the corridor and closed the door behind him.

"Are they alive?" Claude asked.

"I knew you would come."

"Meurice, are they alive?" Is Emma alive? he wanted to ask.

Petit Meurice stood protectively in front of the door. "Antoine did not understand. I think we are well rid of him. He did not remember our vow."

Claude put his hands on Petit Meurice's shoulders. "The Simons and the Benjamins are not the Nazis!"

"Le Dom, you will be proud of me!"

Claude shook him by the shoulders. "Are they alive?"

Petit Meurice smiled. "Champagne will not be occupied again!"

275

Emma was dead. He had killed her. He, Claude, had killed her. Claude embraced Petit Meurice in despair. "I should never have left you here."

"I was sad you did not take me with you. I thought often of you and Pierre and Marcel in Paris together. Oh, the good times you must have had! Sometimes, Le Dom, I even thought you had forgotten about me."

"Never, Meurice, I never forgot."

He smiled. "Oh, I understand that now. It was only during the first five or ten years that I wondered. I knew there must be a reason for me to remain in the caves."

"I should have kept you with me."

"I wanted you to be proud of me again. No one has been proud of me since the war."

"Mon ami," Claude whispered. "You know I love you."

"And you know I would give my life for you."

Claude stepped back. "Meurice, I want you to close your eyes."

"Why?"

"I want you to think of something. I want you to think of the happiest day of your life."

Petit Meurice closed his eyes. And then he smiled. "It was the day I saved you! I can see myself carrying you in from the vineyard. I remember as though it were yesterday."

"It *was* yesterday, Meurice. I remember it too." Claude reached into his pocket and took hold of the gun. "I want you to see it clearly in your mind. It is happening now. It was very early in the morning."

"I remember the birds singing. The ground was wet. There was still smoke over the mountains."

"I remember the sky, Meurice. It was morning, but I could still see the stars."

"I thought you were the enemy."

"I called out to you, 'Help me, I am a Frenchman. Help

276

me!' " Claude pressed himself against Petit Meurice's chest. "Can you feel me in your arms as you carry me?"

Petit Meurice smiled. "Yes, I can feel you in my arms," he said excitedly. "It is happening all over again. 'I will save you, Frenchman. You will be safe soon.' "

Claude took the gun from his pocket. "I shall never forget you, Meurice. You are a hero."

Petit Meurice's eyes were tight shut. "We must hurry, Frenchman. I know a place. Deep in the caves. We will be safe there."

Claude began to cry as he put the gun to Petit Meurice's heart. "It is all right. Put me down." He pulled the trigger. Petit Meurice fell to the ground. Claude knelt next to him. "Rest for a moment, patriot." Claude was sobbing as he leaned over him. "You are a defender of France. A true hero. I am still proud of you, Meurice. You must never forget that!"

Petit Meurice looked up at Claude. His eyes began to flutter. He could barely catch his breath. Putting a hand on Claude's shoulder, he pulled him close. Just before he died, a small smile crossed his lips. "No, no! They can't take that away from me!"

Claude reached over and closed Petit Meurice's eyes.

After pulling the latch behind marker number 9, he opened the door. Dwight Simon was slumped in a corner. Lily Simon lay next to him against the bars. On the other side of the cell, Clifford Benjamin was face up on the floor. Emma Benjamin was sprawled across his body.

Claude reached out and grabbed on to the bars. In his rage, he began to shake them.

"Well, it's about time!" Lily whimpered. "Where the hell is the '42?"

Thursday

CLAUDE refused to look into the cameras as the reporters swarmed around him. They had been waiting all morning outside the Louis. "One picture, Claude," Etienne urged. "Please."

"Picard," one of the reporters shouted as Claude pushed his way to the car. "Give us a smile! They're going to use your face on all the travel posters!"

"Claude," Etienne pleaded, "you are a national hero. This is a national event. You cannot do this to me!"

Claude took Etienne's arm and pulled him to the curb. Gaspar held proudly on to the door of the Presidential limousine. As the flashbulbs popped, and photographers ran around to get a picture of Claude inside the car, Etienne smiled and waved, shouting from the window, "D-u-v-e-r-t!"

As they drove toward the Elysée Palace, Etienne opened

281

and closed every compartment on the lap desk and bar. Claude stared silently out the window. It was a sunny afternoon and the St.-Honoré was deserted. There was no traffic. Salesgirls stood in front of empty boutiques and chatted.

"Isn't it a wonderful day?" Etienne asked, looking out the window. "It took me only three minutes to get down the Champs." He pointed to the empty cabs lined up at a taxi stand. "It is a pleasure to see those bastards waiting for us, for a change!" Etienne turned to Claude. "I do not understand you, mon ami. You look as though you are to be shot instead of decorated. I don't mind telling you, as grateful as the President and I were that you saved the Simons and the Benjamins, we were glad you did not save them any sooner." Claude looked up at Etienne. "I mean, it was not easy to arrange for the export . . . uh, departure of so many. To have to arrange for them to come right back . . ." Etienne raised his hands. "I do not want to think of what a horror that would have been!" He began to laugh. "But all is well that ends well. The city was evacuated. The tourists were delivered. The Americans were saved. And a Frenchman is about to receive a medal!" Etienne smiled. He slapped his hand hard on Claude's knee.

The pain was very comforting. It confirmed a reality Claude feared was lost. There was indeed a time before the Simons and the Benjamins. Another time. Another Champagne. Another France. He did not even grimace at the pain. He was too grateful for it.

Etienne held open the door to the East Reception Room on the first floor of the Elysée Palace. Everyone turned and applauded. Claude stepped into his own worst nightmare. Perhaps he was dead. Isabelle applauded. Pierre applauded. Marie-Thérèse. Le Comte. Robert. Nicolas. Edouard. Emile. Even Marcel. He looked from face to face, having to reconfirm that they were not mere look-alikes, but that both ends of his life had intertwined to strangle him.

"Don't look so surprised, Claude," Isabelle said cheerily. "Thirty-five years haven't made *you* any younger either."

"I'm sure you remember me." Le Comte shook his hand. "Although neither I nor my champagnes are celebrated for aging well. We have at least survived, Claude. Let us be grateful for that."

Edouard stepped forward. "It was incredible that Meurice was behind it all." He looked past the words into Claude's eyes. "We know, Le Dom, how much courage it took to do what you did."

Claude turned away. He clasped Edouard's hand tightly, then nodded and patted both Robert and Nicolas on the shoulders.

"You have saved us once again," Robert said softly.

Claude smiled as he came to Marcel. "From Strasbourg?" he asked, embracing him.

"I do not understand all this," Marcel whispered.

Claude did not answer him. Marie-Thérèse threw her arms around him and kissed him. "Oh, Le Dom. My hero. It is *you* I love."

"Le Dom," he smiled. "Le Dom? No. He is not here. I am sorry. But instead of Le Dom there is only Dom Quixote." Claude looked at Pierre. "Don't you agree?"

Pierre was smirking as he shook his hand. "I thought it would be appropriate to bring together this group you had not seen in so many years. I was so impressed with your story of how Meurice was caught that I suggested this little reunion."

"You are very thoughtful, Pierre."

"You must remember that when you are back at work tomorrow."

"I will not be coming back," Claude said.

283

"Claude, do not let this get out of perspective," Pierre said.

Marie-Thérèse grabbed hold of Claude's arm. "But I have already written to Dwight that I was leaving him! You cannot be serious!"

"No, I cannot be serious. But still, I shall not be back."

Etienne shouted breathlessly. "He's coming! Le Président! Attention! Attention!"

Preceded by the flashing of cameras, the imposing figure of the President of France stood in the doorway. Claude looked directly at his executioner. Following the instructions of the photographers, the President walked across the room and posed near a door to the garden. Etienne grabbed Claude by the elbow and pushed his way through the crowd.

"Monsieur le Président," Etienne said loudly, "I have the pleasure to introduce to you my dear personal friend, Claude Picard."

Claude waited to be acknowledged. "Monsieur le Président," he said, nodding and shaking his outstretched hand. He thought back to the way Meurice had described his meeting with De Gaulle. *The way you wear your hat . . .*

The President of France leaned over and held Claude by the shoulders. Then he kissed him on both cheeks. "Claude Picard," he said sonorously, "the Republic of France is in your debt today. And I understand this is not the first time you have served your country well. I have been told of your efforts during the Second War. You have again saved your country from a madman."

The way you sip your tea . . . Claude spoke softly. "Meurice Rochet was a patriot. What he did, his plan, could only have come from the heart of a patriot."

The President of France nodded. "Yes. I understand. But we do not govern by the heart. We do not live by the heart."

284

The mem'ry of all that . . . The President's aide handed him the blue, white and red ribbon from which hung the medal. After clearing his throat to alert the cameramen, the President of France began to speak. "It is with great pride that I present you, Claude Picard, with this decoration for valor. Your daring rescue of the hostages has put the nation in your debt. This act of heroism has proved to the world that France has now, as always, an outstretched hand with which to greet visitors from every corner of the globe. It is because of you, Claude Picard, that we shall expect to receive ever-increasing numbers of welcome travelers from abroad. God bless you for this legacy."

The executioner put the noose around Claude. As the cameras whirred and the bulbs flashed, as he felt the weight of the medal on his neck, Le Dom died. He would, like Meurice, be buried in Champagne, to be recalled upon occasion between heartbeats, or as a momentary afterthought. No more than that. But, thank God, no less than that. *No, No! They can't take that away from me!*

"OKAY, Daisy. You're on!"

Daisy Rogers looked into the television camera. Her million-dollar face was serious. "I'm sitting in the Salon Murat at the Elysée Palace. It's here, in this very room (PAN AROUND ROOM) that the French Council of Ministers meets every Wednesday. And it was here, only yesterday, that the French Government was faced with the most bizarre ransom demand ever received. (TIGHT SHOT ON DAISY) Unless all tourists were evacuated for a period of forty-eight hours, these people (PAN ALONG SIMONS AND BENJAMINS) would die. I'm sitting here with noted travel writers Lily and Dwight Simon, and Emma and Clifford Benjamin. They're going to tell you just how they felt. I'm also sitting here with the man who saved their lives. (MEDIUM SHOT ON

285

PICARD) And he's going to tell you how he did it. (TIGHT SHOT ON DAISY) My name is Daisy Rogers. And live by satellite from Paris, France, you're about to go with me . . . *Behind the Headlines!*"

"Cut. Thirty seconds. Somebody wipe the Frenchman. He's sweating."

Claude sat like a prisoner as someone mopped his expressionless face. To refuse the interview would have been inconsistent with his role as hero. He stared ahead, wanting only to look at Emma. He said nothing, wanting only to speak to her.

Emma could not take her eyes from him. She knew what he had done. She wanted to tell him she knew. She wanted to tell him it didn't matter.

The Simons and the Benjamins, with their monumental hangovers, didn't have the strength to refuse the demands of the American Ambassador and the French Prime Minister that they appear. Considering the effort and expense in saving their lives, no one could argue. Daisy Rogers was the grande dame of TV interviewers. People watched her because she had a reputation for asking tough questions.

"Be honest with me," Daisy urged them. "No matter what I ask, you'll be okay if you're honest. And don't get angry. I'm only asking what every fart in Kansas wants to know."

"Ten seconds!" Daisy took a deep breath and put her notes away. "You're on!"

Daisy smiled at Lily. "I want you to tell me, Lily, how someone who's been through the absolute hell you have during the past twenty-four hours can look as put-to-gether as you do. Who does your hair?"

"There's a little woman named Lily Simon who comes in every day," Lily said brightly. "I tell you, darling, I learned early on, while we were still in the theater, that I couldn't always depend upon finding a hairdresser everywhere we went. And to be honest, in those days we didn't always have the wherewithal to pay for it."

"But now you do, Lily. For millions of Americans you're the symbol of the savvy traveler, someone who cares enough to spend for the very best."

"Thank you, Daisy."

"Lily, I want you to tell me how you felt being kidnapped by a madman who forced you to drink over a case of champagne, and share a community powder room without even a door for privacy."

"Well, to be honest, Daisy," she sighed, "I suppose there are people out there who've gone through worse."

"Did you really think you were going to die?" Daisy asked.

"Well, the first time I had to use it, yes. I did. It's awesome what the human spirit is capable of withstanding."

"Dwight, do you think this crazed killer acted alone?"

"No, Daisy. I don't. It's my theory he was part of a much larger conspiracy."

"Would you explain that to our audience?"

"Of course." Dwight smiled. "You see, I believe someone was seeking revenge for something candid we wrote in our book, *Simon Says*. We've never pulled any punches, Daisy dear, and it's my belief this entire episode is based upon a grudge."

"How does it feel to be so powerful that someone would try to kill you merely for rapping their restaurant?"

No matter what the dangers, we will continue our fight against mediocrity."

"And now let's turn to the Benjamins," Daisy said. "You're the beer-budget part of this champagne tour. How do you feel about what happened, Clifford?"

"Unlike the Simons, we've always tried to help our readers enter a community as though they were a local. It's our belief that travel isn't a one-sided experience. We think the people being visited stand to benefit as much as the visitor himself."

"Then how do you explain the ransom demand? Why do you think someone wanted to stop you Penny Pinchers as well?"

Clifford thought for a moment. "I don't. I agree with Dwight. I think someone was out to get *him*."

"And you just happened to be there?" Daisy asked. "What does that kind of coincidence make you feel like, Emma?"

"I feel very lousy, Daisy. My head is killing me. My stomach. My feet. Everything. And I don't have a little woman named Lily Simon coming in to do my hair, as you can see. But I can tell you, I understand what these people must have been feeling. You know, tourists are really uninvited guests. The people of Paris or of any city aren't asked whether they want their streets filled with strangers. Not that I think anything's wrong with it. But nobody asks them. It just happens to them. They have no choice. It's very provocative when no one asks what you want."

Claude looked across at Emma for the first time. Why wasn't she wearing the watch? Hadn't Antoine followed his order? How else could she know that he loved her?

Daisy turned to Claude. "And what about you, Claude Picard? You're the man of the hour. I should explain to those in our audience who might not know, affluent tourists in Paris often sip a Tequila Sunrise while swapping stories of how the famous concierge at the Louis Q got them the last seat at a sold-out opening, or the best table at a packed restaurant. Tell me, Claude, how did you feel when this insane beast called to tell you he had kidnapped four of your very favorite guests?"

"Meurice Rochet was a hero of World War Two. He fought bravely with the Résistance to protect his country. He was my friend."

288

"And lucky for us he was," Dwight said.

"Tell us what happened, Claude."

"I received a call from Meurice. He wished me to share his pride in what he had done. I took the first train to Epernay, certain he was holding them in a secret room we had discovered during the war. I tried to persuade him to set them free. He was angry at my wanting to help them. He called me a traitor, a cheat, a liar, a fraud. He took out out his gun. We fought. I killed him."

"We'll be right back after this message," Daisy said, smiling.

"Cut. Thirty seconds. Stand by on minicam remotes."

Daisy lit a cigarette. "It's a terrific spot. You're all going to sell a lot of books." She looked at Claude. "These people have a lot more than their lives to be grateful to you for."

"Ten seconds." Daisy coughed and put out her cigarette. "You're on!"

Daisy looked into the camera. "That's only part of the story. You met the Simons and the Benjamins and the hero who saved their lives. Let's go out now into the streets of Paris. Let's go . . . *Behind the Headlines* and hear what some Parisians have to say. First, we'll take our live minicam into that bastion of fashion, the house that Coco built. Gloria Mason at Chanel."

"Daisy, I'm standing at the counter where only a few days ago, I would have had to wait in line to buy one of these lovely silk scarves. And today? Tell us, Lucille Toulon, how many customers have you had today?"

"I have had no customers today."

"And how do you feel about that?"

Lucille shrugged. "It is very boring to stand here and have no customers."

"Tell me, Lucille, if your job were like this every day, and if you never had any customers, would you still want to work here?"

"No. It would not be interesting to work here."

"Well, Daisy, that's what it's like for one Parisian shop-girl. It would not be interesting to work here, she said. And I agree. This is Gloria Mason with a live minicam unit at Chanel."

"Thanks, Gloria. We go now to Arnold Sawyer, who's standing by at the Café Norma on the rue de la Paix. Arnold?"

"Daisy, I'm standing here at the Café Norma on the rue de la Paix. Now, the Norma is generally mobbed at this hour of the day. But as you can see, there are only two people in an outside area that seats over two hundred. Let's see if we can't talk to this gentleman here. Sir, are you a regular patron at this café?"

"No, no. I am on the television? It is my first time here."

"Do you live in Paris, sir?"

"Yes, of course I live in Paris. I live around the corner. I have lived there for twenty years."

"And you've never been to the Café Norma?"

"No. I could never get a seat. Whatever time, night or day, it was always crowded."

"And how do you feel now, after twenty years of not being able to find an empty chair at the café around the corner?"

The man shrugged. "It is very depressing." He pointed to the man at the other table. "That is my landlord sitting over there. I do not need to come here to see him. Not at these prices. Garçon! L'addition, s'il vous plaît!"

"Waiter, I wonder if you'd mind coming over here for a minute. We're live on satellite back to the USA. Can you tell our viewers how you feel about a Paris without tourists?"

The waiter cleared his throat. "It is very bad for the tips." He pointed to the man at the far table. "Over there is my landlord. He will not leave me anything."

290

"He is your landlord too?" the first man asked.

"Yes," the waiter said.

"But he is also my landlord. Where do you live?"

"I live around the corner."

"No! I do too. At Number 73."

"But that is where *I* live!"

"Daisy, this is Arnold Sawyer on the rue de la Paix."

"Thank you, Arnold. We're going now to Dave Bennett at the noted restaurant, Le Musée. Dave?"

"Hi, Daisy. I'm standing here with Armand Valençay, owner of the Le Musée restaurant. Armand, tell me, how many lunches have you served today?"

"None."

"Why is that, Armand?"

"It is because this country is being run by Communists. No one else would have given in to the demands and said to hell with management. I am going to sue the Government for restraint of trade! Do you think I can afford to keep a staff with no one to serve? They are all trying to ruin me!"

"Why don't you have any French customers?"

"A Frenchman would never pay these prices," Armand said proudly. He looked directly into the camera. "For God's sake, bring the tourists back before I go out of business!"

"Daisy, this is Dave Bennett at Le Musée."

"Thanks, Dave. Speaking of the tourists' coming back, for our final remote we're going to Driscoll Harris at the Arc de Triomphe. Driscoll?"

"This is Driscoll Harris at the Arc de Triomphe. As you can see," he shouted above the hammering, "there are stands being erected here to greet the tourists when they return tomorrow night. This enormous grandstand is only one of dozens being put up at key points throughout Paris. With the city empty of tourists now for less than twenty-

291

four hours, there's a growing nostalgia in the air. On my way here I passed vendors who usually roast chestnuts. They were selling American, British and German flags. There are signs going up everywhere. 'Welcome Back, Tourists! Bienvenue!' By noon tomorrow, Daisy, authorities expect the stands to be filled, and the streets lined with thousands of joyful Parisians welcoming back their friends from overseas. This is Driscoll Harris on the eve of a celebration that's expected to rival the liberation of 1944. Daisy?"

"There you have it. Will we ever really know who all the people were behind this incredible plan? Maybe not. But we do know one thing: the plan failed. They may have moved the tourists out of the city physically. But they didn't manage to move them out of the hearts of the Parisians. This is Daisy Rogers saying You'll have to travel far and wide to find a warmer welcome than you'll get in Paris. Au revoir for now. And merci beaucoup for coming with me . . . *Behind the Headlines!*"

Friday

$\mathcal{A}$S the ornate elevator doors opened, Murphy yelled, "Freeze!"

Dwight and Lily groaned as they saw the crew of photographers and publicity people in the lobby of the Louis Q. Between the gritted teeth of a forced smile, Lily said, "Oh, God!"

"Don't 'Oh, God' *me,*" Murphy warned. "Remember Paragraph 36. We are permitted to photograph you during working hours insofar as our documentation does not prejudice or cause to be prejudiced the services you are evaluating." He smiled meanly. "I remember how fond you are of quoting Scripture."

"And what is it you're documenting now?" Dwight asked between weary smiles for the cameras.

"The resurrection!" he replied.

"Dear Murphy," Lily spat. "Here's one for you. 'He who

lives by the paragraph shall die by the paragraph.' It may be of interest to know you're about to be slapped with a two-million-dollar suit for not having provided adequately for our safety."

"Yeah!" he said grinning. He took an envelope from his pocket. "It's sensational!" Murphy turned to one of the crew. "Caption the elevator shot with something about the Presidential escort waiting outside to take them to the airport, switching the itinerary to start in Bordeaux and that crap." He looked back at Lily. "Sweetheart, with all the publicity, I'm riding on a comet. It doesn't matter what you want to shove up my ass. All you can do is send me up higher!"

"The publicity works for us as well," Dwight said. "You won't dare tamper with our recommendations. You've got the world looking over your shoulder."

Lily tightened her grip on Dwight's arm as she kissed him on the cheek. "Oh, darling, I do feel as though we were the Curies and the Brownings all in one!" She turned to Murphy. "Not even you can spoil it!" She waved Murphy's crew aside and walked into the lobby. "Pierre, darling," Lily implored, "can't you throw this riffraff out?"

Pierre turned to Murphy. "Monsieur—"

"Save your breath," Murphy said. "I already got what I wanted. Outside, you guys, on the double. We want to be sure and catch Eleanor and Franklin as they get into the limo." Murphy smiled at Lily. "In case you were wondering, I'll never settle!" He waved the envelope in front of them. "This is the best present you could have given me. You're gonna win. And I'm gonna get more coverage than the discovery of America!"

"I am very sorry, Madame," Pierre apologized.

Lily shook her head and started toward the concierge's desk. "Where is Claude?" she demanded.

Pierre sighed. "Ah, I have sad news to report. I am

afraid Claude is not well. The strain has been too much. I have insisted he take some time to rest."

"What a dear you are, Pierre. But you musn't coddle the staff," Lily said. She approached a very nervous Henri. "Don't slouch, darling. Oh, I fear I have my work cut out if I'm to break you in properly."

"Good morning, Madame. You are looking radiant."

"Well, at least the raw material is there. Now, darling . . ." She opened her purse and took out a batch of papers. "There are a few little things I want you to do while we're gone." Lily began tossing papers onto the desk. "By the time we get back, I want the menus from these restaurants. Get me the addresses of these new shops. These people should be called and told about reversing the itinerary. Poor dear, the Baron was expecting us tomorrow; you call and explain. This is a list of books I want you to get for me. And we must have reservations at these places when we return. And before I forget, address and mail this note to the Mayor of Roquefort. You better take the cheese he sent out of the room. You may have it, darling. It's absolutely untouched. Now," she said, turning to Pierre, "last, but not least, send this cable to my publisher." She watched as Pierre stiffened. "It goes to Charles Evron in New York. Charlie, darling, roll them presses. Stop. We've allowed a stay of execution for the Louis Q. Stop." And then she added emphatically, "For this edition. Stop. Love, Lily."

"Madame! Monsieur! I am so very grateful," Pierre began.

"Never mind. You deserve it. You run a good inn here." Dwight smiled as he slapped Pierre on the back. "Durac, I want you to move us into a different suite. We don't ever want that one again. But be very careful packing our things. Just to keep you on your toes, there's something we've left behind."

Pierre put a hand to his brow. "Mon Dieu, they are already packing. I must warn them," he said, picking up the telephone.

Lily put her arm in Dwight's. Her eyes twinkled. "Did you really? What a clever trick! What did you leave behind?"

Dwight kissed her. He looked lovingly into her eyes. "All our cares and woes!"

CLIFFORD and Emma were not smiling as they came out of the Louis. Murphy's crew hovered uneasily as he kept urging, "Smile! C'mon, you two. Smile!"

Emma had not seen Claude since the press conference. She had been waiting for some word from him. At the very least, she had expected to see him before they left. Clifford put down his duffel. He reached over for Emma's.

"C'mon, you guys!" Murphy said. "You got a nice big limo to take you to the choo-choo. Give us a break!"

Clifford stood for a moment scowling at the enormous black car with an American flag on one fender and a French flag on the other. He reached for the door, but the driver opened it first. Emma looked into the lobby for a moment as though she had left something behind. She shrugged her shoulders and got into the car.

Murphy stood in the open doorway. "Listen, you two, the Simons are suing NAA for two million in damages. "I'm telling you this as a friend. I think they have a damn good chance of winning. Don't be dumb. Get yourself a lawyer and slap a suit on us!" They stared at him blankly. "Think about it," he said, closing the door and holding up two fingers. "Two million!"

The Simons and the Benjamins had agreed to reverse

the itinerary so that they would start in Bordeaux and finish up in Champagne. This meant inverting the transportation arrangements to arrive in Bordeaux by plane and train. Cancelling the tour had been suggested, but all NAA would allow was a postponement. The decision was made to get it over with as quickly as possible.

Clifford and Emma did not speak all the way to the Gare de Lyon. They barely managed a pleasant smile when greeted by photographers. Like most European railway stations, it was an enormous steel-and-glass structure under which spilled the constant ebb and flow of departures and arrivals. As they made their way through the crowd, Clifford walked next to Emma. He carried his duffel on one shoulder while she dragged hers along the ground. They walked slowly down the platform toward the Second Class cars.

Clifford turned to her. "Emma . . ."

She shook her head. "Don't." She put her fingers to his lips.

"I love you, Em."

"Cliffy, don't."

The conductor called, "En voiture! En voiture, s'il vous plaît!" People began waving goodbye.

"Em, are you sure?"

"Yes."

"En voiture! En voiture!"

Clifford picked up his bag. "You'll be all right?" She nodded Yes. "Emma," he began helplessly, "I don't know what to say."

She looked up and touched his cheek for a moment. Forcing a smile, she leaned up to kiss him. "As they say in Argentina, Cliffy—Auf Wiedersehen!"

The engine began to hiss and chug. Emma turned quickly and walked back up the platform. Tears streamed down her face as she passed between shouts of "Au revoir," "Bon voyage," "Je t'aime" and "Adieu!"

Emma handed her duffel to the man in the checkroom. When he asked her how long, she shrugged. He muttered, made her pay in advance for two days and gave her a claim check. She stopped in the middle of the station. Emma was pushed and jostled as though standing in the center of a whirlpool. She stared at the check. Very slowly, she tore it up and watched the pieces fall.

"Come with me."

The man looked just like Claude. The same blue eyes. The same thick black hair. He took her arm as Claude would have. He even smiled the same way. She followed him to the rear of the station and up the ornate staircase. Neither said a word. When they reached the entrance to the restaurant, she put her arms around him and leaned her head on his chest. They held tight to each other, and then they kissed.

They sat quietly at a table in front of the two-story window that overlooked the entire station. Le Train Bleu, a Belle Epoque restaurant with carved wooden paneling, brass fittings and fifteen-foot-high maroon draperies, had just opened for the day. Through the window they heard the blurred voice of the stationmaster. They sat listening to the departures and arrivals as though synchronizing their lives. They held hands gently. Finally, they smiled.

"You missed your train" he said.

"I looked for you at the hotel. I wanted to say goodbye."

"And now you must say hello."

"Hello."

"Hello, Emma."

They looked up, startled, as the maître put a bucket of ice with a bottle of champagne on the table. "Avec mes

300

compliments, Claude," he said softly. They began to laugh. Claude took the maître's elbow to reassure him he did not mean to insult a friend. Their laughter subsided once they were alone with the champagne.

It was a long time before Emma reached for her glass. She stared into it. "It's just grape juice and sugar."

"I have heard it makes people feel good."

Emma smiled. "Then maybe I'll try it. I'd like to feel good."

Claude turned to look at the label. There was to be no mercy for them. It was Pommel et Bonnard. He stared into the glass, watching the bubbles rise to the top.

A tear fell down Emma's cheek. "I don't think you're supposed to cry when you drink champagne."

"Emma," he said softly, "I love you."

She began to laugh and cry. "As soon as I understood about the watch, I knew I was all right. I knew I would be safe."

"I was honest with you, Emma."

"I know. I know you didn't hate me. You hated Emma Benjamin. I understand."

Claude sat back. He pushed away the untouched champagne and stared down at the trains. "I have left my job," he said.

"Me, too."

"What will happen now?"

"Cliffy can handle it without me. Murphy's had too much free publicity to make a fuss. I've got plenty of money." She smiled and leaned toward him. "Do you know that I am really very, very rich?"

"I am too. I sold everything to a dealer."

"Your room?" she gasped. "You sold the room?" He nodded Yes. "The paintings? Even the books?"

"Everything."

"Oh, Claude."

"No, no. It is all right. The dealer was a friend. I got a very good price."

"But that room . . ."

"It was a room filled with the past." He paused a moment and then leaned toward her. "I was sure he had killed you."

Emma caressed his hand and quickly changed the subject. "What will you do now?"

"I don't know. I have made my last reservation." He smiled joylessly. "Perhaps I will buy a copy of your book and travel." He turned to look out at the station. "What about your husband?"

"I still love him. He still loves me. But we will have to fall out of love with each other."

"And while you are waiting?"

"I don't know." She smiled and patted her bag. "Everything I have is here. In my bankbook."

Claude took an envelope from his pocket and smiled. "This is what I have left of France."

"The only clothes I have are those I'm wearing."

He put his thumbs under his lapels and shrugged. "My wardrobe."

"I don't even have a place to sleep tonight."

"Nor I."

Emma reached across the table to grab his arm. "Please don't buy my book!"

"There is only one alternative."

Emma smiled. "I know."

"Are you sure, Emma?"

"No." She pushed his glass in front of him and took hers. "Not yet. There is still one ghost to go."

"But Emma—"

"I want to drink champagne as we stand on a terrace overlooking the Bosporus."

"Is that where you want to go?"

"I want to drink champagne as we watch the sun set on the Taj Mahal."

He smiled. "Is that where you want to go?"

"No." She leaned across the table. "You know where I really want to go?"

"Where?"

She whispered, "Mecca!"

Claude laughed. "It is impossible to get into Mecca!"

"I know."

"Mecca!" he said. The name reverberated in his mind. "Mecca! It is impossible!"

Emma held up her glass. She waited for him. He hesitated and then clinked glasses with her. They drank. Now there was no turning back.

Emma stared out the window. "There is only one man who can help us" she said.

"Who?"

"I have heard of someone called Le Dom."

Claude sat back. "There is no such person."

Emma leaned across the table. "Le Dom could get us to Mecca."

"Emma, it is impossible! We cannot get into Mecca!"

"I know." She leaned over to kiss him. "That's why I want to go."

Claude smiled and poured more champagne. "It could take weeks. We would have to go by land."

"I have all the time in the world."

"There are arrangements that would have to be made. In Tehran. Or Istanbul. I would have to find . . ." He looked at Emma, finally understanding. "You would go through all of this to save Le Dom?"

"I want him back. I want you back just as you were."

"I love you, Emma."

"Then take me to Mecca."

Claude narrowed his eyes. He looked out the window at the clock and then down at the trains. He pulled Emma out of her seat. "We must hurry!" They ran from the restaurant.

Emma shouted after him as they nearly flew down the stairs. "Where are we going?"

"To Track Seven."

"But why?"

"Because that is where the train leaves for Geneva."

"How do you know that?"

"I used to be a concierge!"

Claude ran down the platform, dragging Emma behind him. She was laughing. They kept bumping into people. Emma blew kisses to everyone. Steam was rising from the engine as they pushed their way through the crowd. He lifted her onto the last car as it was pulling out of the station.

They were breathing heavily as they watched the Gare de Lyon fade from the horizon. Emma looked up at Claude as Paris began to drift away. "Is it really impossible?"

"Impossible." He kissed her gently and smiled. "The moment we arrive in Geneva, I will call Omar. He can tell me where to find Hassan. And then . . ."